One More Chance

Brand of Justice
Book 12

Lisa Phillips

eBook ISBN: 979-8-88552-278-6

Paperback ISBN: 979-8-88552-279-3

Published by: Two Dogs Publishing, LLC. Idaho, USA

Cover Design by: Sasha Almazan and Gene Mollica, GS Cover Design Studio, LLC

Edited by: Lost Canyon Press Editing, Janice Boekhoff

One More Chance

Chapter One

Phoenix, Arizona
Friday, 11:13 pm

Kenna raced up the last couple of steps and pushed the bar on the door to get out onto the roof. Desert wind blew at her face, sending her hair back. She slid a hair tie off her wrist and secured it all in a ponytail. She needed to focus, not worry about tangled hair in her face at the wrong moment—or why she was far more winded than she should be from running up eight flights of stairs.

She couldn't worry about that right now. Her problems could cost someone their life.

Terri Fleming stood at the far end of the rooftop, shrouded by the night sky and backlit by the city skyline. Kenna strode over there, trying to make some noise so the woman wasn't startled. If that happened, then she wouldn't be jumping, she'd have fallen because of Kenna.

She stopped about ten feet behind Terri, who stood on

the ledge that was meant to keep people from falling. "Ms. Fleming." She kept her voice soft.

Terri's white blouse fluttered around her in the breeze. She had on tan linen pants and black ballet flats. "Don't come any closer!" Her short salt-and-pepper hair didn't get in her eyes, which meant she could likely see the crowd gathering below.

People out late downtown, probably after an evening of drinking. Now most had their phones out, and a few were yelling, "Jump! Jump!" Which just made Kenna want to throw something down there to get them to disburse. Instead, she said, "Terri, can we talk about this?"

"What's to talk about? It's over!"

Kenna took a step closer to her, already sweating even though she was dressing for the weather now. It was so hot in Arizona she didn't have much of a choice. She'd opted for chino shorts and a white graphic tee, over which she had on a thin, short-sleeved salmon-colored jacket that wasn't meant to be buttoned or zippered. Its only function was to hide the holstered weapon at the small of her back, among other self-defense items that were on her person. Converse on her feet, of course. She never knew when she'd have to run up several flights of stairs to convince a woman in a bad spot not to jump off a roof. No point being caught in sandals or heels.

"If you're still standing it isn't over." Kenna took another step toward her.

In the distance, she heard police sirens. Flashing lights reflected off a building a block or two down the street. Cops. Probably firefighters and an ambulance as well, because everyone had a part to play in resolving a situation like this.

But Kenna was the one who was here right now.

"I mean it, Terri. It isn't over until you've given up, and how does that help set the record straight?"

"I'm the one who designed this building. Marshal stole everything from me. He took my design, claimed it was his, and never once mentioned that he was starting his own business with *my* design."

Meanwhile, Terri had been skimming from the business she and Marshal Hapsworth had started together. Funding a lavish lifestyle and healthy savings accounts while her regular paycheck went to funding her retirement at hyperspeed. Instead of turning her in, Marshal had double-crossed her and opted to play the long game of revenge.

For five years, he'd been secretly running a competing business solo. Getting this building up and running. Callously undermining Terri, because she'd been skimming from him, by constructing a building she'd designed in a part of the city where Ms. Fleming never traveled to as part of her daily routine.

As soon as she'd realized what Marshal had done, she'd also realized she couldn't go to the cops. She'd hired Kenna under the guise of preparing to sue her business partner and needing evidence to prove her case.

It hadn't taken Kenna long to figure out what was really going on.

Kenna watched the first cop car round a corner onto this street. The crowd below started to yell louder. Because they knew the situation would be resolved soon? They wanted their live stream to go viral with something epic—a woman tumbling to her death—before the cops shut the whole thing down.

"Terri, we can't prove what Marshal did if you take your own life."

"I'll go to jail for embezzling from the company."

"But you won't get justice," Kenna said. "No one will know that you designed this amazing building. We might be able to talk to the prosecutor about a reduced sentence. You know I used to work in law enforcement. I have contacts, even here." She wasn't going to mention that her new husband was the Special Agent in Charge at the Phoenix FBI office. "I can help you get through this, but you have to trust me, Terri."

The cops would be up here in minutes.

Unfortunately, the wrong cop could send this whole situation sideways fast.

She tugged off her jacket and laid it on the ground, then pulled her weapon and its holster from the back of her belt, which she put on the jacket. Fully visible. Making it immediately evident she was now unarmed. She took two steps to the side so she was out of reach of the weapon.

Kenna could hear the cops coming up the stairs, pounding feet and loud conversation.

A second before the door opened, she spread her hands out to the sides so that they would see right away that she had no weapon in her grasp.

The door flung back and hit the wall.

Kenna held her focus on Terri. She couldn't grab Ms. Fleming if she started to fall, not from this distance. Also, Kenna didn't have the strength in her arms to hold a person up most of the time.

She had even less these days, when every part of her body felt sluggish each morning and she had to drag herself out of bed. Slow starts, as if her body had to rev its engine up to full power. She could do the same in the afternoon if she took a long nap.

"Ma'am, step away from the edge." The first cop was uniformed but with sergeant stripes on his short black sleeves. The highest ranking officer on scene right now. He approached with steady steps.

But who was the guy talking to? Maybe both of them? Her T-shirt fluttered in the hot wind, which didn't cool her off much. "Terri, I need you to climb down for me so we can figure this out."

"It's over," Terri said. "I'm going to jump."

The cops spread out, moving closer to Kenna and her client. Terri faced the street, so she couldn't see them, but that command presence police officers had sometimes felt like a physical thing that hung in the air.

Below them, the crowd had started to chant, "Jump! Jump! Jump!"

The sergeant said, "Terri, is it?"

"I'm not talking to cops!"

"I'm sure your friend here would like to hear what you have to say."

"She already knows too much. It's over!" Terri screamed. "It's so over that I'm going over, and then it's done."

Kenna took a step toward her. "Terri, please don't jump."

"You just wanna get paid!"

Sure, Kenna had an unpaid invoice on her accounting software, but that was hardly the point. This woman was determined to end her life. No matter what the situation, that would be a tragedy. "This isn't about money. I want everyone to know what Marshal did to you and to your company. Which means I need *you* to tell your side of the story."

"You didn't do your job if you need that. You were supposed to find evidence!"

Kenna said, "People need a story. Not facts. A story is

what changes someone's mind, and it's how we learn the truth."

The sergeant came closer, catching sight of her gun on her jacket. He looked at Kenna with raised brows.

"I'm a private investigator. Ms. Fleming is my client, and she's going to get down off that ledge so we can figure out a solution to all this."

The sergeant asked, "What do you say, Terri? Do you want us to help you find a solution?"

Below, the crowd renewed the chanting. *Jump! Jump!*

"There is no solution."

The sergeant moved close enough to grab her. Kenna caught the attention of the closest uniformed officer and pointed to her forearms. In the dim light of the rooftop, maybe he hadn't seen her scars, the ones that were visible and ugly in the daylight. That was the thing about darkness and shadows —it hid far too much that would be plainly true in the light. Darkness obscured that truth and shrouded it in mystery.

Kenna's job was to bring those things from the darkness into the light.

She waved the cop over, and as he passed her, she whispered, "I can't grab her."

She turned back to the ledge. "Terri, don't do this. Please. I've seen someone die before because they lost hope and took their own life. I know how much it hurts when you have nothing but despair, but you have to know there is *always* a reason to keep going. What about your niece, Charlotte? What am I supposed to tell her? You'll be altering her life in a way she might not recover from. There are people who care about you. If you love them, you need to do everything you can to stick around."

"I know about your boyfriend and that serial killer,"

Terri said. "This is just about you not failing again. You don't care about me. You just want to save yourself the grief. I don't care."

Kenna's heart squeezed in her chest. She had a gold wedding band on her left hand these days. That life with Bradley felt like decades ago, even though it was just a few years. "You should care. This is your life we're talking about. If you give up, then there's nothing I can do to help you. And yes, I'll have to live with that for the rest of my life."

"I'm not going to jail."

"That's not up to you, Terri. You can't wipe it all away. Marshal needs to face justice, and I'll find you the best lawyer I can who is an expert in clients that have been *suspected* of embezzling." She added the last part for the cops' benefit so they understood what she and Terri were talking about.

"I have lawyers. Not that they ever did me any good before. I don't need Marshal dead. I need him to be the one in jail."

Kenna frowned. "We can figure this out. But you have to come off that ledge and trust me, the way you trusted me to take your case."

A fire truck pulled up on the street. Someone got on a bullhorn to tell the crowd to disburse—as if that was going to work. The show wasn't over, but hopefully, it would be soon.

"She's right," the sergeant said. "You're the one who has the power to figure this out."

Or the power to end it, but he didn't say that aloud. Kenna wouldn't have either.

"We need you to step down."

She could see in his eyes that he was about to step in, and she braced for it. "Terri, step down."

The two cops—the sergeant and the guy she'd waved over—glanced at each other. Kenna spotted a hand signal in the dim light, and a nod in response from the officer.

Everyone else started to approach as well, almost silent in their movements. If someone's life wasn't on the line, Kenna would have wanted to be here just to watch.

In a split second, the two closest officers both grabbed Terri's wrist with one hand and a handful of her shirt with the other. Startling her. But she couldn't do anything about it before they swung her back off the ledge. She fell onto her back on the ground, kicking and screaming. Mostly at Kenna.

There wasn't anything she could do to help or to hinder them. Once Terri calmed down, Kenna could try and talk to her again. See if she really could assist in what happened to her next.

The sergeant waved at his people by the door to the stairs. "Get the paramedics up here."

Kenna went for her jacket.

"Not so fast, PI."

She straightened. Other officers took over with Terri, assisting the paramedics who ran over with duffel bags and a folding chair that had wheels. Kenna turned away, and the sergeant ushered her a couple of paces from the group around Terri.

"Sergeant Hernandez." He had dark hair, tan lines on either side of his eyes as if he wore sunglasses a lot, and a wedding ring on his left hand.

"Kenna Banbury." She'd kept her maiden name for business but changed everything personal to the last name Jaxton.

"This woman is a client of yours?"

Kenna nodded. "I have a business card with my information on it, if you'd like?"

When he nodded back, she dug it out of her pocket and handed it over. "Banbury Investigations," he read from the card, then said, "I'm assuming you have another card that's your permit for that weapon?"

"Of course." Jax's job meant she needed to be on the right side of the law at all times. She'd never had much problem with that, as long as the cops left her alone to do her job. It was just that some of the people she worked with —her team—had more gray-area methods of working.

A suited man came out the door onto the roof. Red hair with a wave, streaked with gray. Suntan lines from sunglasses on either side of his eyes as well. Badge on his belt.

She waved. "Detective Jordash."

The sergeant said, "You guys know each other?"

Jordash joined their huddle. "Ms. Banbury provided some relevant information on a local businessman, Marshal Hapsworth." He glanced at her. "We just arrested him an hour ago."

"That's good news." Probably not a great time to tell Terri, though.

"First thing he did was tell us everything Ms. Fleming has been doing. Probably just to save face."

"If he goes down, they both go down," Kenna said.

Jordash nodded. "Something like that."

"I'm going to make sure she has a good lawyer."

Jordash said, "I still can't believe she hired you to investigate him, knowing full well you'd find out what she did." He shook his head, a disbelieving expression on his face.

"Maybe she had the same idea," Kenna said. "If she was going to go down, she wanted him to go down as well."

"Here?" the sergeant said.

"She designed this building, and he stole the idea. Claimed it as his own."

"And these are the cases you take now?" Jordash tipped his head to the side. "There weren't any missing kids or killers in this one. Doesn't really seem like your speed."

"We all do what we gotta do to pay the bills."

The two of them chuckled, and the sergeant said, "It doesn't pay the bills, but you are going to make a statement to one of my officers about all this. And hand over everything you have on Fleming and this Hapsworth guy."

"I know the drill."

The sergeant smiled. "I'm sure you do, *Kenna Banbury*."

Whatever that meant. Sure, this wasn't Kenna's normal case. But it was done now, and she had a few more on her desk that needed her attention. Not to mention she needed to sleep. Her body was starting to drag, and she hadn't done much but stand here on this roof.

But this was a new chapter in Kenna's life, and she was going to embrace it.

Chapter Two

MONDAY, 7:13 AM

Kenna stared across the breakfast bar at her nemesis, the offending creature she was supposed to share her life with. Not the husband she had married two months ago. No, he'd made good on what should've been a throwaway comment but had turned out to be very real threat about getting an animal.

"Jolene, get off the counter."

The light gray cat swished her tail, prowling around looking for trouble like her namesake. Probably waiting for Jax to show up and coddle her. *Meow.* Jolene swished her tail.

"Are you talking to the cat?" Jax wandered in wearing his work clothes. Slacks, and a buttoned shirt tucked into his belt. Her husband opened the dishwasher and upended his mug, putting it on the top rack.

He glanced at her as he closed the dishwasher door.

Slowly.

Kenna rolled her eyes. "Put it wherever you want."

"Because you'll rearrange it later?"

She chuckled, shaking her head. Married life was fun. Like trying to merge two laundry styles. And debating the best configuration for the dishwasher. Was he really going to complain if she could fit more dirty dishes in there than he managed to? She wasn't the one who'd shrunk a perfectly good hoodie last week.

Jax wore a gun holstered on his hip, but with the position he had now, he rarely had occasion to pull it out. As the Special Agent in Charge of the FBI's Phoenix office, he had more of a managerial position, though he never complained about the bureaucracy. The guy was way too good at politics and getting things done to have an issue.

In fact, the job suited him well. So did the town house they now shared, with her RV parked in the tall bay on the side of his garage. Sure, she was going to complain about things on occasion just to keep him on his toes. Only a little, though. Just enough for them both to know she was paying attention and fully aware of the change in her life.

Kenna leaned back on the bar stool, resting against the back. She was dressed for her job in lightweight black pants that were supposed to be cooling and a white tee that was loose enough she could keep a gun at the small of her back. Trying not to look as tired as she felt, which probably didn't work. Her husband was far too astute. Over the last couple months of being married—spending more time together than they had since they met—he could read her even better now. And he'd already been able to see through her.

"*Your* cat is on the counter again."

Jax came over and kissed her, running his hand between her shoulder blades. "I thought Jolene was *our* cat." He scooped Jolene off the counter and set her on the floor, then went to the cupboard with her food.

"Does anyone own a cat? I think cats own you." And she much preferred dogs, which, of course, everyone already knew. "She doesn't like me because she knows I won't let her be the one in charge."

Jax chuckled, setting down the bowl of cat food. "Easier to leave a cat alone all day when I'm at work. Especially with occasionally having odd hours."

"Don't ruin my story with your logic."

Jax shot a grin at her, but it quickly turned into an assessing gaze. "Doctor's appointment?"

"It's at eight."

"Do you want me to call out for a couple of hours so I can drive you?"

"I'll be okay." Truth was, she worried that the moment she stopped regularly driving, she'd have trouble finding the energy to start again. She slid off the stool, trying to keep it from looking like she had to drag herself around. Her body felt...heavy. That was the only way she could explain the lethargy she felt. It didn't help that food failed to taste good and most things left her nauseous, but she wasn't pregnant.

At least, so far, she hadn't had a positive test.

Kenna took a package of two steaks from the freezer drawer at the bottom of the fridge freezer and put it in the sink.

"Sure you don't want me to go with you?" He knew there was plenty she wasn't telling him. But it wasn't as if she planned to keep the results of any tests from him.

"I'll call you as soon as I'm done." She moved to stand in front of him, sliding her arms around him. She lifted up on her toes and kissed him. "Promise."

He slid his arms around her. "I'm sure everything will be fine."

"I don't need fine. I need answers."

"I know." He kissed her again. "Gotta go or I'll be late for a meeting." But he didn't move or let go of her. "Love you."

That meant, *I'm so glad you're here now, I'm still glad we got married, let's go on vacation, I don't want to go to work because I'd rather stay here with you,* and a whole lot of other things. Enough to make her smile. She dragged her hands up his chest to his cheeks and kissed him, replying the same without words.

"Someone has to be the breadwinner."

Kenna gasped, laughing when she caught the playful look in his eyes. He knew well enough she didn't need anyone to take care of her. After all, they'd combined their finances as soon as they got married.

"Speaking of." He bent to grab something from his work backpack. "Don't tell anyone I gave you this." He handed over a manila file stuffed full of papers and newspaper clippings. "It's a cold case. A legend in the Phoenix FBI office, or a myth. Everyone seems to have a theory about what might've happened."

"What's the case?" She set the file down, working out when she would have time later to look at it between her appointment and grocery shopping. Princess Jolene needed more treats, and Kenna needed more of the energy drinks she'd been living on these days.

"Right around July 1972, a Mafia boss, Lorin Barone, who was the subject of an investigation, disappeared. On the same day, one of our agents, Walter Collins, who was the lead in investigating him, disappeared as well. Along with a hundred thousand dollars in gold that was never found. No one knows what happened to them or where they went or where the gold is. They just vanished."

Her brows rose. "Thanks."

Jax chuckled. "Have a good day, dear."

She rolled her eyes and hung around in the kitchen while he headed out to work. Her phone was where she'd left it on the end table in the living room, where she'd been listening to the Bible while Jax took his shower and got ready. Maizie had called once already this morning. Kenna finished getting ready, poured coffee into a thermal cup full of ice, and armed the alarm before she went out to her car.

She opened the garage door and turned the air-conditioning to full blast while the interior cooled off. It might be morning chill, but this was Arizona summer. Being outside after nine in the morning was like stepping into a furnace.

She called Maizie on the way out of the drive and sipped her coffee as it rang, heading to the entrance of the complex. The two pillars that flanked the drive in and out had a security guard shack on the left side and plenty of palm trees on either edge.

Maizie said, "Hey."

"Morning." Kenna rested one hand on her lap on the straight roads, giving each a break in turn. "You didn't tell me earlier...how was your night?"

"I got my English paper done."

"That's great. What about history?"

Maizie made a noise. "Let's not belabor the point here."

Kenna chuckled. "Summer classes are a good test of whether you'd like college in the fall."

"Or if I'm going to be a model student or a slacker," Maizie said. "I'm still getting used to the name Maizie Jaxton coming up on the card reader when I sign in to class."

"I know what you mean, though I don't know if only changing my driver's license and my name at the bank is making it worse or better."

"What about the doctor's office?"

Maizie was still talking about how they both took the Jaxton family name when Kenna married Jax because Jax and Kenna had legally adopted Maizie. But she had more important things to talk about with Maizie. The teen was already eighteen, legally an adult, and they'd talked at length about her moving in with them. In the end, Maizie had opted to stay in the Airstream in Colorado rather than invade the space of two newlyweds. Not that they'd have minded.

Still, the girl had all the care she needed where she was. Kenna would've liked to have Maizie with her, but spending time alone with Jax was never a bad thing. She didn't want anything about their closeness as a married couple to remind Maizie of the horrific parts of her childhood as the captive of an evil man.

Kenna said, "I'm headed to the doctor's office right now to find out the results of all the tests."

Silence was her only answer.

"Jax gave me a cold case. I'll upload all the pages this afternoon. Want to help me with the research?"

"Why did he give you a cold case?"

"He probably thinks I need a good distraction." Which, to be fair, she likely did. With all the angst she'd been feeling surrounding what was wrong with her, she could use a juicy distraction. One that had nothing to do with her father, her history, or international criminal consortiums who called themselves *Dominatus*. The kind of group she couldn't find a way to take down, no matter how long she worked on it.

"If you need something to do, I have a history paper you can write."

Kenna laughed. "Not on your life, kiddo."

"It was worth a try."

"I'll upload the cold case file *after* you're done with your history paper."

"Ugh."

Kenna smiled to herself. "Did you find anything out about the medical center?"

The insurance she should have as Jax's spouse didn't kick in until ninety days after the wedding, so it hadn't started yet. With her kind of enemies, she hadn't wanted a doctor where her records would be official, so she'd opted for a specific medical center. One that had her on a rougher side of town in front of a rundown strip mall. The store next door was empty, boarded up. "I should rent an office. Hang a shingle."

"Whatever that means."

"Set up an office for Banbury Investigations. Like with a sign out front."

"You have a website."

"Okay, Two Thousands," Kenna said, scared to even think about the year Maizie had been born. "But back in the *nineteen hundreds*, when we had to do things *before* the invention of the internet, we lived on a more...local level."

"Sounds boring."

Kenna parked the car but didn't turn off the engine, so the air-conditioning continued to blow on her. She drank some more iced coffee and watched traffic go by on the four-lane road. A chain hotel sat on the far side. The strip mall housed her doctor's office, which was a twenty-four-hour medical center that let people pay cash and use whatever name they wanted. There was also a Russian grocery store, and beside that was a children's consignment clothing boutique.

Maizie continued, "Unlike the dark secrets of that medical center."

Kenna frowned. "What are you talking about?"

"Your doctor? Nicola Santorini? She's connected with the Mafia in Las Vegas. I had to show Stairns so he could explain it all to me, but he put it together right away. The Santinos are a huge crime family in Vegas, and she did a decent job keeping her life separate from them, but it's never completely foolproof. You can't bury everything. Not when so much is online nowadays."

"And the medical center is part of it, or just Nicola?" If the doctor had changed her name and moved to Phoenix, maybe she wanted nothing to do with the rest of the "family." Kenna knew the Santino family—or she had known one member. At the time, she hadn't even realized there were more of them. What happened in Vegas had stayed there when Anthony Santino died on the same night Kenna killed the FBI Director. She'd also killed the man who'd kept Maizie captive.

Maizie had escaped with them.

None of them had ever looked back.

"The medical center is funded by a foundation, and on the surface, it's this philanthropic cause. Helping people who can't afford treatment or insurance and who don't qualify for help to get adequate medical care."

"And below the surface?"

"The foundation is backed solely by the Santino crime family. They use it to launder money."

Kenna blew out a breath. "Maybe Nicola has no idea."

"Maybe she does good, and there's no reason to rock the boat."

"I guess I'm gonna find out."

"Call me back after."

"Sure thing, Maze." Kenna climbed out of her car, bringing her cold coffee with her. Heat hung in the air, surrounding her, making her want to seek out the nearest cold pool so she could soak away all the aches she had. No longer just the injuries to the tendons and muscle in her forearms, this was deeper. And bad enough that she barely even thought about her forearms now because her entire body made her want to curl up on the floor and do nothing. Take a nap. Maybe cry a little.

If this was what chronic illness felt like...it *sucked*.

Kenna needed to find out what was going on with her body. Okay, fine. She needed to find out what *Dominatus* had done to her when they held her captive two months ago. Smart money had been that they'd impregnated her with one of their genetically modified embryos. Considering she was one of those herself, she couldn't really hold it against the child if that happened.

But there had been nothing.

At least, not so far. Which made it more and more unlikely every day.

All the wild theories her mind wanted to come up with as to what they'd done to her raced through her thoughts. She could be patient zero in a deadly pandemic. A test subject for some new research project they had going on. Or she'd been genetically altered somehow.

Whatever the answer, it put her future with Jax in serious jeopardy.

When she figured out what they'd done to her—and who was responsible—heads were going to roll.

When she was two steps from the front door of the medical center, the window to her right shattered, and two people flew out in a tangle of limbs. A plus-size woman in a pair of dusty overalls hit the ground in a spray of glass with Kenna's associate Bruce on top of her. The former CIA agent wrestled with the woman like he was fighting for his life.

Kenna reached toward the small of her back for her gun, but neither Bruce or that woman had a weapon. She didn't draw hers. "Bruce."

He glanced at her, holding the woman's wrists with one hand, his forearm across her collarbones. "Kenna, good to see you."

The woman wriggled one hand free and punched Bruce in the side of his head. He slumped over, and she shoved him off.

Kenna held up her hands. "Not so fast."

The woman scrambled up, agile in a way that meant she was a serious threat.

Why hadn't she brought a stun gun? "Let's just take a sec and—"

The woman ran at her, crazed and screaming.

Kenna had no time to do anything but turn and present her shoulder to the woman. She slammed into Kenna and nearly knocked her flat on her behind, but Kenna kept her feet planted. The woman's cry cut off, and she clutched her chest, fell back, and hit the ground.

Out cold.

Chapter Three

Bruce blinked, his focus settling on her. "Hey."

She walked over to him and almost held her hand out but caught herself before she did. Just a reflex, the intent to help him up versus the reality of her forearms. "I see you found yourself a case."

"Open and shut. Only took me five minutes." His tone was easy, but the look on his face when he moved reminded her of how recently he'd been shot and left for dead.

The past few months, he'd been recovering, bouncing back but not as fast as he wanted. He probably wasn't completely back to fighting fit. Even if he'd just tried to prove differently to the world—or to himself.

The front door of the medical center flung open, and a nurse in black scrubs, her dark hair in pigtails, rushed out.

"Should I call the cops?" She glanced between Kenna and Bruce as if unsure who the perpetrator here was.

"No."

At the same time Bruce said that, Kenna said, "Maybe."

He shot her a look.

She shot him one right back.

They both lived on thin ice with local police departments, him more than her. Neither needed to get on cops' radars or catch the notice of federal police if they could help it. She'd connected with too many cops over the weekend, but that was what her life happened to be sometimes, more so now that she was married to a fed.

Bruce was a former CIA agent, burned by his government and left in exile in the UK for years before Kenna negotiated his return to the US. Now she was sort of responsible for him and whatever he did, though she didn't want to be.

The guy had discovered his former partner at the Agency was the one who had burned him, and Bruce had spent weeks digging into the man's life. He'd formulated a plan to get revenge, which Kenna preferred to think of as justice, but as soon as he'd moved to pull the trigger on the plan...the guy up and disappeared.

Completely.

The nurse looked between them, then rushed over to the woman in overalls lying on the concrete, unmoving. "Did you kill her?"

"How would I have done that?" Not because she couldn't. More because Kenna had no idea how that would be possible right now. "I only shoved her with my shoulder."

Bruce assessed Kenna. "She went down pretty hard. You good, boss?"

The nurse didn't look over from her evaluation of the patient, but she definitely stiffened upon hearing that. Yeah, so they were connected. That was more of Kenna's problem than anyone else's.

Kenna touched the heel of her hand to her forehead, her thoughts swimming, sending her equilibrium off-balance.

Someone asked, "Do you need to be seen?"

She lowered her hand and looked at Doctor Nicola Santorini. Dark gray slacks and low-heeled black shoes, a white buttoned shirt, and a doctor's lab coat over it. A tiny gold chain rested around her neck. She had dark brown hair, almost black, pulled back into a ponytail with loose strands around her head. Doctor Santorini was probably in her mid-forties but had no husband or children in her life. Just her medical practice.

"I had an appointment, but..." She waved at the woman on the ground.

"We'll get to you." The doctor went to her patient and crouched, speaking with the nurse. She flinched at something the woman said, then pulled a cell phone from the pocket of her lab coat and called 911. She asked for an ambulance. When she lowered her phone, Doctor Santorini said, "Care to explain why this woman's sternum is caved in?"

Kenna's mouth dropped open. She didn't have any explanation. Wasn't that why she was here? For the results of her tests.

For answers.

Kenna said, "She ran at me, and I blocked it. She fell back."

"That doesn't explain this." Doctor Santorini sat back on her heels. "This woman needs to get to a hospital fast. She needs surgery." She brushed back strands of hair from her face. "How did you *do* this?"

Bruce tugged on her arm. "You don't have to answer that. You don't have to say anything."

He drew her away from the accusations, toward the front door of the medical center. She turned to him. "Why don't you tell me what happened?" She lowered her voice. "You're the one who threw her out the window."

"She gave me no choice."

Kenna lifted one brow. "I'm not the police. You don't have to defend yourself with me. You already know that."

She expected the plain truth, no spin. Bruce had been a spy for decades, so telling the plain and simple truth was something they'd been working on. Especially after he handed her over to their enemy a few months ago. Sure, if she'd have been apprised as to what he was doing, she would probably have agreed with his plan. But he hadn't run it by her.

Her ragtag band of employees were the friends she seemed to have gathered over the last few months and, in some cases, years. People who'd stuck around long enough to call themselves coworkers but acted more like family. They were who they were. She didn't want to change that.

What she wanted was to be a positive influence in their lives. After all, she'd surrendered her life to the Lord, and now that she was living out the day-to-day of being a Christian, she supposed that meant being evidence for them of what God could do in a person. It was up to them, not Kenna, whether her story convinced them it was worth taking the same step in their own lives.

She looked around. "What happened, Bruce?"

Instead of answering, he held the door for her, and they stepped inside. The first thing he did was look at two kids sitting in the waiting area, both of them pale and clearly terrified. A little girl, maybe six or seven, held her arm tight to her front. Her brother, around twelve years old, sat close to her side. Both were slender, their clothes from a thrift store or older and worn because that was all they had.

"Bruce." Kenna needed an explanation.

"They came in about fifteen minutes ago. The girl is obviously hurt." He kept his voice low, but the kids knew they were talking about them. Both looked like they were gonna bolt. "When she came in, they both reacted. Freaked out like they're scared out of their little kid minds."

"How did you get from there to tossing that woman through the window?"

He had to have come here to watch out for Kenna, knowing she had an appointment. Every few days, she spotted either him or Ramon somewhere in her periphery, though she hadn't seen Ramon in a couple of weeks. Both of them seemed to be working protection detail—keeping her safe. But also maintaining their distance so she and Jax could be newlyweds enjoying their happily ever after.

She hadn't asked her team to watch out for her. They'd simply taken it upon themselves to do that for her.

Bruce said, "She stomped over and demanded they get up. She would've taken them with her, so I intervened, and things escalated fast. She put her hands on the girl, and the kid screamed in pain. I got her off the kid and over to the door. Told her to go. She tried to punch me. I stopped her. We tussled. Probably too close to the window because we went through it."

Speaking of...

Kenna looked out right as a black-and-white police squad car pulled into the parking lot for the strip mall. Two officers climbed out.

Kenna figured she'd probably end up being taken in for questioning. First, though, she wanted to find out the rest of what was going on. She wandered over to the kids, who were huddled beside each other on waiting area chairs.

She crouched in front of them, keeping her distance, just in case they didn't want their space invaded. "Hi, I'm Kenna."

They both stared at her. The boy, the older brother.

The protector. He stared right back, as if challenging her before he even knew what she wanted. This kid lived his life on the offensive.

The little girl hadn't quite learned that lesson, which was probably why she wound up being the punching bag. The one who had been injured. She was the weak link. She looked at her brother, then at Kenna, and said nothing. Her gaze strayed to Bruce, over Kenna's shoulder, with a little bit of awe in her expression.

"That's my friend. His name is Bruce." She kept her tone and her expression soft, as if she was sharing a secret. "He used to be a *spy*. Now he keeps people safe. Me, or anyone who needs it."

The boy's gaze whipped over to Bruce, a little disbelief in his expression.

"That's what I do as well. I help people when they need it."

"We don't need help," the boy said, no faltering in his tone.

"Everyone needs help sometimes. Even Bruce."

Behind her, he said, "It's true, kid. We all need help sometimes."

"Like when we get hurt." She motioned to the girl, careful to keep it easy and not accusatory. "Or when we're here to see the doctor, like me." She looked at the little girl. "Did you get hurt?"

The little girl nodded.

Kenna smiled. "You came to the right place." She included her brother in that because he'd done the right thing by getting help for his sister. "You haven't done anything wrong."

The little girl's eyes filled with tears. "I burned the mac and cheese."

Her brother stiffened.

"That sounds like an easy thing to do. You made a mistake. I was making cookies the other day, and I forgot all about them," Kenna said. "They looked like lumps of charcoal, all black and burned. The house smelled like a campfire all day."

The girl bit her lip.

The door opened, and Kenna glanced over to see the cops come in. When she looked back at the kids, they were at that ready-to-bolt point again. "You haven't done anything wrong," she repeated. "And you came to the right place." She tipped her head to the side. "You don't need to be afraid of the police."

"Mommy says they're pigs." The little girl flinched like she hadn't meant to say that.

Kenna said, "Their job is to keep you safe. They're not going to hurt you. The police are here to keep all of us safe." She focused on the boy. "Did your mom hurt your sister?"

He pressed his lips together tight and nodded.

"Is that woman outside your mother?" Kenna pointed at the window.

He croaked out the word, "Yes."

The little girl sniffed.

"Does she hurt you?"

The boy said, "Lila is hurt."

Kenna nodded. "The doctor can help her."

"He helped us." The kid motioned to Bruce with a lift of his chin. "He kept her away from us." He looked at the window, where an ambulance had parked with its flashing lights reflecting on the unbroken glass of the door. "Is she dead?"

"No, honey."

"Shame." A tendon in the kid's jaw flexed.

One of the cops cleared his throat. Kenna touched the little girl's knee. "We'll take care of you, okay?" Not really a question, and she didn't wait around for an answer. She stood and turned to the cops. "These two don't fall through the cracks."

The cop lifted his brows. Officer rank, and his name-plate said *Albertson*. "Is that right?"

His partner, a younger guy, said, "Seems like they already did. So let's fix that." He went to the kids and crouched as she'd done.

Officer Albertson didn't move. "Ma'am, I need you to answer some questions."

Kenna nodded, looking around for Bruce. Where did he...? The guy was gone. Nowhere to be found. While her back was turned, in front of cops. She needed to put a little bell on that guy.

Fatigue washed over her, and she hadn't even done all that much so far this morning. The persistent heaviness of her body that seemed to have crept up on her slowly over the last two months was her most prominent symptom. The nausea was a secondary factor.

She needed her test results.

But until she could get those from the doctor, she slumped into a chair on the far side of the waiting room. Officer Albertson asked her a few questions, and she gave him some basic answers. After all, she'd only shown up and then defended herself. The whole thing had been barely a couple of minutes from start to finish, so what more was there to say?

Kenna glanced over at the kids, who were talking to the younger cop. The boy's attention drifted to her. She gave him a smile, fully intending to check up on them in a few days. She'd meant what she said to the cop—that they didn't fall through the cracks. Sure, it had effectively been a threat. He just didn't know that.

The doctor came back in with her nurse, both of them removing protective gloves. Doctor Santorini shook her head.

"Is she...?" The implications of the doc's expression send an icy shiver down her spine. Kenna bit her lip.

"She's in a bad way." Santorini sighed.

Her nurse went behind the front desk and spoke to the older woman sitting there with her headset on. Had that woman seen where Bruce went?

Kenna said, "The girl needs to be looked at."

"She needs an X-ray, something I can't do. We should get another ambulance here."

"Good call not putting her in the ambulance with the woman who did that to her."

Santorini's expression flashed with surprise, then hardened. "She is going to a different hospital entirely, then."

Officer Albertson said, "My partner and I will escort the kids to the hospital and make sure they're taken care of." He grabbed the radio on his shoulder and said to his partner, "I'll call it in."

It didn't take long for them to encourage the kids into the police car so the little girl could get an X-ray somewhere that was equipped with the tech. Kenna crouched in the open back door of the cop car to speak with them both before they left.

When the officer shut the car door, he said, "We'll take care of them."

Anything she responded with would probably sound like a threat, like *Make sure you do*, so Kenna simply nodded. "Thank you." Still, she watched them drive away until they were out of sight.

She headed back inside the medical center and found the doctor behind the front desk.

"You'll need to find a new doctor's office." Santorini folded her arms.

"I didn't start that fight."

"You finished it, though. That woman might die as a result of a crushed sternum. You caved in her chest." She shook her head.

"At least tell me how I managed to do that."

The doctor frowned. "What do you mean?"

"Before you kick me off your patient list, maybe you could tell me what's wrong with me. How I could've done that."

Santorini looked at the computer screen behind the desk and tapped a few keys. "Kenna Banbury."

She nodded.

"Everything came back normal."

"So tell me how shoulder-checking that woman means I caved her chest in." Desperation leached into her tone.

"There's no need to get angry." Santorini straightened, looking nervous.

Was she really scared of Kenna? "I'm not angry." She shook her head. "I want to know what's wrong with me. Because there's nothing *normal* about this."

Santorini looked at the screen again. "You have elevated calcium levels."

"And my weight." Jax had bathroom scales, and she'd stepped on them a couple of weeks ago. Now she did it every day. Trying to figure out why she felt heavy.

Because she *was* heavy.

"What about your weight?" Santorini checked the screen.

"Explain how I'm thirty pounds heavier than usual, but

my clothes still fit fine. I'm no bigger than I've been in a long time, but I weigh that much more? How is that possible?"

"Well, as we age..."

Kenna frowned. "How can I be that much heavier, but no bigger?" It was ridiculous that they had to do this in the waiting room, but given the doctor's scared expression, she stayed where she was. "There's no way this is normal."

She hadn't told Santorini about being captured by the *Dominatus*. Probably, the doctor would think she was nuts.

Just thinking about it made her breathing speed up and her heart race. "Explain how there's nothing wrong with me."

"If you're feeling anxious about changes that are happening in your life, I can give you a recommendation for someone to talk to. Treatment of a different kind."

"You mean therapy."

Santorini said, "I can give you a referral. There are some excellent psychologists in this area. Any one of them can help you work through your fears."

"You mean the medical condition I obviously have. One that made me heavier. Stronger."

"The mind can be powerful."

"So I imagined caving that woman's chest in?"

Santorini folded her arms. "It's time for you to leave. There's nothing more I can do to help you."

Chapter Four

By the time Kenna reached Fulcher Park, the sun was high in the blue sky, not a cloud in sight. A haze of heat bubbled off the asphalt of the parking lot as she walked the path over to their meeting spot.

Clouds sounded good right now. Nice and pleasant fifty degrees, and a hot cup of coffee. She'd been drinking it iced since she got married. Jax had pointed out they both needed to make *compromises.* Which was fine for now, but this winter, he'd be compromising somewhere with three feet of snow. If she had to deal with Arizona palm trees and relentless warmth at Christmas?

Nah. That was just wrong.

She brought her iced coffee and found a shady spot under some trees where there was a memorial bench for a fallen police officer who'd been shot in the line of duty. About as soon as she'd settled onto the bench, Bruce appeared from behind the trees and sat beside her.

"You left the doctor's office." She stared across the kids' playground. The splash pad area was bustling with children in bathing suits and swim shorts, their parents standing watch around the perimeter. She could see all the way to the expansive parking lot and across it to where there were a few restaurants on the other side of the street.

"I had things to do." He stretched out his knees, shifting in his seat until he found a comfortable spot.

He'd sat beside her with at least two feet of space between them. So CIA. Clandestine meetings in public. Handoffs and vendettas. "You left the medical center."

He ignored that. "What did the doctor say about your test results?"

"You don't want to know that the cops are taking care of those two kids? Maybe I don't like how it escalated so fast and so violently"—or what she'd done to resolve the situation—"but you did the right thing in protecting them."

He shrugged, and his craggy face and that few days of gray stubble shifted. "I know I did the right thing. Like how I know that...woman? She probably won't make it. Very sad. Those kids will be better off without her."

"If she succumbs to her injuries, it's going to be me who is held responsible." Didn't he realize they'd arrest Kenna for injuring her in a way that led to her death? She wanted to reach over and wring Bruce's neck, but she'd already used a lot of energy today. There wasn't much left in the tank.

"Turns out I know a good lawyer."

Whatever that meant. Kenna let out a long sigh.

"What did the doctor say?"

She explained the short version that she was getting older, probably had anxiety, and was likely overinflating the entire thing, considering the test results only showed elevated calcium. "How can there be nothing wrong with me?"

He shook his head. "Doctors don't know everything."

"They did something to me." Saying it out loud sent a tremor down her spine.

What she wanted to do was curl up in a cold room with hot coffee and cry herself to sleep. But what would that serve? Feeling sorry for herself had never been her thing. Self-pity wasn't going to help her, but she needed to say something out loud. In a way, it would be like exorcising the thought.

"The minute I get even a hint of happily ever after, it gets taken away."

"Is it really going to change things between you and Jax?"

"I don't want to be useless. He deserves the woman he fell in love with."

"In sickness and in health, remember? It's a part of life."

Kenna pressed her lips together and made a face. "I don't like it."

He chuckled, shaking the bench. "Good thing there's nothing wrong with you because you make a terrible patient."

She gasped. "You take that back!"

He laughed.

She listened to it, enjoying the moment. In the middle of being certain they'd done something to her—because why do nothing when she'd been in their grasp?—she could take a second and appreciate what she had. Kenna had never been the kind of person who was always waiting for a better tomorrow. Now that she had what she hadn't even admitted she wanted for a long time, and she was finally enjoying her happily ever after...

"I'm waiting for the other shoe to drop. And it might've happened with that woman." She winced. "I caved her chest in with just my shoulder. How could I do that?"

He patted her shoulder. Left his hand there and gave it a gentle squeeze. "Doesn't feel odd to me. Maybe they did surgery on you. Put in metal joints and stuff. Like Wolverine."

Kenna rolled her eyes. "I don't think I'd have been walking around the next day. I was achy; I wasn't superhuman."

"I guess there's no point in telling you that you shouldn't let what you don't know destroy your happiness."

"Maybe I need to hear it anyway." She glanced around, watching other people enjoy a warm day. Even if she was sweating and wanted to get inside to some air-conditioning. Take a nap. Call Jax and tell him about her day. Make dinner so they could eat together when he got home from work. "I have to go to the store."

"Domesticated Kenna." Bruce chuckled. "Heaven help us all."

She frowned.

"You can leave in a minute."

"What?" She would leave when she pleased, and he had no say in it whatsoever.

He lifted his chin. She looked in the direction he indicated and spotted two women walking toward them. Slender, wearing professional clothes. Completely out of place in a city park. Maybe they were on an outing on their lunch break, getting some fresh, extra-hot air before going back to the office.

Except they were headed right for her.

"Is there a meeting on the calendar I'm not aware of?"

"Hear them out."

She glanced over at him, figuring there was no point in arguing now. Or making a scene by leaving. These two women gave her a vibe. "Members of the resistance?"

"I didn't ask."

Which meant he figured yes but wasn't about to force them to admit it.

She got up, not wanting to remain seated and be at a disadvantage with them standing over her in their power suits with their professionally blown out hair. They hid their strength well, but she spotted telltale signs in the way they moved.

Signs that they could very well be the children that her enemy, the organization *Dominatus*, created in their labs. Crafting genetically superior children and implanting them in high-achieving women whom they had kidnapped for the purposes of breeding. The whole thing was an insane story that she would struggle to believe if it wasn't for the fact she was one of those children.

She stuck her hands in her pockets, which drew up her shoulders and reminded her of that woman. The boy and his injured younger sister, Lila. Wishing his mother was dead so the terror and pain could be over.

She slid her hands out just as the first woman approached, sliding sunglasses to the top of her head. She carried a leather briefcase. The woman with her seemed to be an associate, or she was a bodyguard with a fantastic ability to come across as unthreatening.

The first woman stuck her hand out. "Lisa Romeo."

"Kenna Ban—Jaxton." Maybe she should double-barrel her name, so she could be Kenna Banbury-Jaxton. They shook hands.

The woman's eyes widened. "That's quite a grip you have." She motioned to her friend. "This is my associate, Beth Potter. We're from Hann, Anthony, and Associates."

"Lawyers?" She glanced at Bruce. How had he found

these women? Or had they found him? "What can I do for you?"

"Typically, we specialize in corporate law, but once in a while, we take on specific cases." Ms. Romeo opened her briefcase and drew out a file. "Several years back, we were working one involving a medical research company and the cutting-edge work they were doing with genetic modification. Our client's information will remain confidential. However, it's pertinent that you know she was all set to testify against the company and disappeared the night before."

"Disappeared?" Kenna would take a missing person case right now. Even if she had the cold case that Jax had given her this morning. Anything she could work from her laptop while she rested in bed sounded great. Like ordering a pizza and falling asleep halfway through the third slice while snuggling against Jax's warm chest—

She cleared her throat. "Do you have any idea who took her?"

There was a chance the witness got cold feet and left of her own volition, but if they were talking to Kenna, it was far more likely she'd been taken. Probably killed, since it had been several years.

Ms. Romeo continued, "Despite the fact she was under guard and at a safe house, our security was breached, and the guards were murdered. The witness has never been seen since."

"And you want me to find her?"

Ms. Romeo shook her head and handed over the file. "Actually, we want you to testify."

Kenna opened the front cover and found a photo. A grainy black-and-white image of a Caucasian man in a lab coat with no hair.

Her mind recalled events from just a few weeks ago. She was held captive by a senator, who had been part of *Dominatus*, until her friends killed him and rescued her, along with Jax's sister and mother. She'd seen this bald man. For a few moments, she had woken up in a hospital bed with him standing over her, surrounded by other medical personnel.

"You've seen this man?"

Kenna lifted her head and looked at the woman. "Do you know who he is?"

"Everything we know is in that file."

Kenna's chest tightened, her breaths coming faster now.

Bruce took the file from her hands. "She accepts."

Kenna wasn't going to be told what she was doing. None of them got to decide that for her. "I'll think about it."

These people might come off as resistance, as working within *Dominatus* to take it down, but what if they weren't? They could be lying. What if they were the same people who'd held her captive? Targeted her. Making the right move here didn't just affect her. Her friends had been caught in the crossfire. Jax's family. All of them were vulnerable because Kenna had found out things about her past that her parents never had any intention of telling her.

Her dad, the man who'd raised her to be an investigator.

Her birth mother, or the woman she had believed gave birth to her.

Only one was alive now, and she hadn't seen Amara in weeks. Had no idea where she was or what she was currently doing to take down this evil group. She'd been helping Kenna's sister, who was more like her cousin, recover from being held captive by the same people. Zeyla had been used as an organ donor, and last Kenna had heard, it was slow going with her recovery.

Kenna's parents had long ago agreed to raise her away from everything that she had invited back into her life—or which had been thrust back upon her. Whatever they'd wanted for her life, it hadn't happened.

But the point was that she got to choose. Her road was hers to travel.

Ms. Romeo nodded. "All we ask is that you consider it."

Ms. Potter said, "As you can probably imagine, our firm is committed to seeing justice for our client. No matter how long that takes."

"I'm sure you are." Kenna wasn't going to commit to them or refuse them on the first pass, despite what Bruce had said. Instead, she would turn all this over to Maizie, her tech whiz, and see what she came up with. They needed to do a deep dive on the law firm and each of these lawyers, who she'd have immediately pegged as assets for the resistance, double agents inside *Dominatus*. Problem was, they could just as easily be real agents, not the ones actively trying to undermine the master plan, making them very much a threat.

Not just to Kenna's happily ever after.

Trying to figure out where their allegiance lay made her exhausted.

"Do you know what he did to me?" She motioned to the file. "This doctor."

Ms. Romeo shook her head. "I'm sorry, we don't. Right now, we don't even know where to find him."

So, showing Kenna the file had been a long shot. A way to find out if they had the right guy—if Kenna would have a personal reason to want to nail this guy.

They'd come here on a gamble. Because of Bruce?

Either way, it paid off because she had recognized him right away.

Bruce was more closely connected to the resistance than Kenna. After all, he'd worked with them off and on over the past few years since the CIA had burned him. If she had to guess, he'd sought out her mother Amara and gone after her romantically. According to him, they'd had a *moment* back a few months ago. But it was better not to get involved in Bruce's personal life if she could help it.

He might know these women, even though he'd said he hadn't asked whether they were resistance. He was absolutely the kind of guy who went for plausible deniability.

She shook their hands again, careful not to squeeze too hard. As soon as they were out of earshot, making their way to a car that pulled up to the curb, she turned to Bruce. "How did they contact you?"

"I found them. Did some research on people actively trying to hit back at *Dominatus*, even if they don't realize that's what they're doing. They popped on my radar after their witness gal disappeared." He cleared his throat. "Someone found her, by the way. I had Ramon make a trip to Palm Springs last week. The cops there found her in pieces in a landfill. DNA was a match to what the law firm had on file, but they'd taken out her teeth and cut off her fingers and ears."

"Trying to hinder the police from IDing her?"

He nodded. "Cops didn't know the law firm had a record of her DNA."

"Does the law firm know you accessed their records?"

His lips curled up into a smile that lit his eyes. "Their security system was a challenge. Ramon didn't think I could do it."

Kenna let out a long sigh. "Did you find anything in there that I should know about?"

"We only got what we were looking for. We didn't

invade their privacy or anything." He shrugged. "I'll send the file to Maizie. You've got groceries to buy, right?"

"This conversation isn't done." He'd kept far too much from her. While she wasn't the kind of boss who micromanaged the people under her, she expected them to at least fill her in on what they were working on.

"I expect nothing less." He actually gave her a little bow. "Have a good night."

She watched him walk away with the file, which, she had to admit, did mean it would be uploaded to Maizie faster than Kenna could do it. Having other people help her out was...helpful. Okay, she was tired. It might only be two in the afternoon, but she was fully done for the day.

Whatever was wrong with her...it sucked.

She was so far past drained she couldn't think straight but managed to haul herself around the store and get a few things. As much as she would be able to carry from the car into the house.

Kenna wrestled it in the trunk of her car, and thankfully, the grocery store was barely ten minutes from the town house. She slid into her driver's seat, thinking how great it was going to feel to crawl into bed and take a nap.

Someone walked in front of the car. Probably her mind coming up with an odd apparition because of her fatigue. The person had on white scrubs and an odd, almost porcelain mask. She flinched. The nightmare image affected her to her core. This was not the kind of person she wanted to meet in real life, or even in her dreams.

Something sharp touched her neck. She gasped and reached for it, but her hand never made it that far.

Everything went black.

Chapter Five

"I'm home!" Jax's call rang through the house.

Kenna stared up at the ceiling, coming awake while she listened to him make his way through the house. She shifted on the bed. Fully clothed. Not even under the covers. Instead, it seemed as if she'd slept on top of them.

He appeared in the doorway. "Hey." Soft words, and a soft expression to match. "You took a nap?"

She lifted up far enough to look at herself. A sting of pain pricked her neck and the inside of her left elbow. But that wasn't what caught her attention.

"With my shoes on?" She wiggled her feet and kicked them off, leaving her in her socks. But it didn't fix the problem.

He came over. "Time to get up, or you won't sleep tonight."

Jax held out his hand, and she took it with her right, sitting up. She looked at the scar on her forearm.

He said, "You're out of it. Must've been a good nap. I've been trying to call you for the last hour, but you didn't answer."

She shook her head and looked down at the inside of her left elbow. A red mark, like the spot where a needle had been placed. She'd seen that before through surgeries and being captured by *Dominatus*.

"They did something to me." She shivered, trying to think. "I was in the parking lot outside the grocery store. I felt something." She touched her neck, shifting her hair aside and tilting her head. "Is there a mark on my neck? I think someone stuck me with a needle."

She felt his fingers on the skin of her neck, and he rubbed the spot. She hissed.

"I don't see anything on your neck."

"Someone stuck me with a needle." She showed him her arm. "Look."

Jax crouched in front of her. "You might've scratched yourself. Maybe you had a bad dream."

She looked at the alarm clock on the bedside table. "How is it nearly seven?"

"You slept hard, and now you're feeling disoriented. Give yourself a second, okay? Then we can figure out what happened. Maybe you cut your arm earlier."

None of that made sense, except the disorientation. Everything in her objected to the suggestion she was just confused about her afternoon.

"I know what happened. I was kidnapped." Kenna pushed off the bed, using his shoulder for leverage.

Getting up was a whole lot easier than it normally was, leaving her off-balance. With the heaviness she'd been feeling giving her so much lethargy, as if she wasn't strong enough to carry her own body around, she was more used to having to force herself to move.

She looked down at her arms and legs. "I feel better."

"See." He stood. "Give yourself a few minutes. Your brain will catch up to being awake."

Kenna rolled her shoulders and shifted her weight from one foot to the other. "No, I mean I feel better. Maybe better than I have in a month."

"That's good, isn't it?"

"It's suspicious." She headed for the kitchen, not wanting to fight with him if he really thought she'd just slept hard and dreamed vividly. There was no dreaming the mark on the inside of her elbow. Someone had done something to her in the grocery store parking lot, and she'd lost nearly three hours of time. "How can I not remember driving myself home? Why did I fall into bed with my shoes on?"

"It's possible you were extremely tired."

"I was, but that's not it. I don't drive around on autopilot like I'm unconscious." She looked around the kitchen, trying to figure out if anything was odd. Her keys weren't on the hook where she always put them. She went to the garage and hit the button for the trunk of her car. No groceries.

Kenna checked the cupboards and then the fridge. "Did you put the groceries in the fridge?"

"I only got home a couple of minutes ago. I haven't done anything."

She grabbed a can of juice from the fridge, shook it, and popped the top. Downed the whole thing in just a few gulps, thirsty and hungry at the same time. In fact, she was ravenous. "Why am I starving?"

"Did you eat lunch?"

She had no idea. "I went to the doctor's office, then met Bruce in the park."

"I heard about the kids and that woman Bruce tussled

with. Maybe the adrenaline took more out of you than you realized."

"And maybe I was kidnapped." She showed him her elbow. "Otherwise, how do you explain this?"

"I can't." His expression darkened. "I believe you if that's what you think happened, but we need evidence if we're going to run with a theory."

"Fine." She wandered to the alarm panel. "This was deactivated." She tapped through to the history. "At three thirty-five."

"Is that when you got home?"

"The groceries were put away." Had she really done all that and forgotten about it? Kenna patted her pockets. "Where's my phone?"

"Where's Jolene?" He started to turn away.

Kenna called out, "Can you call my phone so I can find it?"

She went to the living room while he checked the bathroom. After they'd looked in all the rooms and he'd checked for Jolene under the bed, Kenna started opening closet doors. When she opened the hall linen closet, a thin door that held a slender set of shelves inside the small space, Jolene hissed at her from the top shelf. "Jax!"

He appeared at the end of the hall.

"She's in here."

"Did you shut her in the closet?" He reached in and lifted the cat down, setting her on the floor where she trotted off.

She didn't need to get mad at him for suggesting it, but she kind of wanted to. "Why would I have done that? She's only going to mess up all these clean sheets and towels."

"Okay, dumb question. Sorry." He looked at his phone. "Your cell is still ringing."

"I don't hear it." Kenna walked through the house. "Keep it ringing."

She didn't want to miss it because the call had gone to voicemail when she walked right past it. She opened the door to the garage, since that was the only other place to look, and heard the faint sound.

Inside the car...

She crouched and reached under the driver's seat, digging out her dusty phone. "It was under the seat." The call ended, and she wiped it off on her pants. She really did feel better. She was moving more easily, and her body didn't feel so heavy. If someone had taken her this afternoon and done something to her...they'd made her feel better. "This makes no sense."

Jax retrieved the steaks from the fridge. "I'll go fire up the grill. We can eat and figure it out, maybe?"

He probably thought she was going to snap out of this funk if he gave her food. Which, to be fair, usually did work.

Maybe whatever had happened at work today meant he didn't have the bandwidth for the threat of *Dominatus* right now. Which was fine, unless she really had been kidnapped by them this afternoon. That wasn't something either of them could ignore.

Or, at least, *she* couldn't.

He set the packaged steaks on the counter and went to the back patio door. She loved sitting outside in the evening watching the sunset, finally able to share her whole life with Jax. It was part of her happily ever after that she was here full time, not just with her RV temporarily parked in the garage.

He loved his job at the FBI, even if he might have wanted to quit a few times to go on the road and solve cases with her. His work at the bureau gave him access to channels that would be useful in the fight against *Dominatus*.

Kenna called Maizie, who picked up after a couple of rings. She put the phone on speaker and decided to make potatoes, because they made everyone feel better.

"Quiet afternoon?"

"Not exactly." Kenna explained the events of the past fifteen minutes. "My arm hurts where they stuck me with a needle. Can you check—"

"The security cameras. Good idea."

Even before she'd moved in, Jax had installed security cameras inside the house in the kitchen and living room and outside in the front and in the backyard. If she'd supposedly deactivated the alarm when she got home at three thirty-five, there would be no movement logged inside after that because it was set to turn off when she got home. Otherwise, every movement through the house would be constantly tracked and sending notifications to both of them. But it was possible the footage showed something from inside the house.

"Grab your laptop. You can look at the same time."

"Thanks, Maze." Kenna had to make the circuit of the house twice to find where her laptop was, discovering it on the lower shelf of the end table in the living room. "Why is this here?"

She had no idea when she'd put it there or the last time she'd looked at it.

This whole thing was off. Was it her or something that'd been done to her? How was she supposed to figure it out? She sat at the breakfast bar and prayed while her laptop turned on, asking for wisdom.

"Click that."

A window popped up asking for her permission for

someone to remotely log in to her laptop. Kenna accepted the request, and her mouse started moving. Windows opened, and Maizie logged on to the site for the security system.

"I want to see when I came home."

Maizie said, "The outside camera should show you pulling into the garage."

Which meant Jax would have had an alert that she got home. "What time?"

Jax had more information than she did about what had happened to her this afternoon, considering the notification would have told him that she had arrived hours ago. Apart from the groceries being put away, or maybe including that, everything seemed like it added up to her being so tired she had been on autopilot.

But none of that explained the needle mark on the inside of her arm.

Aside from going and getting more blood tests, she couldn't know what they'd done to her. And even if she did that, who was to say the results wouldn't be just the same as the previous round? Nothing was wrong with her except elevated calcium levels.

She sipped more juice, watching Maizie scroll back to three this afternoon. "There it is."

Maizie hit *Play*, and Kenna's car pulled onto the drive. The car stopped in front of the closed garage door, then the door started to roll up.

Jax came back into the kitchen, got a tray and wire rack, and opened the steaks. He laid them on the wire rack and seasoned the meat.

She couldn't really enjoy watching him do that because she had no idea what had happened to her. "I always hit the garage door button when I pass the mailbox. Why would I wait until I was on the drive? If I was out of it, I could've plowed into the garage door and destroyed it."

The car pulled into the garage.

"There's interior footage until the alarm turns off, right?" She wouldn't say, "until I turned the alarm off" because right now she wasn't convinced it had been her in the car.

It would be convenient if this was a ruse. If someone else had brought her car home, unpacked her groceries, and then later—while the alarm was off—put her on the bed so she woke up here at home.

A nice, neat answer to her questions.

But when had life ever given her nice, neat answers?

"Here it is," Maizie said.

Jax washed his hands and came over, drying them off on a kitchen towel. He tossed the towel beside her phone on the counter and stood beside her, one hand braced on the edge of the tile.

She leaned against his side and watched. A woman with dark hair, who looked a whole lot like her, entered the kitchen carrying bags of groceries. Actually, that was all of the bags she'd had in the trunk of her car. The woman never looked at the camera, keeping her head turned away as if she knew where it was and intentionally avoided it.

She moved around the kitchen, putting things away with efficiency.

"I carried all that?" Her arms had been as heavy as the rest of her when she loaded it all into the trunk.

"Looks like it."

"I couldn't get it in the trunk all at once. I had to load one or two bags at a time, and I switched off hands."

"Why would someone pretend to be you just to put your groceries away?"

Kenna looked at him. "You don't have to say it like that."

A tendon in his jaw flexed.

Maizie said, "Maybe we don't know why, but we know what happened."

Kenna looked at the phone, even though she couldn't see Maizie. "What do you mean?"

"Look at her shoes."

The screen shifted, and the image zoomed in on the woman's feet. "Heeled boots."

Maizie asked, "Do you even own a pair of shoes like that?"

"Nope." She looked at Jax.

All his attention remained on the computer screen, a frown drawing his eyebrows together. Even if he hadn't entirely believed her, she still valued the fact he was here.

She gestured at the screen. "That isn't me."

He said, "Maizie, scroll it back."

The woman moved around the kitchen with Jolene standing at the edge of the image. The cat was clearly not happy. Probably why she'd ended up in the hall closet—this woman got so tired of the cat that she stuck her in there.

"I can tell by the way she's moving that isn't you. Not just because you move more slowly than that now." He pointed at the counter. "What is all that?"

Maizie asked, "Are those papers?"

Sprawled across the surface of the counter, some of them ripped and rumpled. The Kenna impersonator had set the groceries on top. "The cold case file." Kenna looked around. "Where is it?"

"She unpacked the groceries and then turned off the alarm. Making it look like you got home." He looked around as well.

She got up to pace a little and think and take her can to

the trash. Which turned out to be the answer. "The papers are here." She tipped the trash over so he could see the torn pages of his file along with the grocery bags in the trash. "They wanted to deceive us, but they didn't focus on the details."

Jax folded his arms across his chest. "Someone was in this house."

From the phone still on the counter, Maizie said, "The cat shredded the file after you guys left this morning. Jolene must've been mad because she went right for those papers and destroyed them. After she was done, the motion alerts stopped, so the camera doesn't record anything else until that woman came home."

"And there's nothing showing when I actually got here?" Kenna tried to think.

Jax said, "Exterior cameras should've shown movement if you were brought in later."

"Checking."

"Text with what you find." Jax hung up the phone.

She shoved the trash can back under the sink and shut the cupboard door, turning to find him in front of her.

"Are you okay?" He hesitated, then slid his arms around her.

"No, not really. But at the same time, I feel better than I have in weeks."

"I don't like this."

"Me, either. But I want answers. I'm not going to pretend nothing is happening to me."

"But your test results showed nothing?"

She told him about the elevated calcium levels. "I'm not going to let this go, even if I don't ever get answers. I'm going to investigate. They did something to me, and I want to know what it is."

Jax didn't say anything.

"Say it, whatever it is. Isn't that the point? Whatever you're thinking or feeling, we deal with it together. Right?"

Jax kissed her, lingering with his nose alongside hers before he pulled back. "They can do whatever they want, manipulate whatever they want, and it seems like there's nothing we can do about it."

"I know you didn't sign up for this. It isn't the start to a marriage that you thought you were going to have, but—"

"Kenna, that's not it." His expression softened. "I knew things wouldn't be normal with an enemy like ours." He dipped his head for a second, then lifted his face so she could see the torn expression there. "How am I supposed to protect you if I'm at the office all day? Even with your team, our enemies still get far too close. They were in our house." His arms tightened around her. "There's nothing we can do to stop them."

She lifted her chin. "We can try."

As far as she was concerned, they were going to regret making her feel better.

Kenna might just have the energy to work this case.

Chapter Six

She muscled open the slider, holding two plates loaded with salad and potatoes. The last two things they needed to complete this meal.

Jax held a spatula in one hand, an open half-drunk bottle of beer on the side of the grill. "Thanks, Ramon. I appreciate it."

She set the plates down on the table and pulled the forks out of her back pocket.

"Got it. Bye." Jax hung up, setting the phone on the table next to the plates and her can of prebiotic soda. "Steaks are done."

She nearly sat, realizing that had become her default for the past few weeks. Slumping into the closest chair because she was so drained she didn't have the energy to do anything else.

Kenna reached above her head, stretching her arms, and bent both ways. The groan she let out felt good.

"You do seem like you're moving better." He set a six-ounce steak on her plate, then lifted his and deposited the ten-ounce on his. "I don't want to assume you're good, though."

"So far, so good." She sat then, and he said a prayer for their meal. "How's Ramon?"

"He's worried about you, so he's gonna wrap up the case he's working in Palm Springs and make his way here."

Ramon seemed to have been purposely giving her and Jax space after they got married. Maybe he assumed that if she stayed with Jax at his house and only worked a local case, she'd stay out of trouble. Maybe have time to be newly-weds without all her coworkers hanging around. Possibly, figure out what *Dominatus* had done to her.

Then she'd seen him a few times, watching out for her.

Bruce said he'd gone and found the woman the lawyers lost.

The sun was just setting on the horizon, turning the sky pink and orange. That view, plus having a good meal and her husband beside her, made the evening about perfect. Nearly perfect enough she could forget everything else.

Except when she reached to cut her steak and saw the pink dot on the inside of her arm, with slightly blue bruising on one side of it.

She sighed. "I really want to know what's going on."

"We know you lost time, and we know someone else unloaded the groceries, cleaned up the mess of shredded paper the cat made, and shut her in the closet."

"Making it look like I just came home and took a nap." She ate a bite of steak that was groanworthy. "Which makes me wonder if that's happened any other times in the past two months."

He ate a bite of his meal, saying nothing. Enjoying the silence, or not wanting to start a fight. Life wasn't ever going to be perfect, but talking it through was better than not. Right?

She glanced over. "What are you thinking?"

Jax took a sip of his beer and sat back in the chair. "It's easier to keep it to myself rather than unload and cause you to have to carry that weight along with everything else."

"I want to know."

"And I don't want to burden you with my issue."

That was going to put them at an impasse. There was no resolution to both of them wanting to support the other but going about it differently. Their intentions were for good for each other. They just disagreed on how to go about it.

"I feel good today. Better than I have in weeks." Kenna leaned back in her chair, shifting her knees toward him so she faced him a little better. "You, a great meal, and the sunset. Hit me with it. I want to know how you're doing with all this."

He stared at her. "You're going to think I'm crazy."

"With our lives? I find that unlikely." She smiled.

He smiled back, but it didn't last long. "I was...actually kind of hoping." He paused. "That you were pregnant."

"With a *Dominatus* baby?"

He shrugged.

"You were hoping I was having a baby." Having a child might not be conducive to the kind of life she lived, working cases. Not being on the road all the time, settling here, had changed things. But did that mean she was ready?

Maybe she would never feel ready to go down that road.

He asked, "Why not?"

Kenna chuckled. "There are always reasons why not."

"And a whole lot of reasons why as well. There are a lot

of reasons for and against it. Ours. Theirs. It's an innocent baby that deserves to be safe and cared for."

"Doesn't mean we have to jump into that right away. If we have kids, I should probably retire from private investigation. Become a consultant or something."

"You wanna get a nine-to-five gig?"

She shrugged. Her thoughts went to those kids from the medical center this morning. They'd need to be taken care of now that their mother was—hopefully, for their good— out of the picture. "Maybe we could adopt."

"I've thought about that." Something shifted in his expression, and he looked almost nervous when he asked, "Were you hoping that you *weren't* pregnant?"

She would've been actively preventing it now that they were married, but the risk to a baby in the event she'd been impregnated by her enemies meant her options were limited. "I was prepared to embrace it if it happened. Even knowing it would be a child that was genetically altered like me. No way was I going to let an innocent baby suffer just because they wanted me as an incubator. I would've given my life to protect that child. And knowing them, it would have been a very real possibility."

"There's a whole lot of honor in you, Kenna Jaxton."

Her lips curled up at the edges. "Unless I'm fed up and tired and, let's face it, probably hungry and *so over* the whole thing. In which case, you'll find me all up in their faces screaming bloody murder about how they're ruining my happily ever after, controlling my life, and I don't like any of it."

"You're better at living in the moment and rolling with the punches than anyone I know."

She wrinkled her nose, taking a sip from her soda can. "I don't want to get punched anymore. I've had enough punches." She glanced at him. "Isn't life just supposed to be plain sailing after you get married? I didn't think I got the angst and problems package. Did you?"

He smiled around the rim of his beer. "In this life, you will have trouble?"

"I'm all for *taking heart*, but some peace would be good."

"Peace in the storm?"

"No, no storms. I want at least a week of quiet and feeling like this."

"Mmm. I could take a few days off. We could get lost somewhere no one will find us." His tone sounded wistful, almost dreamy.

"That sounds like an invitation I want to accept."

She hadn't been so self-absorbed as to not realize he was carrying different kinds of burdens. Having to work. Knowing she didn't feel good. Worrying, as she was, that it could be something serious or that she was pregnant with a baby he'd raise as his own but would always know wasn't his.

"Even if you wind up pregnant?"

Kenna sighed. "Anytime is a good time to be pregnant."

"Is that really true?"

Maybe not, but that wasn't her point. "While married. When it's you and me. I can say that honestly now, because I've lived the story where things got out of order. But what I mean is, anytime is a terrible time as well."

"I don't follow." He shook his head, taking another bite of steak.

"There are always reasons it might be inconvenient or heartbreaking or the wrong time. But the trade-off is something beautiful. A life that connects us. A child we made that we can raise together."

"Lord willing."

She nodded. "People take it for granted, I think. It seems like an everyday occurrence, and for some people, it just happens easily. Others have to fight for years to get pregnant. The road is long and hard and painful or even heartbreaking."

"And you've seen both sides of it."

"I have." She looked at the wide expanse of sky behind the house. "I've done the wrong thing and had the best results, or so I thought. I've been as low as a person can get, and now I'm happier than I have any right to be. But with a cloud over my head. I'd rather just enjoy it."

"Life doesn't come with no worries."

She knew what he meant. "Really? Let's sell everything we have and move to Aruba. Live in a hut on the beach. Then you can tell me you still have worries."

He chuckled, finishing his meal.

Kenna snagged a couple more potatoes and stood. She went over to Jax's chair and slid one knee beside his hip on the cushion. She leaned the other knee on the other side and didn't quite put her weight on his lap. She didn't want to squish him with her recent weight gain—the additional mass she'd accumulated while remaining the same size.

Didn't make any sense to her, but it was what it was.

He set his hands on her hips and pulled her fully onto his lap. *Guess he doesn't agree.* She settled there with his arms around her. Hers resting on his shoulders with her fingers linked behind his head. "Now I remember all the things we need to talk about."

He shook his head. "No talking."

She chuckled. "Sorry, it doesn't work that way."

Before she was even finished saying that, he'd tugged her close against his chest and kissed her. Kenna pushed everything out of her conscious awareness except for the feel of her husband and the moment they were sharing right now. All of it went on hold while she reveled in the feel of his lips against hers.

She rested her forehead against his and touched his cheeks. "You'd make a great father."

"Anytime. You just say when."

Kenna kissed him again, enjoying that he wanted to raise a family with her. *Anytime.* She could get on board with that. On one hand, why should they put their lives on hold just because of a dangerous enemy? But on the other hand, having a child would make them so much more vulnerable. These people were deadly serious, would stop at nothing, and might snatch any child they had. Kenna might be too weak to stop them.

If only she could be strong enough to protect her family, no matter what happened.

The sliding door opened, and someone came out.

"Don't mind me." Bruce stepped onto the patio, carrying one of Jax's beers, and took Kenna's seat. "How are you folks tonight? No more kidnappings?"

She sighed, shifting on Jax's lap to face Bruce. Jax tugged her so she leaned her shoulder against his chest. "Oh, you know. Same old. Enjoying a quiet evening in. Just the two of us."

Bruce sipped the beer. "Don't blame you. It's nice out here."

She sighed. Jax chuckled, and she felt it under the palm of her hand—the one braced on his chest. She was probably squashing him, but he didn't seem to mind. He could shift her off him at any time. She kind of liked it right here.

"There's no more steak," Jax said. "We only defrosted two."

Bruce waved a hand. "I already ate. Then Maizie called and told me the story of your afternoon. And I thought this morning was exciting."

"No one got thrown through a window here," she said.

Bruce grinned. "Night is still young."

Kenna frowned. "Is there a reason for your visit?"

"I installed some more sensors, more cameras, took care of some other business. Maizie is rebooting your security system. Once it's live, I'll get out of your hair. But we need a plan for this doctor guy." He took another sip of beer. "First thing tomorrow, let's roust the guy out. Make him tell us what he did to you."

"You're all in with this law firm?"

"I looked into them. They're practically famous—in certain circles, anyway." He sat back in the chair, looking at the yard. "You guys should put in a pool out here."

Jax said, "The neighborhood has a community pool."

"You could fit one in here." Bruce waved at the grass. "It would be more private."

She asked, "Can we get back to the subject at hand?"

Bruce glanced over. "You mean how to take down these sons of—"

"Yes, that. We have a lot of work to do. First thing, not tonight. We need a full background on this doctor, and I need to look into a cold case."

Jax said, "The cold case can go on the back burner. Your health is more important."

She heard a trace of worry in his tone and didn't like it.

"We also need to talk to that doctor lady," Bruce said. "'Cause if she falsified your test results or was paid to tell you that you're fine, we need to know."

"She probably has nothing to do with this." Kenna figured that given how quickly they'd kicked her out and told her not to come back, it meant they were good people. She was the threat to them as far as they were concerned. "I want a follow-up on those kids, though. Make sure they're placed with a good family."

Nicola Santorini didn't need to be in the line of fire just because they'd brought the woman into this. If Nicola had nothing to do with it, then Kenna wouldn't make her a target.

"I have an initial report on the doctor guy," Bruce said. "Top of his class at Harvard medical. Forty years ago now. Since then? Nothing. The guy has been completely off-grid. No employment record. Not listed as practicing anywhere."

"So he isn't a licensed physician." Great. She had some hack, who'd started with promise but now operated with no oversight, messing with her while she couldn't fight back. "I'm feeling the need to dissociate with a cold case."

"I'll take a vacation." Jax squeezed her hip. "We can work it together."

Bruce saluted them with his bottle. "Bon voyage. I'll take care of the doctor while you're gone."

"Thanks for offering." But he knew she wasn't going to do that.

Bruce made a face. "Figures you'd say that."

"I want to know what he did to me."

"I can find out for you." Bruce shrugged. "Ramon will help. And Maizie. You take some time off and don't worry about it."

She sighed. That did sound extremely tempting. "We'll see."

She was about to tell him to get lost when his phone buzzed, and he looked at the screen. "Reboot is done. I'll get out of your hair." Bruce eased out of the chair, and she heard his hip pop. He groaned out a sigh. "I could use some of that mojo of yours. The kind that caves someone's chest in."

She pressed her lips together and didn't look at Jax. "Bye, Bruce."

"Have a good one." He closed the slider behind him.

Jax asked, "You caved a chest in?"

"I thought you heard about what happened." She shifted on his lap and still didn't look at him. "You knew about the woman and the kids."

"I'm definitely taking time off."

Chapter Seven

Kenna reached up and scratched her nose, only half awake. Her arm moved faster than she expected, and she smacked herself in the face. "Ow." She started to sit up, bracing against the weight on her chest. But it wasn't her. The weight was the cat. "Jolene, get off me."

Meow.

She shoved the cat to the side and saw the clock. Not even six in the morning. Usually the time Jax woke up, but given he'd opted to take the day off, he was fast asleep beside her.

She slid out of the bed, padding softly to the door so she didn't wake him and grabbing her robe on the way. Jolene walked ahead of her down the hall. The cat hung out in the bathroom, meowing the whole time Kenna took care of pressing business. The cat waited expectantly in the spot where her bowl was placed until Kenna had mixed wet and dry food and set it on the floor.

Jax had ground the coffee beans and filled the pot the night before, so she hit the button and went to her favorite spot in the living room, where she had her Bible on the side table.

She curled her feet under her, getting in the Word before she picked up her phone.

Whatever emergencies might be on that device, things she'd have to face once she looked at her messages and emails, she would be better equipped to deal with them after she'd absorbed what God had to say.

Her mind wandered to their conversation yesterday. Jax had been so worried about her and hadn't shared his concerns—or that he'd been hoping she was pregnant. He had intentionally not given her more to carry, adding his burden on top of the worry about what was happening to her but keeping it inside. It turned out they'd both wished that she was pregnant, accepting that as a very real outcome of her time as a captive.

The coffeepot beeped. She headed to it, poured herself a cup, and drank it while she stared out the kitchen window.

"You got up." His voice sounded like gravel.

Kenna turned to see Jax walk in, sweatpants low on his hips and no shirt. Hair mussed from sleep and a crease on one cheek.

He commandeered her coffee and took a sip.

"Sacrilege," she breathed.

He wound his arms around her hips and lifted her, sitting her on the counter and moving to stand between her knees.

"What are you doing?" She lifted a brow.

"Saying good morning."

"Good morning."

He smiled and leaned in to kiss her. Things were getting interesting—and she'd almost forgotten that coffee existed—when her phone rang from the breakfast bar counter. He growled, "Ignore it."

He must be happy that she felt better and that he had the day off. She was willing to forego any work on cases at all and spend the day just enjoying each other's company. A much-needed Sabbath to recharge and just hang out. Or a short interlude before the day got going.

After a shower and a plate of bacon and eggs, she finally called Maizie back.

The video call on her phone connected, and she saw Maizie in the trailer, her blond hair loose on either side of her face. "Hey, what's up? I've been going through the file those lawyers gave Bruce. You're going to want to hear this."

Jax wandered over and set a cup of coffee on the breakfast bar where she'd slid onto a stool. He leaned in and kissed the side of her neck while Kenna tried to get the phone to stand upright.

"You guys." Maizie blushed.

Kenna smiled.

Jax said, "Morning, Maze. What was in the file?" He settled onto the stool beside her, and she moved the phone so Maizie could see both of them.

Maizie glanced to the side, her focus going distant. "A full file on the doctor. Bruce said you guys talked about that. There's a collection of news articles from papers with dates spanning forty years. Some guy moved a car and saved a child. Another guy saved a bunch of people from a fire, carrying two or three at a time to get them out of the burning building."

"Wow." Jax leaned against her shoulder, and she shifted so her leg was against his.

"I know. There's also a long research paper about modifying RNA to control osteoblasts and osteoclasts."

Kenna sipped her coffee. "What does that mean?"

"Elizabeth and Craig have that. They're going to figure out what it's about."

The couple took care of Maizie, who lived in an Airstream in their backyard. Retired and living in a remote Colorado cabin, they could watch out for the teen full time, and Elizabeth was a trained counselor. Craig Stairns had been Kenna's boss at the FBI years ago, back when she'd been an agent. Now he unofficially worked for her team at Banbury Investigations, and his skills meant he was on hand to protect Maizie when needed.

The teen said, "I looked some of it up, but I was confused. I don't think I'm destined to be a nurse or doctor. But RNA is ribonucleic acid, which is a molecule. It's a messenger that carries genetic information."

"And they messed with mine. I need you to dig up a coroner's file. Bruce will know which one I'm talking about. Tell him we need the witness exhumed and for tests to be run to see if the same thing was done to her."

Jax shifted, probably because he had questions, and she hadn't managed to fill him in on everything.

"Anything else?" Maizie typed on her computer.

"You tell me." Kenna drank some more coffee, even though she should switch to water at this point in the day. "Nothing on the exterior cameras?"

"Nope, but the lawyers reached out this morning. They want to know if you've had a chance to look at the file and if you're willing to come in today. There's something else pertinent they need to talk to you about."

"Not wasting any time on this, are they?" She sighed. "Call and tell them we'll be there as soon as they have an opening."

"Got it."

They signed off and hung up. Kenna finished her coffee and slid off the stool. "Guess we have an appointment."

Jax smiled. "You're definitely feeling better."

"It's nice not feeling weighed down and exhausted."

"Don't use it up fast. Just in case it isn't going to last."

She figured he had a point. "It's hard to tell, but I get what you're saying. We can take it easy today, even though that sounds incredibly boring. Which means I need another copy of that cold case. That way, I can do some research later if I need to rest."

"You're going to work the case? I figured you have enough going on that maybe you didn't really need it."

"I always need a case." She kissed his cheek and went to grab her socks and shoes from the closet.

Just a reflex, but the sentiment hung on in her mind. She did always need a case, and mostly it was just what she did. What she always wanted to be doing. For a long time, it had been what defined her, what kept her going and kept her sane.

If she didn't have a case to solve?

Just weeks ago, she'd have said her value wasn't much beyond her ability to investigate crimes. Maybe at one point in the past, she'd have said she was nothing without it. These days, with being married and having a thriving group of friends who helped her out, things were a lot different. But being an investigator still defined her.

Meeting Jax, saving Maizie, and finding each of her friends had changed her life. But who she was would always be wrapped up in the way she'd been raised.

Taking this cold case and working it was about being who she was.

Saying to the *Dominatus* that they couldn't control her life. She was still going to do what she did, and they weren't going to change her. It felt good to thumb her nose at the big bad company. Like standing up against a bully.

She found Jax in his office, taking papers off the printer. "Ready to go? Maizie said the lawyers are available."

"Ready." He stuffed the papers into an empty file and brought them with him, grabbing his keys.

She got in the passenger's side, flipped open the file, and leafed through the pages to read the cold case information as he drove across town to the office for Hann, Anthony, and Associates.

A Mafia boss had gone missing. At the same time, an FBI agent disappeared, and the gold the Mafia boss had supposedly stolen from another Vegas casino owner at the time had never been found. She looked for the Santino name, but it was nowhere in this file. Not that she'd expected it to be connected to the same family as Nicola Santorini. She wouldn't have been surprised if it had been, though.

She skimmed the page. "Did the bureau talk to the casino owner?"

"Airtight alibi. He had no idea what happened to either of them. He also said the gold wasn't stolen, but that it was a payment for something."

"So he wasn't looking for it and didn't care that it was gone?" She flipped another page. "If it was up for grabs after their disappearance, maybe he went after it later."

Jax said, "Or he's the one who killed them both and took back his gold. But the man the bureau had embedded undercover in his casino said he didn't have it and wasn't going after it. He didn't care at all, apparently. He wanted nothing to do with it. The statement said he actually thought the boss was scared of something or someone else, so he was staying out of it."

"Very interesting."

Jax pulled into the parking lot.

It turned out there were more lawyers on the payroll than the two she'd met at the park. The law firm had a huge office, six stories tall, which took up the entire corner lot in the commercial park. The exterior was all black and glass.

"Impressive."

"Hmm." Jax shut off the car.

"What?"

"I don't know yet."

She figured he had some idea, so as they walked together across the packed parking lot to the front doors, she asked, "What *do* you know?"

"They found you. How easy is that? Not only did they find you, but they know something happened to you?"

She explained that she figured it might've been Bruce who approached them, regardless of what he'd said to her. "They had a picture of the doctor, and I recognized him right away. I know it's him that did...whatever it is he did to me."

Jax nodded. "That's what I'm worried about."

"I still think they're resistance. They just have that look about them."

The doors swished open ahead of them. Kenna blinked against the brightness of the expansive lobby that stretched up at least three stories with balconies overlooking from the floor above. All of it was bright white, even the couches. Even the fake plants in the corners were white and the artwork on the walls.

They headed to the receptionist, a shock of color in this ocean of stark whiteness. Strawberry-blond hair, blue eyes, and a green dress. She had a matching suit jacket on the back of her chair and a headset that covered one ear, the mic resting along her cheek.

"Welcome, Ms. Banbury." She looked at Jax. "Special Agent in Charge Jaxton." Nodded. "I'll inform the partners that you're here."

"Thanks." Kenna turned from the woman and put her back to the counter. She raised her brows to Jax. "This place is obviously a front."

Jax gave her a knowing smile, as if he thought her being mischievous was adorable.

She leaned over the reception desk toward the woman. "What is this place, really? I mean, this isn't just a law office. Is the resistance operating in Arizona? Another fake company with no real clients, and the people you do deal with...it's heavily weighted toward your agenda."

Kenna looked at her nameplate on the counter. "Taylor Newport? Is that even your real name?"

The receptionist tapped a button on the desk phone's keypad and spoke low into her headset, but Kenna couldn't make out what she was saying. Probably calling for security or reporting to them that Kenna was already acting unhinged.

She needed them to think she was a wild card—someone they couldn't control. But maybe not this early, when she hadn't even found out what they wanted with her. They might have information on her lost time from the day before and why she felt better today than she had in weeks.

These lawyers knew who the doctor was. He'd been there when that senator captured her a couple of months ago, before the wedding. What else did they know?

This was like fighting a battle blindfolded.

Jax shifted and looked up at the balcony. Something up there was drawing his attention. "Couple of cops are here."

Kenna spun to see but didn't recognize either of the uniformed detectives. They weren't any of the cops she'd met so far in this town. "I should check on Terri."

"Huh?"

"The woman from Friday night. They took her to the hospital, but under arrest." She lowered her voice so the receptionist, Taylor Newport—if that was really her name—couldn't hear what she said. "If these lawyers want anything, they can agree to represent her in exchange."

Why were there cops here?

This wasn't a good sign. Especially not when the cops looked over the railing from the floor above and spotted them, then immediately moved toward the stairs. As if they'd been waiting for her.

Kenna's phone rang in her pocket. "Why does this smell like a trap?"

She pushed off the reception counter, and her phone rang again. When she pulled it out, she saw it was Maizie calling. Kenna swiped the screen. "Give me a reason to ditch this meeting, Maze."

"The doctor you saw yesterday, the one who ran those blood tests? She's missing. So is the woman you and Bruce tussled with. The doctor never got home last night, and the other woman, the kids' mother, literally vanished out of the hospital. They're both gone."

Chapter Eight

The doctor and the mother.

Both of them missing.

Kenna pulled a chair out and sank into it across the table from the two detectives, both men. The older one, with dark hair and a little gray on the sides, was Detective Orlando. The other was Detective Pendleton, who had blond hair and light eyes.

Kenna's self-proclaimed lawyer, who'd introduced herself as Heather Pickett, sat beside her. She had brown hair, pulled back and pinned up, and blue eyes. Apparently, it didn't matter that they'd never met. This woman was here to represent her. Or to ensure she didn't reveal too much about what might very well be a resistance operation?

The lawyer's motives weren't clear.

So long as Kenna didn't end up in jail for something, she was willing to compromise. Maybe.

The blond officer, Detective Pendleton, opened a notepad on the table in this sparse conference room with zero personality. Probably by design. He cleared his throat and asked her a few basic questions. Her name and date of birth and whether she had a valid private investigator license in Arizona, which she did now. "What brings you to Phoenix, Ms. Banbury?"

"I live here now."

That made the two of them perk up.

She glanced between them. "What's this about?"

Pendleton said, "I have two different police reports from the last few days with your name on them. Are you... working a case in Phoenix? Maybe something that the police should be aware of?"

"Something that would get a doctor and a patient mysteriously kidnapped?" Kenna wasn't going to mention her own mysterious kidnapping—assuming that's what had happened to her yesterday—at least, not at first. She might need the information to corroborate something she said to them, but likely it would only invite more questions.

Both of their eyebrows rose.

"I'd love to act surprised to hear that Doctor Nicola Santorini and...the mother of those abused children—I don't know what her name is—have both gone missing, but the fact is my office assistant called me just a moment ago while I was in the lobby and informed me."

"Because it's relevant to your case?" Pendleton asked.

So far, her lawyer hadn't intervened in anything Kenna said. Heather sat beside her, making notes in shorthand on a legal pad. At some point, she might cut Kenna off or advise her not to answer a question. Hopefully, before she incriminated herself. It was all a guessing game, though.

"I don't currently have a case I'm working involving the doctor or that woman." Kenna explained about Friday night and how she'd been paid by Terri Fleming to investigate her business partner, then discovered that Fleming had also been embezzling money from the business. "I had an appointment at the doctor's office yesterday."

"Regarding what?"

Kenna said, "That would be private medical information."

Heather lifted her chin, ready to argue on Kenna's behalf.

"Very well." Detective Pendleton nodded. "Ms. Banbury, where were you yesterday between four fifty-two and midnight?"

"Most of that time, I was with my husband." She figured the fact Jax was FBI would add credence to her alibi, even if they'd insisted he not be present for this conversation.

"And the rest of the time?"

"Jax didn't get home until almost seven, and before that, I was sleeping."

"Alone?"

She nodded.

Pendleton said, "So, no one else can confirm your whereabouts during that time?"

"I can tell you what time the security system was deactivated when I arrived at home. I believe it was around three thirty."

Heather glanced at her, then made a note on her legal pad.

As far as all of them should be concerned, it was Kenna who'd come home then. She knew it wasn't her, and Jax might not lie under oath.

Okay, fine. He definitely wouldn't lie.

More likely, he'd say it *appeared* to be her that entered the kitchen. Only if the cross-examiner picked up on the tiny note of him hedging would they ask further questions and get to the bottom of the fact it wasn't Kenna. She had no idea where she'd been nor when she was really brought home.

"I must have been completely exhausted because I hardly remember getting home, and when my husband showed up, I was only just waking up."

Hopefully, that answer was going to satisfy these two.

Time to change the subject. "How did the mother manage to leave the hospital? Wasn't she under police custody? Do you have footage that shows her being taken out or leaving of her own volition?"

The older detective shifted in his seat. "Are you attempting to imply that it's the fault of the officer watching her?"

Heather touched the table in front of Kenna. "My client is certainly not commenting on the professionalism of the Phoenix Police Department. But if she's being accused of kidnapping or some such crime, she has a right to ask questions. The answers to which will enable her to defend her case."

"So she can explain how she caved a woman's chest in, and only hours later, that woman has gone missing from the hospital?" Pendleton asked.

Kenna said, "What reason would I have to take her from police custody? I only met her that morning. The first thing she did when I attempted to defuse the fight between her and another man was rush me, forcing me to defend myself. Aside from those seconds of contact, I haven't spoken to the woman or ever met her in any way. I don't even know her name, and I never saw her again after that incident at the medical center."

"Right," the older detective said. "This 'other man' you mentioned. An associate of yours, I presume? The cops who responded said you told the children he was a spy."

"They were scared kids. It seemed like a good way to distract them." Truth.

"He disappeared before they could get his information or talk to him about what happened."

Kenna said, "I have no idea where you'd find him now." Which was also the truth.

Her lawyer said, "It's not my client's responsibility to do the police's job for them. You expect her to hand over this person?"

"They know each other, don't they?" the detective asked.

Kenna said, "I'm not sure I'd say I really know him." Also not untruthful.

The lawyer touched the table again, so Kenna stopped there.

Heather said, "We asked you here as a courtesy to ensure from the outset of the investigation that the police department doesn't waste their time looking for the wrong suspect—my client. As we've done that, and she's explained that she had no contact with either of the missing women after yesterday morning, I believe this conversation is at its end." She stood. "My associate will see you out."

The door opened, and another woman, a brunette, stepped in, holding the door open. "If you'd come this way."

"Thank you, Tina." Heather collected her things, slipping her notepad into a briefcase on the floor and effectively dismissing the two detectives. Such a power move.

Kenna managed not to smile because it would look too much like gloating.

The cops didn't like being told the chat was over, but they didn't argue either. When they were gone, Kenna and Heather went out into the hall.

Kenna asked, "Where did you guys stash Jax while we were talking?"

It probably would've looked too much like she felt she needed defending to have both an FBI agent and a lawyer in the room with her.

Heather said, "This way. I believe he's speaking with Ms. Romeo."

Kenna smelled coffee but didn't know where it was coming from, and no one offered her a cup. Heather took her to a corner office one floor up with a slender woman at a desk out front, speaking on the phone.

Heather asked, "Is she in?"

The woman nodded, covering the phone with her hand. "You can go in," she whispered. Then she said into the phone, "I've explained our position thoroughly."

Heather opened the double doors into the office, and Kenna saw Jax was sitting at one end of a leather couch. Lisa Romeo sat on an armchair to the left, and both of them had mugs in hand.

He smiled when he spotted her. "How did it go?"

Kenna shrugged. "Not much I can say to help them, apart from convincing them to scratch me off their suspect list." She slumped down on the couch right beside him, and he handed over his mug. She took a long drink from his coffee and handed it back.

"Keep it. It was for you."

She smiled at him. "What are you guys talking about?"

Jax motioned to the lawyer. "Ms. Romeo was explaining about the disappearances of those two women being a federal matter."

"Is it?" She glanced between them.

The lawyer, Lisa Romeo, seemed like she might be in charge of this whole operation if the size of her office was anything to go by. But who knew? Maybe all of their offices looked like this.

Ms. Romeo said, "Special Agent Jaxton's access to the case, if it was under the jurisdiction of the FBI, would only be a benefit."

"To whom?" Because these lawyers needed to explain whose side they were on before Jax would do them any favors.

"We're all working toward the same end."

Kenna had heard that speech before. "So we should work together? That's usually not an arrangement that works out to my benefit."

"You got Bruce out of it, didn't you? And you met your mother." She set her cup on an end table. "How is Zeyla doing?"

If these lawyers were actually part of the resistance, they probably knew more than she did about her cousin—sister—whatever she was. "Zeyla was moved to a long-term care facility so she can continue her recovery. Physical therapy, things like that. I'm hoping we can get together in a few months when she's on her feet."

"How wonderful."

It was impossible to tell if this woman was being sincere or not. "Did you ask me here so you could ambush me into making a statement to the police?"

"Of course not. That was simply a box we could easily check off. All part of the service."

"Do you take pro bono cases?"

"Terri Fleming?"

How did she know exactly what Kenna had been thinking? Unless Taylor Newport at the reception desk had overheard and passed on the throwaway comment Kenna had made.

"We're already looking into Ms. Fleming's case. She currently has a public defender assigned to her, but if one of the associates decides to take the case, then that's what we'll be doing."

But not because it would make Kenna owe them a favor.

Kenna took another swig of coffee. "So what was the other reason you asked me here?"

"I assume you've filled your husband in about the doctor you identified? And read the file we gave you about Doctor Buzard?"

Kenna shrugged. "I didn't really have time to read the file after he kidnapped me yesterday." But Maizie was on it, hence the morning update.

The lawyer actually flinched. "Excuse me?"

"I lost some time yesterday. I was drugged and dumped back at my house later. Now I feel better than I have in weeks with no explanation except for a needle mark on the inside of my elbow."

Ms. Romeo lifted a phone from beside her mug and tapped out a message, more forcefully than necessary.

"Guess your people didn't inform you of that."

"We don't have you under surveillance, Kenna. We'd like to work with you to take down the doctor."

"I have the information you gave me, some of which was a little confusing since I don't know how it relates." Aside from a basic rundown on the doctor, there had been a genetic research paper and news articles of astounding feats.

Nothing like crushing someone's chest in with one shoulder check. Thankfully, Kenna hadn't killed the woman because she hadn't known what she was capable of. That would've been awful.

"Is the disappearance of the doctor and that woman yesterday connected to this Doctor Buzard guy?"

Ms. Romeo said, "We aren't certain, but we're looking into it."

"Anything else you'd like to share?" Kenna asked.

"I'm still reeling from the idea of you being captured just yesterday by him." She set a hand on her front. "And you say you're feeling better?"

"For now, at least."

Jax squeezed her shoulder.

Ms. Romeo said, "My people will work on the more recent missing persons. If you could follow up with the people in the file, we would appreciate it. The men referenced in those newspaper articles are men we believe the doctor experimented on during his time in covert government work. They may have been some of his original subjects, and if that's the case, they might be able to help you understand what was done to you."

She'd probably just been hoodwinked into doing what they wanted her to do.

But what else was new?

"You're going to look into Nicola Santorini and that other woman?"

Ms. Romeo nodded.

At least the kids had been taken somewhere safe by those two cops. Everything else wasn't turning out to be quite so simple.

Kenna stood, and Jax did the same behind her. "Okay, I'll admit I do want to know what happened to me. Enough to track down these guys."

The lawyer nodded. "Then we're in agreement."

Chapter Nine

"This is where they live?" Jax stepped into the retirement home's main building beside her.

She took in the décor of the lobby with its vaulted ceiling. The whole place had a hospital vibe, and the plants looked fake. Some facilities opted for the log cabin décor, which was preferable to this one that looked like it was for colonoscopies and asking invasive questions. But it was a toss-up as to which of those activities was worse.

Kenna shivered. "This place reminds me of a rehab facility I stayed in just outside of Reno."

He looked at her.

"After what happened in Salt Lake City, the first time, my arms needed physical therapy, and it meant being an inpatient."

He gave her a soft smile, then his attention shifted over her shoulder. "Come on, Dad. The nice people are waiting."

She glanced back, trying not to grin, and spotted Bruce.

The buttons of his shirt were offset, misaligned so one side hung lower than the other. A Hawaiian shirt—not something all that unusual for him to be wearing—but the amount of hairy chest he showed was different. That, and the gold chain around his neck.

He wore linen pants and loafers with no socks. She bit her lip to keep from smiling and headed toward the desk at the far end. The cheesy knickknacks on top made it seem as if this was a budget hotel mixed with a medical facility. She said quietly to Jax, "This place doesn't know what it's trying to be."

"All five of them are registered as living here, according to Maizie. But the names are so generic they're all clearly fake names."

They'd driven over from the lawyer's office because why waste time when there were leads to work and missing people to find? The two disappearances probably weren't connected, but it was possible. After all, they could have been targeted because of her. She was the thing that connected them to this Doctor Marcus Buzard.

After they'd called Bruce and explained the plan, and gotten him to agree to meet them here, Jax had ranted for a while in the car about what he wanted to do when he got his hands on the doctor. She'd told him that meant he should get his FBI people on it, but he didn't want to put any of his agents or analysts on a personal problem. Even one with such a potentially wide-reaching impact.

This was a problem the whole world faced, even if most of the people on the planet had no idea that a secret organization sought to direct people's lives. Countries. Businesses.

The moment Jax got official FBI people on the case, it would get flagged by *Dominatus*, and their enemy would know exactly how close they were to uncovering the truth.

And taking them down.

"How can I help you?" The guy behind the desk wore

khaki slacks and a white shirt with a bow tie. He had a name tag that read *Sigil* pinned to his shirt.

Jax said, "Mr. and Mrs. Watson. We have an appointment for a tour." He motioned to Bruce. "This is Mr. Abrams, my father-in-law. We're looking for a long-term care facility for him and his wife."

They'd explained to Bruce that he didn't need to act senile or combative about the prospect of moving to a care home. But she wouldn't put it past him to come up with an act so he could stomp around a bit and draw attention to himself. He probably figured that meant people would pay less attention to Kenna and Jax.

"Of course." He lifted a clipboard from the desk beside the ancient desktop computer and walked to the end of the counter. "I'll give you a quick tour, then you have a meeting scheduled with our general manager, and at the end, we can take care of any pesky paperwork."

"Great." Kenna smiled. "I've never liked that official stuff, anyway."

They followed him down the hall, and Bruce squeezed between Kenna and Jax to walk right behind Sigil. "Does this place have bingo? What about trivia night?"

The employee hugged his clipboard. "We have plenty of amenities as well as a full calendar of activities for you to enjoy during your stay here."

"Oh," Bruce said. "Well, I don't want to be busy all the time. And will those things be loud? I need my beauty sleep 'cause if I'm real tired, I have nightmares about the time I spent locked up in a French prison. They don't treat you very well in those places. Not that there aren't worse ones. Now Russia? Boy, that gulag is a bad piece of—"

Kenna cleared her throat.

"Sorry. Forgot I'm not supposed to talk about all that

'classified' stuff now. I'm losing my marbles." He hissed. "My bad. Isn't that what the kids say these days?"

Jax choked on a laugh.

Kenna nearly slapped them both up the backside of the head.

Sigil looked like he saw the need for some damage control. "While we have residential rooms inside the main building here, we also have a number of cabins in the outlying areas of the property where we invite any guests who need a little more...space to reside. The activities and amenities are available to anyone, as much—or as little—as they'd like."

"Good, 'cause I'm feelin' some mini golf." He slapped Sigil on the shoulder.

"We do have mini golf." Sigil coughed.

"That's what I'm talkin' about, Turkey!"

Sigil pushed out the door, and Bruce followed. The employee looked at them as they exited, so she couldn't make a face at Jax and wordlessly communicate how ridiculous Bruce was. Though, admittedly, the guy seemed to be thoroughly enjoying himself. And he was entertaining.

She smiled politely at Sigil. "Thank you."

Jax put his hand on the small of her back. "I love mini golf as well. We'll have to visit dear old dad and play a few rounds. Keep him company."

Bruce entered a white gate about waist height surrounded by a picket fence. Inside was a pool area, but there was no water in the pool. "Not sure this'll do."

Sigil said, "Our pool is currently being refurbished and upgraded. It should all be completed in just a few months to create a state-of-the-art facility for water recreation, therapy, and entertainment."

"That's what I'm talkin' about, Tur—"

Kenna took his arm and led him on. "I'm glad you like the place so far, *Dad*. I think you could be happy here."

She hurried him through the rest of the tour, though she tried not to make it look obvious. He insisted on inspecting the cabin bathroom so he could check out the "john" he'd be using. Then they circled back through the main hall.

Most of the residents were in there eating lunch. Bruce yelled, "Stuart!" across the room and scurried away, apparently noticing someone he knew. Maybe? He ended up in the meal line with a tray, so he was probably just hungry.

"Your father will be well taken care of here." Sigil still hugged his clipboard. "If the two of you would like to meet with the manager while your father-in-law is enjoying a meal?"

She wanted to scan every face in the meeting hall herself and try to find the collection of five older men who were supposedly other victims of the doctor who'd messed with her. She'd seen photos of them from years ago, but didn't know their real names. However, Bruce could more seamlessly mingle with the residents, and his spy skills would come in handy. He was supposed to tell them afterward if those men were here, and then they'd figure out how to talk to them.

For now, they had to finish out the ruse before they could leave.

Sigil took them to the main building and a rear office on the ground floor. "The manager will be right with you." He pointed to a sideboard. "Help yourself to beverages from the fridge."

"Thank you," Jax said.

After Sigil shut the door, she said, "Now I'm hungry. I bet Bruce won't bring me anything from lunch."

"Maybe he'll put a pudding cup in his pocket for you."

"I can hope."

Jax chuckled, sliding his arms around her waist and nuzzling her nose. "Are all your operations based around access to food?"

"No." She tipped her head to the side to think about that. "Maybe."

He let go of her. "I'm going to see what's in the fridge."

She sighed, looking around at this office. "There's nothing on the walls except this weird print that looks like it came from a doctor's office in the nineties."

"This whole place is a total throwback." He crouched in front of the fridge.

"Don't people usually put their college diploma on the wall? Or personal stuff on their desk?" She walked around the desk and crouched. "There isn't even a computer. The monitor has a cord that just hangs down under the desk."

"Everything in this fridge is frozen, like it was left in here with the thermostat turned far too cold." He straightened, frowning.

"This is supposed to be us pulling one over on this retirement home." She set her hands on her hips. "Why does it seem like this isn't what it seems?"

Jax looked around, then pulled out his phone. He frowned. "I have no signal."

Kenna didn't bother checking if she had any. She went to the door instead and discovered it was... "Locked." She glanced at Jax. "Why is the door locked?"

The handle tingled. It took her a second to figure out what was happening, and she got her hand away a second before a spark arced between her skin and the door handle. She hissed. "Ouch. That stung."

"We're locked in?"

"And the door is electrified." She shook her head. "I

guess there could be some kind of electrical problem in here. But it seems far more sinister."

"Look for another way out, but be careful what you touch."

Kenna nodded, wandering the room. File cabinet beside another file cabinet. No window. A single door.

She turned around.

Jax had his head under the desk. "There's something down here." His body jerked, and he bumped his head on the underside of the desk. "Ouch." He backed up and stood. "It was a spider." His cheeks had pinked.

"I'll kill it for you if you want."

He chuckled. "It's already dead. Did you find anything?"

Rather than saying no, she said, "Maybe." And turned away, only to hear him chuckle.

"Whatever it is, I'll kill it for you."

Kenna grinned to herself, looking back at the file cabinets. She opened a drawer, but there was nothing in it or in any of the others. She grabbed the top corners and muscled it over, wiggling it on the corners and fighting the drawers when they slid toward her.

"Huh." Jax grabbed the cabinet and shifted it a little more. "We need to move the other as well."

"It's just a panel. It might be nothing."

"You're more curious than that."

Kenna shook her head. "Didn't curiosity kill the cat?"

"Jolene will be fine. If we can get out, we're going in."

"Assuming there's an in to go to." She pushed on the panel and found it slid to one side. About three by three feet. She climbed in because she spotted a wooden set of stairs. She flipped on her camera flashlight. The stairs ended at a closed door several feet below. When she looked back at Jax, he had his gun out.

"I'll go first," he said.

"My hero."

Jax kissed her. "I know you're joking, but I don't care. I go first."

"Is this one of those macho, protective guy things?"

"Yes."

"As long as you give me some of your fries, I guess it evens out in the end."

"Glad you agree."

She admired the breadth of his shoulders in the light of her flashlight while making her way down behind him. Getting a little distracted. But he was her husband. There could be a million ways that might go wrong. Anything could happen to either of them. Health scares. Bad guys. Accidents.

She could choke on a peanut tomorrow and croak.

No one knew what the future held. Unless she suddenly developed precognition or clairvoyance—or whatever word meant she could see the future—as a new ability along with the strength she seemed to have. That could be cool. But it could also feel like a curse.

A terrible gift.

Better to trust the Lord with the future she wanted, which included the man God had given her.

He hesitated at the bottom, reaching for the handle. "Just locked." He let go. "Not...whatever happened upstairs."

"It felt like it was electrified." She touched his shoulder, eased by him, and tried herself. "I guess we could go back upstairs and try to break the door down somehow. Get out that way."

"Sure, but this is date day, and you're treating me to the full Kenna-on-a-case special."

She grinned. "Glad I amuse you."

"I like seeing you do your thing."

A sarcastic comment bubbled up, but she pushed it down. This might not work, and then she'd look like a fool. So, she said nothing and backed up a step. Slammed her shoulder into the door and snapped it free of the frame and the lock holding it shut.

The door splintered.

"Yeah, like that."

Kenna was focused too intently on the room beyond the door to make a snarky comment back. There was plenty of time for the two of them to banter. "See if you can find a light switch."

"One that isn't going to shock me?"

She couldn't resist saying, "If you're lucky, I'll shock you later."

He chuckled. "Shine your light around. Make sure there's no one in here and nothing dangerous." Another light flipped on behind her. "I see a light switch."

"We're clear."

He flipped it on. She scanned the room, then tapped off her light. He still had his gun out.

Not that he'd need it in this empty room.

It was a living area with a kitchenette to the right. An ancient tiny TV set that was probably black and white. Aging couch with threadbare arms. Recliner, in a similar condition. Coffee table. All of it looked like the set of an old nineteen fifties TV show.

"This looks like..." She couldn't put her finger on it.

"A nuclear shelter."

"Right. One of those that was built in the fifties during

the Cold War. Everyone thought they could stockpile cans and survive the fallout if they just stayed inside long enough." She'd seen a documentary about one once.

"Under the retirement home."

"I mean...maybe they didn't even know it was down here. Maybe they never moved those cabinets, and if someone knew, they forgot all about it." Kenna shrugged.

And then, the TV flickered to life.

Went black.

Green letters appeared on it. So small that Kenna had to go over to it in order to read what it said. *There's no cure for what you are.*

Behind her, metal slid into place.

"The door is blocked. It's just a sheet of steel." Fear laced Jax's tone.

Kenna pulled her hand back and punched the TV screen.

Chapter Ten

"Kenna!" Jax rushed over to grasp her hand.

She pulled it out of the TV screen, barely able to feel the cuts from the shattered glass screen.

"That's bad. We need a bandage." He led her to the couch. "Sit down. I'll look for a cloth or some kind of first aid kit. Don't get up."

"I'm not going to." She didn't even know why she'd done that.

"Here." Jax raced back over with a dish towel. "Not the cleanest thing, but better than nothing."

"I'm fine." She straightened her fingers, then contracted them. Blood seeped from multiple cuts on the back of her hand.

"Sure. Looks real fine." He sat on the coffee table, wrapping the towel around her hand. "What did the TV say before you took your frustration out on it?"

She pressed her lips together.

"Kenna."

"There's no cure for what you are."

A tendon in his jaw flexed. "And what does that mean for this operation?"

"They know who we are and why we're here, and they drew us down here."

"I think it was a test. To see what you would do."

Which meant he thought he might be a loose end these older men didn't need. Assuming they were directing this, watching, and not back in the main hall having lunch with Bruce. "I don't care. This thing has gone from interesting to mildly curious to *over*." She tipped her head back. "You hear me? It's over."

Nothing happened.

"We're trapped in here unless they decide to let us out." He tucked the end of the towel under the part he'd wrapped around her hand.

Kenna's blood was already seeping through the towel. She slumped back on the couch. "Who cares? Bruce will come looking. What do they think Ramon is gonna do when he finds out we're missing? He's on his way, right? And all our other friends. I didn't even *get* to the FBI realizing you didn't show up for work tomorrow and sending a tactical search party in full gear to kick all the doors in."

Jax said, "That's the spirit."

She let out a breath that puffed out her lips. "Do they have any snacks?"

"Nothing you'll want to eat."

"Darn."

Jax got up. "I'll see if there's a way out."

If this really was some Cold War–era bunker, it probably had bathroom facilities and a bedroom. There could be other storage rooms or a huge pantry with months of food supplies. "Maybe this is some kind of *Wizard of Oz* thing."

"Or a puzzle we need to solve to move on to the next stage."

"No thanks. That always *sounds* like a good idea, but in reality, they're frustrating, and I don't want to."

Jax said, "That's fine because I haven't found anything like that."

A telephone rang. An old-timey ringtone. Kenna pushed up on the couch and looked around, still seated but not in such a reclining position. "Where is it?"

"Here." He pulled open a closet. The inside looked like a phone booth. He grabbed the receiver. "Hello?"

His body stiffened. He turned to her. Held the phone out. "It's for you."

Kenna yelled, "I'm not playing games!"

A panel in the wall slid away at the far side of the room. Jax dropped the phone. "Come on."

"How do I know I even want to go in there?"

"It could be better than in here. Smells like dried cheese in this place."

"Mothballs and old wood."

He went through the panel first.

"At least if there's anyone in there, you can just shoot them."

The panel slid shut behind her, plunging them both into darkness.

"Well, this is fun." Jax flipped on his camera flashlight. "Long hallway."

She peered around his shoulders, her hands on his hips. "Lead the way since you wanted to go first, and we can't go back now."

She should be able to feel the cuts on her hand, but all she could feel was the dampness of the bandage around her injury. If someone was at the end of this ridiculous maze, she was going to ask them why her hand didn't hurt. Had there been something in the glass of the TV?

Or in her?

Everything went back to the doctor. A man who was supposed to have also altered these people the way he had altered her. *There's no cure for what you are.* Maybe they had enough experience with what'd been done to them to know there was no fighting it and no way to reverse it.

She prayed, not liking the way she was feeling right now. Maybe she would always struggle with control—maybe everyone did. It seemed like she should have a handle on things. That she should be able to work the outcome in her favor. But if that was true, then it would remove any faith from the equation.

If she didn't need to trust and have faith, then what good was that belief? She wouldn't need God, in that case, because she would be the lord of her own life.

The door ahead of them clicked open.

Jax went through it, gun first. She had her hand close to hers. Ready to pull it, just in case. But the trust she had in her husband was a great example. Jax would take care of whatever they faced, and he would give it all to protect her. She wanted to do the same for him. That's why she was backing him up with every step.

Light flickered on in the room that was larger than any they'd been in so far. This one was a long hallway, wide enough it might have been some kind of garage or storage room. Now, it had a fake fireplace halfway down the left wall and huge portrait paintings on the other side, hanging up on the double-height wall so the images towered over them.

Men in World War II–era uniforms.

Two or maybe three chandeliers hung over a long table set for dinner.

"Come in. Have a seat. After all, you've made it this far." He had a strong voice, but the man himself was barely five-foot-two. "I'm One."

Three other men stood.

One said, "This is Three, Four, and Five."

No Two.

Kenna glanced at each man. They looked to be about mid-fifties, which was impossible if they'd first been experimented on in the nineteen fifties. That was over seventy years ago.

They all wore jeans and buttoned shirts, some plain and others stripy. Different color hair and skin tones. Three and Five had tanned complexions that told her they didn't live down here all the time. One was the broadest and moved like the alpha. His shiny bald head resembled the doctor's. Four had stark white hair and a ring on his right pinkie finger.

One waved them over and took a seat on the far side. "There is good food, and we have much to discuss."

Jax put a hand on the small of her back. Not ushering her over to the table but supporting her and allowing her to make the decision.

The four men were on one side of the table, all in a row. Two place settings had been laid on the other side.

As if they'd been expected.

"We know who you are." Not that she knew all that was going on. But finally, she had a chance to get answers. "Maybe you could tell us why all of this was necessary when we just came here to talk to you."

"So let's talk." Five grabbed a hunk of bread from a

basket at the center of the table. He pulled off a small piece and tossed it into his mouth. "Before the food gets cold."

She sat, putting both her hands on the table.

All four men stared at her hand that was wrapped in a towel.

"Where's Two?" she asked.

One lifted his chin, motioning to the towel. "What's that?"

Beside her, Jax didn't reach for any food or his utensils. He slid out his phone under the table and unlocked it, keeping his attention on the men across the table.

"I punched the TV," Kenna said. "One, Three, Four, and Five. So where's Two?"

"It doesn't matter." One lifted his silverware and cut a bite of what looked like chicken.

"Potatoes?" Four held up the dish.

She stared at him.

"I thought you liked them." He handed the dish to Five.

One was definitely in charge. The others deferred to him. Seemed like Three didn't say much at all. She turned and looked at the paintings hanging behind her, history looming over the present as if to say, *You should be as impressive as I am.* And yet, the images were of the same men sitting across the table from her.

"You like those?" Four had a smile in his voice.

She shrugged, turning back to face them. "They look like you guys, but it can't be you."

Four gave her a toothy smile. "I had them commissioned. One didn't seem to find them as funny as I did, and I nearly threw them out, but they were up there the next morning. Hanging on the wall."

"So, you all live down here?"

Five looked at his friends. "Does she not know what a Batcave is?"

Kenna said, "I know what the Batcave is." She grabbed a roll and tried to tear it in half. With a towel around her hand, it was difficult.

Jax took the roll and tore it for her.

She buttered it with jerky movements, irritated she couldn't tear it herself. Her forearms felt better than they had in years. But the trade-off might be far too costly.

"He fixed you, didn't he?" One motioned with his fork. "The tendons in your forearms. Maybe you've been ignoring it, but there's not nearly as much pain. You can lift far heavier things. Right?"

He was right about part of it. Since the other day. She'd had a lot more strength and less pain. "Can I?"

Jax turned to her. "Is that true? Your arms are better?"

She lifted her hands and stretched them out in front of her, rotating her wrists. "How am I supposed to know what he did when I was unconscious? I wake up, and I feel differ-ent. I have no answers and no clue what is happening."

"So you came to find us." One took a bite and chewed thoughtfully.

"What did he do to me?"

"Time will tell, I suppose." One shrugged. "That's how it was for the rest of us."

Five looked at him.

Three and Four, on his other side, just ate their lunch. Jax served himself some chicken and potatoes and dug in. She finished her roll, still irritated at the whole thing. Was this really better than being pregnant? Not that she'd have been able to enjoy it with their enemy looming.

She blew out a breath and rolled her eyes, eating some chicken and potatoes while One asked Jax how he liked being the boss at the Phoenix FBI office. They made their way through some small talk, including comments about Jolene. Seemed that Five liked cats.

After she'd scarfed down most of the meal, she said, "Enough chitchat."

Four smiled at her.

"Do you know Doctor Nicola Santorini?"

One wiped his hands on a cloth napkin and tossed it onto his plate. "Not the doctor I thought you were going to ask me about."

"We'll get to him. Answer the question."

"Very well." One sipped his water, then said, "Nicola is our doctor also. The very things that led you to her, paying her under the table in cash and keeping everything off the record, meant that she was ideal for us also." He nodded. "Your instincts were right. She would have done right by you if your friend hadn't confronted that lady."

"You mean if he hadn't protected those two kids?" She figured they knew Bruce was upstairs. "Do I need to be worried about my friend?"

Who knew what the people in the main hall were doing to him. He could be carved to pieces in the empty pool by now.

One waved away her concern.

"I'm not going to stop worrying until I see him."

One shrugged. "Guess you'll have to trust me in the meantime."

Yeah, that wasn't going to happen. "Did you take Nicola? She's missing." Even though Kenna figured they knew, she still wanted to see their reaction. None of them let go of any tell. Even the small mannerisms she'd been getting were gone now.

Four said, "Nicola is missing?"

Now that was interesting. A personal reaction. Concern for the young woman.

Jax set his silverware down. "Since last night. Along with the woman who hurt those kids. She's gone, too."

They both waited to see these guys' reactions to the news.

Four sipped his water, a blank expression on his face. Five didn't move. Three was busy picking chicken from his teeth, and One simply stared at her and Jax.

"Where are they both?" Kenna asked. "Tell us, and we'll be on our way."

"But that's not why you came, is it?"

"We came here looking for you." She wasn't going to hide that fact.

"Because you want answers as to what was done to you." One stared at her, unmoving.

No one else moved either.

"I want to know where to find Marcus Buzard."

One lifted his chin. "So you can kill him?"

Four looked a little uncomfortable at that.

"My business with him is just that," Kenna said. "My business."

One shook his head. "That doesn't work for us."

"Because you need him alive?" Maybe the doctor supplied them with meds or continued treatments they would be forced to live without if the doctor was suddenly out of their lives. Or unobtainable. "How do you contact him?"

"Perhaps you should focus on your case. Leave the doctor to us."

"Protecting him won't help."

One chuckled. There was no humor in the sound and

none on his face. "I wouldn't recommend going up against us. It won't end well for you."

Jax leaned forward slightly. "I wouldn't recommend going up against my family. It won't end well for you."

One almost looked impressed. "Let me guess. The city suddenly decides the retirement home above us needs a full inspection, and a federal investigation is opened into our finances. At least to start with."

Jax said nothing.

"You want to protect the doctor," Kenna said, "that's your prerogative. But I want answers, and I want to know where that woman and Doctor Santorini are."

"*That woman,*" One said. "I'll give you the address where you can find her. We can't allow evidence of what we are to be out in the general public's knowledge. You took a risk. Anyone could have been filming on their phone and caught what you did."

"Is she alive?" Kenna asked.

One pushed back his chair and stood. "This conversation is over."

Chapter Eleven

Daylight seemed harsh after the dim light of that dining room in the basement. Wherever they'd been, she was glad to be out of there. Even if they'd been summarily dismissed. No more conversation. No more exchanging information. Thanks and goodbye. The rest had disappeared through different hatches in the walls, leaving Four to walk them up to the surface.

Kenna had tried to ask him questions, but he hadn't answered. Not even a "goodbye" or "nice talking to you." Not one word.

As soon as they stepped out, he closed the door behind them.

"What did One give you?"

Kenna opened her hand. How her husband knew that man had given her anything with just a handshake was anyone's guess. "A card with a phone number on it. Nothing else."

Jax asked, "Are you okay? I know you were hoping they might give you answers as to what happened to you."

"They also gave us an address."

"You remember it?"

She nodded, pulling out her phone. She sent the address and the phone number to Maizie so her assistant could run down both and then grabbed Jax's hand. "Let's get Bruce and get out of here."

"We're checking out that address? They all but admitted they killed that woman just so she didn't give away anything about you."

"They wouldn't have said they killed someone in front of an FBI agent. That would have led you to arresting them."

"You think I would've been able to do that?"

He didn't like feeling powerless any more than she did. Something else they had in common. "I don't think they're bad guys we need to take down, but they're definitely not harmless."

"Neither are you, and I haven't arrested you yet."

She grinned at him. "What do you think Bruce has been up to while we were led on a goose chase and given the runaround?"

Jax smiled back. "With Bruce, I'm not sure I want to guess."

"Probably a good call."

"You really trust him? I mean, he hasn't exactly let you down before, but you've been in situations where he should've had your back, but he didn't."

"The people I trust are...less than the fingers on my hand." Was he one of them? "I guess there are degrees even of that. Full trust? You. Ryson and his family. Maybe it's just you since I don't see him much."

"We should go visit them at the holidays."

"I'd like that." There were others, like Maizie and

Ramon. People she put a whole lot of faith in. But she'd been burned before.

She squeezed his hand and pulled open the door for the main hall. Moving from the outside scorching temperature into the air-conditioned indoor space made bumps appear on her arms.

"Your arms do seem better with all this."

"I know." She looked down at her forearms while they were tucked in this little entryway together, between the exterior doors and the ones that led into the dining hall. A small alcove with a noticeboard covered with event flyers, one about a missing cat. "I'm trying not to think about it, but they almost feel...fine."

"That's a good thing." He touched her shoulder, his hand sliding over so his thumb could swipe her cheek. "The stronger, the better. Considering you expend your life to help people and right the wrongs of the world. If you can do that with a little less pain, I'm okay with it."

"Even if the trade-off is that evil wins?"

He leaned close. "Don't let it."

"Easy for you to say."

"Then join the FBI. It's what we do."

Kenna rolled her eyes. "Been there, done that."

"You could be a consultant for real, though. Not just because I have the paperwork already."

She pushed through the interior doors. If she did that, it would mean she'd be stuck working his cases and not her own. She would have no autonomy if they dictated what she was supposed to be working on all the time.

Not that working with Jax would be bad. But living and working together? She might not be ready for that. Far as she could see, a man had to have his thing. He might like the idea of her being part of it, but he wouldn't want her there when he had to be the boss, and he'd know she wasn't going to like it.

Jax snagged her elbow, and she nearly ran into Bruce's back.

"What's going on?"

The older man said, "Nothing." He ushered them out. "Time to go, I guess."

They stepped outside and strode to the path that would take them to the parking lot.

Kenna asked, "What happened?"

"I was gonna ask you guys the same thing." He looked her up and down, then did the same to Jax. "You both seem like you're in one piece."

She gave him a rundown of their encounter downstairs. "How about you?"

"Explains why I didn't find them at lunch. Everyone in there..." He paused to shake his head, blowing out a breath. "Stepford. Isn't that the movie?"

"Happy, plastic? Super fake?"

"That's it. Everything's great. It's all wonderful. Meanwhile, they're eating mashed potatoes that taste like sawdust and the chicken was... I don't even know what it was." He shuddered. "There's something wrong with those people."

"Maybe they're just trying to make the best of it," Jax suggested. "But I can call the health department."

"You do that." Bruce nodded.

"Nice to know you care about people." Kenna was almost impressed by it.

"I'm gonna end up in one of those places someday. Lord willing." Bruce frowned. "It had better be a good spot."

"Start saving now. That's all I have to say."

Bruce said, "Maybe I'll just get a cabin in Wyoming and go off the grid. No one needs to worry about me."

"But we are going to worry about you."

"Then come visit. Your feelings aren't my problem."

Jax looked a little offended, but Kenna just laughed. "Leave some instructions on what to do in the event of…"

"Yeah, yeah. I'll give you the password for the safe deposit box. All that stuff needs to come out into the open so people know what's going on. Better if that happens after I'm gone." Bruce took a step back. "Got a job for me?"

"Not right now. Jax and I can check out the one lead we have."

"I'm gonna track down those kids. Make sure they're all right." He looked at her husband. "Keep her safe?"

Jax just nodded.

Bruce wandered off to his car. Jax drove, and she entered the address One had given her into the dash screen map. Those men had been mysterious. Maybe like her, and maybe not. Definitely covering for the doctor. Or they had no choice in the matter, and they had to protect him whether they liked it or not. Either way, they were going to find themselves at odds with her if she went after Buzard to take him down.

She didn't want to put their lives in jeopardy, but justice had to be served. This doctor couldn't continue to operate without someone exposing him. He was destroying lives by working for a deadly enemy with international reach.

If she didn't take him down, who knew what might happen. He could take anyone. Kill without consequences and target whoever he wanted. If she did nothing, it would be at least partially her fault because she could've stopped it.

Her phone rang. Kenna put it on speaker. "Hey, Maze."

"I got an answer on that phone number they gave you, but it isn't one you're going to like."

Jax turned onto the ramp for the freeway, their destination twenty minutes away.

Kenna asked, "What is it?"

"The number comes back as registered to a pay phone in New York City. But the number was discontinued years ago, when the whole network was taken down."

"Do they even have pay phones anymore?"

"All of them were taken down except for a few phone booths and some private phones. The system was dismantled. Who knows how they have access to one of the numbers, if it wasn't just reassigned to a regular phone."

"Access to government resources, or they know someone they can bribe that gave them the number." Kenna had a few other ideas, but that was the gist of it. "They got it somehow, and apparently, it's how we get ahold of them."

"Maybe I should call. Introduce myself."

Hopefully, she was joking. "Let's leave bringing them on board with the team for a while yet. We don't even know if we can trust them."

"But they're like you, right?"

"I have no idea, Maze." No reason to discuss this anyway. Whether they were the same or different didn't matter. She lived her life, and they'd chosen theirs. She probably wouldn't be able to sway them from what seemed like the tenets they lived by.

Rules that had kept them alive for years.

"Anything on the address they're sending us to?" Jax reached over and squeezed her knee.

"Only that it's all over the police band. A pizza restaurant, some kind of franchise place. It burned down last night. The cops are there now because they found something, but no one has said what it is on the radio. Yet."

"Thanks," Kenna said. "We're almost there."

"Keep me posted. Anything else? Stairns just showed up with pizza."

Maizie probably didn't want to be on the phone when she shared her dinner with Kenna's dog, Cabot, who lived with her in the Airstream. The dog who *wasn't* supposed to eat pizza.

"Nope. Thanks, Maze." Kenna hung up. "A pay phone? Seems like an old-school way for people to find you."

"Maybe the number goes nowhere. Or it's a prank number they give out when they don't want someone to be able to contact them."

Kenna let out a sigh. Up ahead, she spotted several unmarked police cars, a coroner's van, a fire truck, and a fire chief's SUV, along with another vehicle with Fire Marshal written on the side.

"This looks interesting." Jax pulled over a distance from the incident scene on a suburb street with a strip mall on one side and a row of apartment buildings on the other. Two lanes of traffic had been reduced to one due to all the emergency vehicles. A couple of police officers stood in the center directing traffic.

The middle of the strip mall housed a wide restaurant with two stories, or it had. Now it was a burned-out shell that hadn't spread to the neighboring storefronts, but she figured they had significant smoke damage. Enough that everything had been shut down.

Jax approached, digging out his credentials. He introduced himself and explained that Kenna was his consultant.

When the cop looked at her, she said, "Sarge."

Jax tried not to react, but she knew he wanted to. It wasn't like she knew every cop in Phoenix.

The sergeant said, "Hernandez."

She nodded. "I remember. How is Ms. Fleming?"

"How should I know?" He motioned over his shoulder at the burned-out building. "Is this your doing?"

"Not so far as I'm aware."

Jax said, "It's possibly connected to a case we're working, but we aren't sure. If we could just have a look around and talk to your guys, that would be great."

Sergeant Hernandez said, "This isn't about jurisdiction?"

"It's not currently an FBI matter."

Her husband, so diplomatic. "Come on, Sarge. Can we look around?"

Hernandez frowned. "You can walk through with me. You don't go anywhere without my escort."

Kenna nearly snapped a salute, but if she did that, they would probably get kicked off the scene entirely. She pressed her hands together in front of her. "Promise."

The sergeant sighed. "I'm gonna regret this." But he went to the front doors, where they all had to put on booties to cover their shoes so they didn't contaminate the scene. "The fire originated in the kitchen, or so the fire marshal tells me. Something about the accelerant used giving off more heat than would've ever been necessary to just destroy the place."

"It was arson?" Jax asked. "That's his ruling?"

"Fire marshal says whoever set the fire intended to destroy what was in the kitchen beyond any chance of us retrieving evidence. Scorched earth. Hot and localized. It was a powerful burn, but it didn't spread quickly. The perpetrator kept it contained so that nothing much else was damaged."

"Considerate." Kenna looked at the blackened interior of the building as they walked through, unable to distinguish tables or chairs. There was an area that might have been a front counter, but it was impossible to tell. Everything had been charbroiled to the studs. It was all black, cracked, burned wood. Nothing left.

"What was in the kitchen that they wanted to destroy?" Kenna asked.

"Firefighters missed it. Whoever it is, they look like everything else in here."

Jax asked, "One victim?"

"No way to ID them. The body was brittle, and the ME is still trying to figure out how to get it out of here aside from scooping the whole thing into a basin."

Kenna winced. "If it happened fast, maybe they didn't suffer."

"I hope so." Hernandez led them into a room in the rear. What should've been the kitchen, most likely. The huge industrial stove was distinguishable, now covered by the hood that had fallen down on it. A brick oven to the right had an open metal grate. It had to be crazy hot in here when the fire was going to cook the pizzas, let alone when this blaze happened.

"Where was she found?" Kenna had to ask, rather than guess.

"She?"

Uh-oh. "The victim." She tried to brush it off. "Force of habit. Most of my cases involve female clients or missing women and children." He couldn't blame her for that, could he? Besides, they didn't know for sure if this really was the abusive mother of those two kids.

"In the brick oven they use to cook the pizzas." Hernandez didn't seem convinced. "Do you know who the victim is?"

They weren't likely to identify her otherwise, given the destruction. There wouldn't be any DNA left to collect. The only way to find out who it was would be for someone to confess.

"We can't be certain."

Jax said, "We don't even know for sure if it's connected. What else can you tell us otherwise?"

Hernandez folded his arms, tightening the sleeves of his uniform shirt over his shoulders. "The restaurant was about to declare bankruptcy and shut down. After this, they'll be able to recoup their losses and get solvent again. The fact someone chose this place to burn and dispose of a body actually did the owners a favor."

Kenna turned away, as if she suddenly needed to look at the room around her. She just needed some air.

The men she had met at that retirement home had taken a woman and disposed of her so thoroughly no one would ever know who she was, and they'd done it in such a way that would help out the owner of this place. They probably thought they were like some kind of Robin Hood do-gooders, taking money from insurance companies and getting the little guy a payout they desperately needed.

She had to get Maizie digging into this to see if they'd done it before.

Chapter Twelve

Kenna slid into one side of a booth, grabbing the menu from between the ketchup and the window. Jax sat across from her so he could see the front door. She could see the window to the kitchen and the archway with the sign Restrooms above it.

The place was about half full. Construction workers at the counter. A couple of uniformed cops at the far end who were done with their meal. A family in the corner, wrangling little kids into eating more than fruit. Two pairs of older men having breakfast.

The whole place smelled like bacon and biscuits.

"Caramel milkshake?"

She looked over her menu at Jax, remembering the first meal they'd ever shared. Years ago, back in Salt Lake City. "That's the day I found Cabot."

He smiled. "You like Jolene, right?"

"She doesn't annoy me as much as I thought she might."

"That means you love her," he said. "Give it some time, and you won't be able to imagine living without her."

"Yeah, sure."

That wasn't too likely to happen. However, that was the crux of her worry about the people in her life. Not the cat. Kenna loved her family, and she had a lot of things now that she'd been missing. If she lost any of them, she might not be able to cope with it. She'd been utterly destroyed before when she'd lost everything.

Was it possible to survive that a second time?

Jax tugged her menu down, but the waitress wandered over. They gave their orders, and when she'd walked out of earshot, he took her menu and stacked them back between the ketchup and the window. "What are you thinking about?"

"Just stuff."

He dumped a half-and-half into his coffee and stirred it. "The case?"

She shook her head and tugged her coffee over. "Life. Family. Loss. Grief. Cats. Milkshakes."

"Days off are a good time for existential questions. The tricky part is taking sufficient time off that you get the chance to wrestle with them for long enough to come up with a solution."

"Why do you have to be so smart?"

"It's part of my charm."

She smiled. "Yes, it is."

He chuckled, not quite so sure of himself here with her than he probably was at work in his job as the boss of the FBI's Phoenix office.

"Thanks for spending the day with me." She moved her hand to the middle of the table, her palm up.

He set his in it, those strong fingers curling around hers. "You're welcome. I'm glad you feel better, but I'd be here if you didn't."

"I know."

"What?"

"I don't want to be a burden," Kenna said. "I want to pull my weight. Actually, more than that. I don't just want to be sufficient. I'd rather be successful in a way that people are impressed with you because of me." She shook her head. "I don't even know if that makes sense."

"I think I know what you mean. Honestly, I feel the same way." He squeezed her hand but didn't let go. "I don't think you're wired to be dead weight in a relationship. But you don't always have to be trying so hard to succeed that it takes everything you've got, and then some, just to try and not let your side down. Otherwise, you're twisting yourself in knots or burning out. Just do what you can."

"That's probably another thing to wrestle with."

"Why do you feel like you have to try so hard?" He tipped his head to the side. "It's not so you can prove yourself to anyone. Is it?"

She shook her head.

"It's because you survived."

Kenna shifted in her seat. "I don't need a therapist."

"Everyone needs a therapist. Especially the people who say they don't need a therapist. Because we all need someone to talk to so we can process out the things we're thinking through and wrestling with."

"I'm dealing with it."

Jax said, "You're also scared to death."

"Like I said, I'm dealing with it."

"I get it."

She looked up from her coffee. The waitress set their plates in front of them. Kenna grabbed her fork.

Jax said grace, praying quietly over their meal. Then he said, "I worry every second that something's going to happen to you or to Maizie. Ramon. Stairns. Ryson and his family. Laney and her family. My parents. But you can't let the fear control your life. You need to *live*. Which I know is something you already know."

"If I wasn't intentionally living, I wouldn't have married you."

"I know." He smiled. "And I'm really glad you did."

She figured marriage was about giving the other person reasons to stay rather than simply convincing them not to leave. Being the thing that kept them invested and what they couldn't live without was far more positive than just resolving the reasons they wanted to go.

Again, with the add-on element that it wasn't about her tying herself up in knots. Overextending herself and burning out "doing" instead of living and enjoying her life.

"You know what it's like to lose everything, and you're scared to death it's going to happen again."

Kenna needed to lighten this conversation, stat. "Why do you have to be *in* my brain?"

The corners of his lips curled up. "I know you. I get you. Even though you live a lot of your life in solitary ways, keeping things to yourself. Not in a bad way, like they're secrets, but you keep to yourself. It's a protective measure."

"But you're not trying to get me to open up."

"If it's important, you'll tell me."

She studied him. Most guys would expect her to open up and might even get pissy when she didn't. He seemed content to let her have autonomy in this relationship. She said, "I want to believe we have plenty of time to get to know each other a little better every day."

Maybe falling in love with each other a little more each day. But she wouldn't say that. It would sound overly sappy. She liked a good romance novel, because she was a quality human being, but being gregarious with her emotions hadn't ever been her thing.

"But?"

"Maybe we won't," she said. "We could have three weeks or fifty years. Or less. Or more. Or something in between. We could have no kids or a whole bunch. Things could go wrong in a million ways. We could both quit our jobs to eliminate as much of the risk as we can, and then one of us could get hit by a car getting the mail from the mailbox. You can't guarantee anything."

"So let's just enjoy the heck out of what we do have. See where it goes."

She studied him.

He held his hand out across the table, like a pact. "What do you say, Banbury?"

She chuckled and took his hand. "I agree to your terms, *Oliver*."

"People have been calling me Jax." He seemed to find it amusing if the look on his face was anything to go by. "It started with Ramon and Maizie, Bruce and Stairns. Now, it's even creeping in at work. They call me Boss to my face, but I've heard them refer to me as SAC Jax."

What could she say to that? "Sorry?"

He shook his head. "I actually like it. Laney used to call me Ollie, and I *hated* it."

She chuckled, but her phone rang before she could say more. She pulled the earbuds case out of her pocket and handed one to him, then swiped the screen while putting the earbud in her left ear. Jax slid the other in his right, though it was probably too small. "Hey, Maze. What have you got for us?"

"A few things. Ready?"

Jax gave her a soft smile. They needed to visit Maizie, or

have the teen come and stay here with them for a few days so they could hang out with their adopted daughter. The more time she spent with good guys who would treat her in healthy ways, the better she'd be able to discern a good man from the kind who would mistreat her. It hadn't even been two years since she'd escaped the sick man who had raised her until she escaped him. Sometimes, it felt like far longer.

Jax said, "We're ready."

Kenna finished the potatoes that had come with her eggs while she listened to Maizie.

"Elizabeth and Craig have finished going over the medical research paper. It wasn't written by this Doctor Buzard guy, but if those lawyers included it, then maybe it covers what he did to you. Basically, this process replaces the marrow in your bones with bone, making them dense to the point they will become nearly solid where they're actually supposed to bend and be flexible—to an extent. Instead, this will make them more brittle. So they can shatter really easily."

Kenna didn't want to reach for her water glass and betray the shakiness of her hands.

Jax had an eye on her, probably trying to gauge how she felt about this whole thing. "Is there a way to reverse it?"

Maizie said, "They told me Kenna should go get a bone density test. To see if that is what he did to her. The process of genetic modification will make your bones denser, but there are drawbacks. They think he sped up the body's natural processes so that she has built stronger and denser bones with no marrow in the center. Problem is, she won't produce red blood cells, which is bad. She'll need a calcium-rich diet or some kind of drug or fluid that is packed with bone-building nutrients."

"Maybe that's what they did the other day. Gave me

another treatment so I feel better." Kenna had to clear her throat, and then she told Maizie about the scene they had just gone to. "Can you find out if there have been any similar cases the police have investigated? Scenes where the body was there but destroyed beyond any ability to identify them or discover how they really died."

"What about people who just went missing? What if they were never found?"

Kenna said, "Keep it to people who inexplicably went missing. Because with those who are regularly missing, there would be too much risk that they might get found. Therefore, we can probably rule them out. We have to narrow it down somehow."

The men they'd just met at that retirement home were the kind who would take care of an issue in a way they could be certain of no blowback. Just like with that fire. They'd wanted to get rid of the evidence of what Kenna had done, so they'd taken and disposed of that horrible woman. No way they'd leave their secrets to chance when someone might discover who they were.

If she went after the doctor for real, would they stop her?

"On it," Maizie said. "I also have a lead for you on Nicola Santorini's disappearance."

Jax's brows rose.

Kenna asked, "What is it?"

"First, Craig found evidence that the Santino crime family has made moves to leave Vegas and go down to Phoenix. Presumably because Nicola is gone, and they want to find out what happened to her. So keep your eyes peeled for them. He said things could get 'sticky' if you tangle with the mob."

"Again." It had happened before.

Jax's lips twitched.

Maizie said, "Nicola has a roommate. It's not official. The girl isn't listed on the lease. But her best friend from high school got into drugs and alcohol. I found a newspaper article about a car crash when she was seventeen. She'd been driving drunk. Thankfully, no one else was hurt, but the friend—her name is Dana Barrett—went to rehab after that. She's been in and out ever since and stays with Nicola when she's doing well."

"You think she might know what happened to the doc?"

Maizie said, "Her cell phone use has her at Nicola's house all afternoon and evening the day she went missing, but no one has seen Dana since. The rehab facility she checks herself into won't tell me if she's there or not."

"We'll check it out. Thanks, Maizie."

Jax said, "Everything else okay, kiddo?"

"Yeah."

Kenna knew that tone. "Do your homework."

"Ugh." Maizie groaned the word. "Your stuff is way more interesting."

"Then it'll be a treat after you've finished your homework."

"Fine." Maizie hung up.

Jax handed Kenna back the other earbud, and she put both in the case.

"You're good with her," he said.

"It's weird having a teen, but I'm not her mother. We're an odd mix of friends and parent and child."

"Maybe that's exactly what she needs. It could be the exact reason why God put you in each other's paths."

Kenna nodded. "I had thought the same thing. But I was actually thinking about all of us, you and me. Us and

Maizie. Ramon—I mean, who else would put up with him coming and going, doing his own thing?"

"Bruce?"

"Let's not get crazy. I don't think he was sent by God."

Jax chuckled. "I do think the same thing about you and me."

"God knew what you needed?"

"It wasn't some SUV-driving soccer mom, ferrying the kids around and meeting her girlfriends for brunch." He lifted his hands. "Not that there's anything wrong with that, if it's the life you want. Everyone gets to choose, and no one should have to live a life they're stuck with just because it's the consequences of their poor choices."

"But that's not you."

"I know it isn't because I tried it once, and it only lasted a few months. I was bored out of my mind."

Kenna grinned. "I'm definitely not boring."

If only he didn't have to deal with *all* the things she'd brought into his life. She could do without the *Dominatus* and the genetic experimentation. But still, they'd handled it all so far.

"I get a partner who understands what I do and why. I get a woman who would go to war to protect the people she loves, who holds people tightly and is fierce. Who values family above everything and knows the value of working together, but who is also independent enough to stand on her own, and I don't have to worry."

Kenna had to clear her throat. The sheen of tears in her eyes couldn't be helped. "I love you."

Jax leaned across the table. "That's the best part."

She wiped the corner of her eye. "Let's go visit a rehab facility, see if we can get some answers."

"Maybe Bruce will pretend we're there to check him in."

She chuckled, enjoying the way he'd lightened the mood. She did that a lot, defusing tension. Setting people at ease. Letting them know it didn't have to be life and death all the time. Things could be light and enjoyable, even in the middle of a tense situation.

She slid to the edge of the bench seat. "Let's go, partner. We've got a case to work."

Chapter Thirteen

"As I said"—the nurse stepped to the side with her back to the door—"if she doesn't wish to speak with you, I'm afraid there's nothing any of us can do."

Kenna nodded. "We appreciate you letting us in."

That had happened thanks to Jax's badge more than the goodwill of the staff here at the Morrow Wellness Center. A fancy name for a psychiatric hospital that turned out to be more upscale than Kenna had expected. It almost looked like a hotel, or a resort, than a hospital. All gleaming fixtures and fresh paint. Ceiling fans and precisely controlled temperature.

But Dana Barrett was still a patient. She'd checked herself in voluntarily, knowing she couldn't leave until she completed the program.

Jax touched her shoulder and whispered, "I'm going to hang out here in the hallway."

Kenna turned her head to him a little without taking her attention from Dana. The patient sat in a high-backed chair in the corner of the room. She had a book on her lap and wore light pink scrubs. Slippers on her feet. Her hair had been brushed, but it hung limp over her shoulders as if it didn't have the wherewithal to do anything but lie there.

"Dana? I'm Kenna." She spotted a wood chair with a pleather seat in the corner. "Is it okay if I sit with you for a few minutes?"

Dana's gaze shifted from the window to Kenna, then to the door. "Kerry, the cat is back. She caught a mouse."

Kerry, the nurse, smiled. "I'll tell the groundskeeper." She ducked into the hall where Jax stood. He would find out what the staff knew, but it could add context to what she learned from the patient.

There might not be much the staff could tell Kenna and Jax when medical privacy rules came into play. It was up to Dana and what she wanted to share.

"There's a cat?" Kenna dragged the chair over and sat facing Dana. "My husband and I have a cat also. Her name is Jolene."

Dana's lips twitched. "Like the Dolly Parton song?"

"I guess." Kenna chuckled. "She is always getting up to trouble." It was important to keep this conversation light, even as much as she needed to press Dana for information. "This seems like a nice place." When Dana didn't respond to that, Kenna said, "They've helped you in the past?"

The woman nodded. She had to be in her thirties. Nicola's closest friend, two people who'd stuck by each other for years even when their lives went in different directions.

"We all need help sometimes. It's great that you have a place to go where you can feel...safe."

Dana inhaled, just a tiny intake of breath. A miniscule, little gasp.

"You are safe."

Dana said, "Yes, because they lock the doors here at night, and there is always someone on guard."

"But that wouldn't be true at your apartment. I mean, there would be a lock. But no one is on guard."

She looked at the window.

"I can understand that." No need to freak this woman out with specifics, though. "I know what it's like to be scared. And I don't mean freaked out. I mean the kind of terror where you're certain you're about to die."

Dana kept looking at the window.

"People don't get it. How scary it is to think you're going to die. Or when you think you've lost someone you love."

"She isn't lost."

"And you don't *think* she's gone. You know she is."

Dana jerked her head in a nod.

"Did you see what happened, Dana?"

She seemed frozen for a second, then she looked at Kenna. "What do the cops care? It isn't like they help Santinos."

"I'm not a cop, Dana. I'm a private investigator."

Dana looked at the door.

"My husband is an FBI agent, but this isn't one of their cases as far as I'm aware." Kenna shifted in the seat, adjusting her position so she came across as open and like she had all the time in the world. "I met Nicola at the medical center where she worked. You've known her for years, haven't you?"

Dana nodded. "You're not a cop?"

"Not officially. I would just like to know what happened to Doctor Santorini."

"She loved that name. It's why she chose it."

"Did you choose yours?"

She wrinkled her nose. "I always thought I should change it. Nicola and I could've been sisters, officially."

"She helped you out a lot, didn't she?"

"Sometimes, I wonder if it's why she became a doctor. So she could help me, or so she'd know what to do. She couldn't be *my* doctor, since we're friends."

"Sisters."

Dana said, "Can't treat a family member."

"I'm guessing she did everything she could to make sure she was there for you."

Dana nodded.

"I'd like to find her. If she's still alive, she may be in danger."

Dana remained silent for a long moment. Finally, she said, "They took her." Tears filled her eyes. "They should've taken me instead. But I'm not worth anything."

"Nicola doesn't see it that way, though. Right?" Kenna figured Nicola would much rather be the one who was taken if it spared her friend more pain. "She looked out for you." Kenna waited a beat and then said, "Did she protect you?"

"She told me to run. But they didn't care about me." Dana's breaths came faster. "They came into the house, and they grabbed her. I screamed. She was screaming and crying. They put a cloth over her mouth, and she went limp. I tried to stop them, but one of them slapped me." She showed Kenna a red area on her cheekbone and gasped back a sob. "I couldn't do anything to stop them."

"Nicola didn't want you to get hurt." The question was, why she hadn't gone to the police? Instead, she'd checked herself into the safest place she knew. "Will you help me figure out who they are?"

"How?"

Kenna kept her voice gentle. "What did they look like? Can you describe any of them?"

Dana inhaled through her nose, squeezing her eyes shut.

"What is it?"

"They had...masks on."

"How many of them were there?"

Dana shook her head. "Five. Six?"

That was interesting, for taking one person. "What were they wearing?" She needed to get to the masks but in a roundabout way. "Can you describe their clothes?"

"That's what was...terrifying."

Kenna waited.

"They had on those white medical outfits. Like old-timey nurses, with the white dresses and the little watch thing on the breast pocket and that white card thing over their hair."

"All of them were women?"

Dana bit her lip. "There were a couple of men in white scrubs. Maybe three. And two women."

"All of them dressed in white medical staff clothing?" A memory sparked in Kenna's mind, but she pushed it aside for now.

Dana nodded, opening her eyes.

"Tell me about the masks."

Fear flashed in her eyes. "They were white and plastic. Maybe porcelain. With round holes for eyes."

"That sounds pretty terrifying." Especially for a person trying to avoid the usual ways she'd have disassociated in order to cope with the high stress in her life. A woman who had suffered for years with addictions had come to exactly the right place—where she knew she'd get the help she needed.

"She told me to hide in the closet, but I just crouched behind the chair. I didn't have time to run. They rushed in and surrounded Nicola. It looked like they swallowed her up. Then she was limp, and they carried her out." Dana gasped. "One of them looked at me. But then she turned away and left with the others."

"Do you have any idea who they were or where they might have taken her?"

Dana shook her head.

Kenna sat forward in the chair, resting her forearms on her knees. "Did she seem worried about anything?" She needed Dana to think through the days before Nicola was taken. "Did she seem different or stressed more than normal?"

"I don't think so."

"What about people in her life? Is there anyone you can think of who might have a reason to take her?"

"I don't know who those people were!"

Kenna nodded. "I know you don't. But pretend for a second they're some kind of theater troupe or the whole thing was a practical joke." She paused. "Is there anyone in Nicola's life who might have done something like that?"

The older men she and Jax had met at that retirement home were the ones who had *disposed* of the mother of those abused children. Had they taken her from the hospital without anyone knowing by using the same people?

She needed to find out if they'd done this to Nicola.

Or if it was someone else entirely.

Kenna continued, "Someone like an ex-boyfriend or a current relationship? Maybe someone in her family?"

"You think it was a joke?"

"I have to ask every question, even the ones that are less likely. I need a place to start looking."

Dana was the one who had seen it happen, and they'd

left her alone. So, they didn't consider her a threat. Or she was irrelevant.

Did this Doctor Buzard guy have a terrifying staff who kidnapped people?

And what did he want with Nicola?

"Is there anyone in her life who might have done this, whether with evil intentions or as a joke?"

Dana sucked in a choppy breath. "I don't think so. Not even her family."

"Is there anything else you can think of that might help me find her?"

She shook her head. "Sorry."

"Don't be sorry," Kenna said. "You've helped. Probably more than you know. Okay?"

She seemed reassured by that.

Kenna chatted for another minute, then wished her all the best and left her to her peace. She found Jax in the hallway speaking with a doctor. The guy had a kind face, but she didn't trust places like this. There was too much in Kenna's past that had put her mental health on a knife-edge. She could easily have ended up confined to a facility, unable to regulate her fears or come to terms with the loss she'd suffered.

There but for the grace of God.

It was absolutely true. She wasn't ever going to take her peace, or her freedom, for granted. Not when things could so easily have gone the other way.

The grace of God had her where she was.

At the same time, the grace of God might be the reason Dana was here. Because this was the best place she could be. And hopefully, the grace of God would allow Kenna to find Nicola despite the odds, allow her to take down *Dominatus* and do so with minimal collateral damage. She had to rely on the Lord because there was no way she could do this on her own. Even with a team behind her.

Kenna's dislike of feeling trapped was her deal. She wouldn't project that fear onto someone else. The kind of person who might need a situation exactly like this in order to feel as if they were in control.

"Thanks." Jax turned from the doctor and walked toward her, making a face. Apparently, there wasn't much that the doctor had said, even if Jax had thanked him. Seemed like it was more of *Thanks for nothing.*

He stopped in front of her.

"It might be a serious long shot, but we need to see if anyone caught Nicola's kidnapping on camera." With the perpetrators wearing masks, they might not learn anything useful if they did manage to find evidence, but they had to at least try. "I think this doctor guy took her."

Whatever he wanted her for, it wasn't going to be good.

Kenna needed to find her.

And fast.

Chapter Fourteen

"Nothing?"

Kenna probably sounded as exasperated as Maizie when she said, "Nothing."

"Isn't that odd?" the teen asked.

They were back in the car, heading to a place where Kenna could get a bone density test. She'd already made the appointment, choosing an out of the way doctor's office. She would have to use a fake ID, and paying in cash would help keep the test results off the radar of the wrong people. She needed to know for herself what had been done to her.

Jax pulled into the parking lot in plenty of time for the appointment. He stopped, leaving the engine running so they could keep talking to Maizie in the cool, air-conditioned interior.

Probably not the day off he'd been imagining, even if it was a normal day for the two of them.

Jax looked over at her, then said to Maizie, "Not super odd. People don't purposely point their doorbell cameras at each other's homes. There were no traffic cams in the area.

No neighborhood surveillance. We knew going over there that it was a long shot."

"I found a couple of cases. I sent them to Bruce so he could look over the files. In one, there's a witness who reported exactly what Dana told Kenna. People in medical uniforms with freaky masks on. The guy is a neighbor, and he happened to be looking out of his window at the time. But the police didn't put much stock in it."

Kenna said, "They never found the missing person?"

"Nope. Scottsdale PD has one listed as a cold case. It's eight years old now."

"Who went missing?"

Maizie said, "Rebecca Hardy. Twenty-seven years old. Husband and one child." Her tone softened, resonating with sadness. "No one ever saw her again."

"And the other one?"

"Similar story, Melissa Graham. She was engaged, went missing just a few weeks before her wedding, but no one found her, and the police assumed she got cold feet," Maizie said. "There's more evidence on Mrs. Hardy. She went missing after a church service one night. She had stayed late to clean up. Next day, the church's administrator showed up and found her car in the parking lot. The driver's door was open, and her keys were on the ground near it."

Kenna asked, "What about the husband? He didn't report her missing?"

"He'd gone to stay with his mother for the weekend and took their child with them. Could be a coincidence, but it might not be."

She looked at the time on the dash. "I need to get inside for my appointment, but can you find out if there are any similarities between these three cases—the two missing women and Nicola Santorini?"

"I'm digging in now."

"Thanks, Maze."

Jax told her bye and hung up. "Ready for this?"

"No." She wasn't going to lie. "I want to know, but I also don't want to know."

"I can understand that."

"Whatever he did to me...it's done. I doubt there's any reversing it. And honestly, why would I want to go back? My arms are stronger. All of me is stronger. I have to learn exactly how much stronger and how to account for it. And what the drawbacks are going to be."

"You think he did you a favor?"

No way to tell. "I just don't want to keep being kidnapped if it means I need treatments. I don't want to be someone who's inexplicably missing or the subject of an experiment. I just want them to leave me alone. Preferably long enough that I can figure out how to destroy them."

Jax squeezed her knee. "That's my girl."

She chuckled, shaking her head.

"You can go in by yourself if you want to. I don't need to be in there."

"I know, but you should come with me and hang in the waiting room at least." Not just because she'd rather not face this alone. It was an odd mix of wanting to shield him from it and knowing she probably needed him there to help her deal with the test results. If only she could handle it herself.

Which meant she should pray that God gave her what she needed to get through this.

It wasn't only about her being sufficient on her own or leaning on Jax and getting her strength from him. What she needed to do was go to God for strength.

"I'll find a good restaurant for dinner after."

She smiled at him, got out of the car, and headed into the doctor's office with her husband right behind her. The waiting room was empty. Within ten minutes, they had her in a gown, lying on a table while the scanner thing moved over her.

Kenna avoided the questions of why she'd suddenly requested the test, opting for an answer about getting older. Sure, she was only in her mid-thirties, but why not get a jump on the next twenty years and how her health was going to change? She'd need a baseline later. The nurse and the imaging assistant didn't seem to believe what she said, but she sounded convinced about her own story at least.

After she'd dressed, they showed her to an office. The nurse stood by the door. "The doctor will be with you shortly to discuss your results."

"My husband is out in the waiting area. Can I go get him? He'll want to be in here."

"I'll show him back." The nurse gave her a polite smile and shut the door.

Even though there were two chairs in front of the desk, Kenna wandered to the credenza and looked at the shelves. Photos of the doctor in a row—framed pictures of him with the governor and then on a cruise with his family. He seemed like a nice guy who kept his figure trim and enjoyed having a tan from his leisure activities.

She couldn't tell much else from his office since it needed to present a professional front. It wasn't as if he was going to leave his dirty secrets on the desktop where a lone patient could snoop. She wiggled the mouse and found she'd need a password to access his computer. So he cared about keeping records secure. Or perhaps maintaining his own privacy.

Hopefully, this doctor wouldn't face any danger from

treating her, even if the last one had probably been kidnapped because of her.

Kenna heard a shuffle behind her.

The door hadn't opened, so no one else was in—

A sharp prick turned into a burning sensation in her upper arm. She twisted, grabbed the outside of her shoulder as she turned...

And came face-to-face with a guy taller than her, dressed in white scrubs and wearing a white mask with holes for eyes.

She rushed at him, but he caught her. Her limbs felt like jelly. He turned her and sat her in one of the chairs.

She tried to speak. No words came out.

Jax. She screamed his name in her head. This was it. They were going to take her from him. This time, she was going to remember every terrifying second of it.

She tried to move, but it felt like being paralyzed—or how she imagined that would feel. Wanting to move but unable to get her body to cooperate. Her mind was convinced she should be able to move if she simply willed her body to do so hard enough, as if her mind had full control over her body. But she couldn't even lift a finger. She could barely hold her own head up.

Her lips wouldn't move any more than her body.

She couldn't get to her phone to warn anyone or call for help. But Jax would know something was wrong as soon as he was brought here.

A door to the side opened, and he walked in. Doctor Marcus Buzard. She'd seen him more in photos than in real life, at least that she could remember. The top of his head reflected the light overhead, and he stared at her with an assessing gaze as he went to sit behind the desk.

Whoever had stuck her with that needle was probably still here, lurking behind her.

The doctor's shoulders filled out the lab coat. He wore a purple shirt with a floral tie under it, along with gray slacks. He settled into the chair, which rolled back a couple of inches.

"It's good you sought out the right kind of testing." He set a tablet on the desk in front of him and swiped on the screen. "It will make it easier for you to follow my instructions if you understand what we're trying to achieve here."

She stared at him.

"Over the past seventy years, my predecessors and I have been endeavoring to provide *Dominatus* with the perfect operative. Considering you are one of their progeny, it seemed you fell into my lap when you moved here with your husband. Certainly made it easier to continue your treatment."

So she'd walked right into a trap. Or the whole thing had been orchestrated. The *Dominatus* might have been pulling strings the whole time, making sure Jax got his job here. Directing their lives so that they'd settle in this city where the doctor already had everything set up.

He wasn't the man in the photos on the credenza, so she figured he didn't operate out of this office specifically. Hopefully, the doctor who did was still alive and not another casualty of this war she'd found herself caught up in.

Kenna tried to inhale, but it was like sucking through a blocked straw. Her head swam.

"You gave her too much, Earnest." Doctor Buzard shoved his chair back and came around the desk to her. He touched two fingers to the underside of her neck. Checking for a pulse.

I'm not dead yet, Buddy.

She wanted to strangle him, but that would have to wait until she could move her fingers. When she had her strength back, he was going to regret doing this to her.

Doctor Buzard chuckled, digging in his breast pocket for a tiny flashlight, which he flicked in front of her eyes, moving it from side to side. "Kenna Banbury isn't scared of us."

He was wrong about that. She simply preferred anger... and action. As far as she was concerned, he could do whatever he wanted to her so long as Jax was kept out of it. More likely, though, he would be the leverage they'd use to convince her to cooperate.

He reached over her shoulder and accepted something from Earnest. Another sting, burning in the outside of her arm, and he used his thumb to massage deep circles on the outside of her shoulder. "Give it a second. I don't need you dying and costing me all that valuable work."

"...kill you."

He chuckled. "I see you can breathe more easily. You may be able to move a little as well, so I'll take my seat back behind the desk. I don't need you scratching my eyes out."

She tried to respond to that, but the words got trapped on her tongue. Earnest laid heavy hands on her shoulders, holding her in her seat. As if she could stand.

He settled back in the chair across the desk. "Each month, you will require additional treatments. You will also need to adjust your diet to accommodate your body's need for additional calcium and some other key nutrients. Your meal delivery service will continue."

She frowned. The service that sent them boxed meals and recipes every week? She'd figured Jax set that up when she wasn't feeling well, and maybe he had, but it turned out to be this guy's doing? She wanted to throw it all out.

"If you don't comply, which is for your own good, failure to follow the instructions will be considerably... uncomfortable."

"It'll hurt."

He nodded. "If you don't comply, we'll be forced to *retrieve* you. Admit you for observation."

"You mean kidnap me. The way you kidnapped Nicola Santorini, Rebecca Hardy, and Melissa Graham."

Buzard actually looked impressed. "Interesting conclusions."

"Are they wrong?"

"What I do is no one else's business."

"Except *Dominatus*."

The hands holding her in the chair flexed, squeezing her shoulders hard enough she winced. Someone else who didn't like hearing that name out loud? Too bad.

"You work for them."

The doctor wiped his damp forehead with the back of his hand. "I provide a unique service. In return, they ensure I'm not disturbed and don't run into anything that might interrupt my research." He swiped the screen of his tablet. "Earnest, we should draw more blood while Ms. Banbury is here. I don't believe we have time to take spinal fluid. That can wait until next time."

"Why?" She needed to know why he'd targeted her. Why she'd been singled out. Just as she needed to know if anyone else in her family were targets. Jax was outside—had they captured him with the intent to experiment on him?

The idea of it made her want to rage. To make sure all the focus remained on her.

Doctor Buzard didn't look up from his tablet. "We don't

need your husband interrupting a delicate procedure. I'd hate to have to kill him. I doubt I'd secure your cooperation after that."

"I mean, why are you doing this?" She wanted to kill *him*, but would she be signing her own death warrant at the same time, and that of those men at the retirement home? The consequences could be disastrous.

She tried to move her fingers and could twitch them, but only barely. It took far more effort than she had.

The doctor sighed. "Earnest? Take the samples."

His hands eased off her shoulders.

She wanted to run but couldn't move. "Jax!" she yelled his name as loudly as she could.

A split second later, a heavy hand cuffed her across the back of the head.

"Earnest, is that any way to treat our guest?" Buzard chuckled, still not looking up from his tablet. Certain that there was no way Jax would come in and disturb them. Maybe he simply believed Earnest would take care of the "problem" if that occurred. "Hmm, interesting."

She wanted to roll her eyes, but Earnest distracted her by tying off a strip of rubber just above her elbow and sticking a needle in her arm. He had a crescent moon scar at the base of his thumb, on his right hand, so she focused on that and not the burning pain on the inside of her elbow.

"Ow." She said it loudly, in Earnest's masked face. He didn't seem to care, though. "Don't quit your day job, Earnest." If only she could tear that stupid mask from his face and see the man hiding underneath.

"Very interesting."

Kenna gritted her teeth as Earnest filled the third vial of her blood. "Care to share, Doc?"

"Your bone density tests."

"It would be good to know if I'm in danger of shattering."

"Your red cell count is down, which is to be expected given that bone marrow is what produces blood cells."

"That's gonna cause me other problems, right?" She needed to get online and search what happened when a person had solid bones with no marrow. That couldn't be a good thing, but it explained the heaviness and fatigue she'd been feeling.

"Not if you continue your treatments," he said. "I'm thinking synthetic bone marrow might do the trick. At least while our stem cell research is still ongoing."

"Great. Sounds great." She didn't bother to keep the sarcasm from her tone. "Let's schedule out some appointments so I know where to be and when."

He smiled at his tablet.

Earnest finished what he was doing and pulled the needle roughly from her arm. He untied the strip of rubber from above her elbow. Kenna focused on her other arm, the left one. Could she...?

Her arm swung over toward him, and she managed to bat his face, catching him enough by surprise that she got purchase on his mask and ripped it down. The face that stared back at her seared in her mind. It was familiar. She wasn't going to forget that pasty complexion, those dark eyes that were almost black, and those meaty cheeks.

She also wasn't going to forget the surprise on his face.

Or the fact this was one of the police officers who had responded to the callout at the medical center. Which meant the doctor *did* have a connection to Nicola Santorini, at least to her practice. There was something odd about his ears, but she couldn't tell what from straight on.

Kenna stared at him. "Gotcha."

He spun away, dropping the vials of blood on the carpet and scrambling to put the mask back on his face.

She glared at the doctor. "Where is Nicola Santorini?"

Resorting to threats wasn't likely to get her anywhere. He obviously had a cop in his pocket, so he wasn't afraid of being discovered by the police. He probably had some other officials somewhere in his pocket, too. Or *Dominatus* took care of those pesky annoyances for him, leaving the doc to do his research undisturbed.

"Where did you take her?"

The doctor lifted his face. He didn't even look at Earnest, who had resituated his mask over his face and retrieved the vials from the floor. The doctor said, "I believe you're missing something important in all this. Two somethings, actually."

"Like what?"

"Instead of firing off questions, you should be thanking me. I've given you a gift."

She stared at him. He could *not* be serious. "You expect me to be grateful? You're insane."

He laughed, pushing his chair back and standing. "I consider that a compliment."

"If you've done something to Jax, I will kill you."

He continued laughing as he headed for the side door.

She felt hot breath by her ear, then the prick of something against the side of her neck.

At last, Earnest said, "This isn't over."

Kenna said, "I'm counting on it."

She knew who he was, but there was no way he could kill her here. That would only cause problems between him and the doctor. But oh, he wanted to.

The feeling was mutual.

"Jax!" she screamed his name again, but Earnest punched her in the head.

Everything went black.

Chapter Fifteen

Kenna came awake swinging. Jax grunted, next to her but not on his normal side. She slept on the left. Why was he over on that side?

She sat up. "What the…"

It all flashed back to her mind. The bone density test and the doctor. Earnest and his face. Other things she couldn't recall right away, which she would need time to process.

Jax shifted on the bed and groaned. "Ouch. I feel like I was whacked on the head."

"You probably were." She flopped back onto the pillow and looked around. This was their room. They were both fully clothed—thank You, God—and she had her shoes on again. "Don't they know you take your shoes off at the door when you come home? Who wants all that street dirt tracked all the way through the house?"

She hadn't been given the results of her test. She'd been hoodwinked into facing the doctor again. As if she was going to thank him.

Kenna rolled her eyes because she could. Because she was allowed to control her own emotions and reactions, and no one could tell her what to do or not do. Whether that guy thought he could control her life or not, it was only if she allowed it. He would never own her.

Jax slid his hand over to hers. "Come on." He sat up, tugging her with him. "We need to flush this from our systems and figure out what's going on."

Now he knew what it had been like for her to wake up after being kidnapped last time, except back then, she hadn't known what had happened to her. It had only been a portion of lost time.

She brushed hair back from her face, the inside of her elbow stinging yet again. "We should check the cameras."

"They're going to be wearing masks. Or it'll look like you and I came home, except for the shoes. But maybe they're going to better disguise their intrusion this time." His tone bled with anger and frustration, emotions that she hadn't heard from him much.

The guy was so steady she sometimes wondered if he had negative reactions at all, but once in a while, it showed through.

Frustration. Fear.

She was looking forward to a lifetime of him peeling back the layers as they continued to get to know each other. In a lot of ways, he was another mystery for her to solve. Maybe even in all the best ways that was why he appealed to her. That and his steady goodness.

She stood in front of him and touched his cheeks, ignoring the assessment her mind wanted to make of how she felt. Right now, this was about him. "Are you okay? Did they do anything to you?"

"I got jumped." He scrunched up his nose, then twisted

to tug up his T-shirt and reveal a red mark on the side of his ribs. "Someone kicked me. I didn't see their face, though."

She couldn't forget the face she'd seen. "Then what happened?"

"I think they knocked me out. I tried to get to you because I heard you call my name." He shook his head. "I'm telling this backward. Feels like my head is scrambled."

Thankfully, he hadn't been hurt worse than that.

He kissed her, quick and hard. An almost desperate note to it, but there was still a whole lot of relief. She hung on, not wanting to let go of him. Feeling the sensation of having him here with her—both of them safe. She'd needed him in that room, and it wasn't his fault that he hadn't been able to get to her.

Neither of them was responsible for this. In some ways, they were more like a pair of mice in some grand experiment—powerless. So she took what he was willing to give. Just to remind herself again, and some more, that she had control over herself. She made the choices here, not some doctor working for *Dominatus*.

When their kiss wound down, both of them breathing hard, neither one let go.

He asked, "What did they do to you?"

Kenna explained about the paralyzing agent and how she managed to fight back. "I saw his face." She had to take a breath. "The doctor called him Earnest, but it was one of the cops who responded to the medical center. They took the kids to..."

Her thoughts stuttered.

"They took the kids." She tightened her grip on Jax's shirt. "We need to find the kids and make sure nothing happened to them. He said I was missing something or some *things*. I don't know. Maybe that's what he meant."

Jax nodded. "Okay, let's call Maizie. See what she can find out."

"I'm going to check the cameras. I want to see if there's anything that we can use as evidence against them." Kenna followed him to the door. "Can you look for Jolene? Maybe they put her in the linen closet again."

"We should also check everything we own for bugs, surveillance devices, and GPS locators. Who knows how closely they're keeping tabs on us."

Kenna shivered at the idea that their private lives were being observed. What happened between a married couple was their business and not for viewing purposes. She didn't need another reason to want to get the doctor, his minions, and the *Dominatus* out of their lives, but if she did, that would definitely be on the top of the list.

"Jolene!" Jax started, ahead of her, and then chuckled.

She heard a meow across the house and went to check it out. When she didn't find Jolene in the room that Jax had turned into a home office/gym, she called out the cat's name again.

Maybe the hall bathroom?

But she didn't see the cat in there or in the shower. Kenna crouched and opened the cupboard under the sink. Jolene jumped out and landed on Kenna's shoulder, scrambling for purchase. "Whoa, kitty."

She stood, holding the cat on her shoulder and wandered back to Jax. "Found her."

He turned to her, the phone at his ear, standing in the kitchen between the dining table and the breakfast bar. He lifted his chin. "Thanks, Maizie. I'm going to call my office as well. Find out what we can about the officers who responded to the call. If one is dirty, we need evidence to bring to the Phoenix PD's Internal Affairs Department."

Kenna grabbed a treat for Jolene. One of the fancy ones. She set the cat down on the back of the couch, where Jolene would be able to see Kenna and Jax, and put the treat in front of her.

"Thanks, Maze. Will do." He hung up. "Is Jolene okay?"

Kenna studied her for a second, watching her movements. Not really sure how to tell. "I think so."

He slid his arm around her and kissed her forehead.

"Maizie is on the case of Earnest?"

Jax nodded his head against hers. "I'll get my laptop and look at the cameras we have."

"I need one of those wands that checks for bugs." Or she needed Bruce. "I'm gonna get some spy help." She found her phone on the dining table and called his number, explaining what had happened.

"I was wondering where you guys were at, but Maizie said you had an appointment and then you both went home."

"I'll have to ask her what time that happened, but I know it'll be wrong." Kenna explained Jax's theory about their lives being bugged.

"I'll be right there. We'll find 'em."

"Thanks, Bruce."

"Don't get soft on me now, girlie. I'm doin' my job." He hung up.

Kenna rolled her eyes, then went to slump onto the couch beside Jax. It was going to be a quiet evening for sure —unless they found out where the kids were. If two children needed rescuing, nothing was going to stop her from doing that.

But if they really were safe in the care of social services

or a family that fostered kids, then she could leave them to their lives.

Kenna curled her legs up, then remembered about her shoes and kicked them off. She tossed the shoes over the back of the couch. They landed in the mouth of the hall that led to the front door. She bent her legs, drawing her knees up so she could wiggle her toes under Jax's thigh while he tapped keys on the laptop.

"Cold?"

She started to shake her head but realized that wouldn't be true. "Maybe." She grabbed a blanket from the back of the couch that she'd used just a week ago—every time she was so exhausted she fell asleep on the couch. Days she couldn't have walked to the bedroom to nap there.

She felt so much better now, but it had been an interesting day.

"They took a lot of blood." He rested the back of his hand on her forehead. "I can make you some tea."

"Coffee would be great."

He chuckled, then said, "There's nothing on the cameras. Not even us coming back in. I think they just shut the system off, so it recorded nothing at the time they brought us home."

Kenna let out a long sigh, curling the blanket around her and leaning her head on his shoulder. "We need evidence. Not just for the doctor but everyone working with him. Any one of them could lead us to the *Dominatus*."

"And you're certain you want to go up against them?"

"I'm not sure we have the resources to go to war with a powerful group that has tendrils across the world, but I'm also certain I can't do *nothing*."

Jax nodded. "I know what you mean. If I jeopardize my job using federal resources to help you, does it really matter? In the grand scheme, we're doing the right thing. Even if it costs my career, there's a whole lot more at stake than that."

"If we succeed, we'll gain a whole lot more." Not that their victory was likely. But who would she be if she didn't at least try? "This is about justice and being able to live our happily ever after without this over our heads."

He nodded. "Right now, it's about this cop you saw and the safety of two children."

"Agreed."

The doorbell rang.

She started to get up, but Jax told her to stay put. He set his laptop on the coffee table. "Bruce was quick."

She watched the hall and heard the door open.

Jax asked, "Can I help you guys?"

She heard a scuffle, then more than one person came down the hall. Kenna couldn't keep twisting to the back of the couch. "By all means, come in."

There were two, then three...then four and five came in. All the men had gray in their hair except for the last two. The youngest were likely in their thirties. All of them wore suits. Shined black shoes—at least the ones whose feet she could see. Slicked back hair. The first man to enter moved to stand sentry in front of her TV unit. She pegged which one was the boss easily because he took the armchair. He had a ring on his pinkie, left hand.

Jax came from the front door, which was a good thing because she would've drawn the pistol under the couch cushions and demanded to know what they'd done with her husband. He came over and stood behind the couch where she sat, putting his hands on her shoulders. But it felt too much like what Earnest had done, keeping her in her seat even with the paralytic drug in her system.

She turned toward the man in her armchair and lifted one hand, lacing her fingers with Jax's. "Like he said"—she tipped her head toward Jax—"can we help you guys?"

"I don't often need to introduce myself, but I'll make an exception in your case."

Kenna nodded. "Obliged."

"I'm Gregorio Santino. These are my associates, family members, and...coworkers."

She glanced around. "And you're in my house because...?"

"You know where to find my Nicola. You know who took her, and you're going to get her back for me."

"Just because I know who took her doesn't mean I know how to find her." Unless she looked for the kids and that led her to the doctor. Could she find both? But there were so many pieces missing to this puzzle. Like why the doctor had been taken or what Doctor Buzard wanted with her.

Nicola could be dead...

Or working for him.

"I suggest you rectify that, Ms.—" Gregorio glanced at Jax. "Mrs. Jaxton."

"You can't pressure me into doing what your men should be able to do." She shrugged, motioning to them with a lift of her chin. Scattered around her living room so they looked imposing. Arms crossed so their upper bodies appeared more impressive. "Surely, you trust them to find Nicola more than you trust me. You wouldn't bring them with you if they couldn't get the job done."

"You're the last to see Nicola before she disappeared."

Kenna shook her head. It wasn't true, but she wouldn't tell him about Dana and what she had seen. Not yet, anyway.

Gregorio frowned. "You will do this for me, regardless. Use your resources to *get the job done.*"

"Just as long as you don't think I'm responsible for this."

"That's your only concern?"

"My concern right now is two potentially missing children." She should have checked up on them. Hadn't Bruce said he was going to do that? When he showed up, she'd have to ask him about it. When it came to Bruce, trust was an elusive commodity. The truth was, she had reason to distrust him. He was the kind of person who played the game but made up his own rules.

"My only concern is Nicola."

"You believe she's in danger?" Kenna needed to know if he had additional information.

Gregorio didn't even move, but there was a shift in him, and it felt like a threat. "You don't?"

"It would be far easier to work together. Pool our resources." Kenna figured that Jax wasn't going to like teaming up with a crime family from Las Vegas, though. "That will enable me to find Nicola more quickly."

"I don't get into agreements with the FBI." He stood. "Not after what they did to my family."

"Then why ask for my help? You know I married into the bureau." Sure, she spoke about it like it was a family. In a lot of ways, that was true.

"Anthony spoke highly of you. He was my father's cousin."

"I'm sorry for your loss." What else could she say?

Anthony Santino had been her father's associate. She'd met him in Vegas the last time she was there—when Maizie had escaped, and Kenna had killed the man who held her captive for years. Santino had been looking for revenge, and he'd been killed by a dirty FBI agent who'd been controlled by a man who believed he had all the power.

"I know who you are and that you tried to help him."

"He told me he made peace with what happened to his family, but he still wanted revenge."

Gregorio said, "That's why you're going to find Nicola. Because you got yourself all in with the FBI, and I figure they owe my family."

Chapter Sixteen

"You knew his father's cousin?" Jax turned from closing the door behind the Santino family patriarch —or so she assumed—and his associates. The men who protected him.

Kenna leaned against the corner of the wall with the blanket wrapped around her. She was freezing. "You met him in Vegas."

"Right." Jax shook his head, then looked at the watch on his wrist. "I thought Bruce was gonna be here soon?"

She went and got her phone, her mind full of thoughts of Vegas crime families and the horrifying situation they'd pulled Maizie out of, which had connected Kenna to Anthony Santino. He had died in the course of her freeing Maizie. At least he'd told her he was at peace before he died.

Kenna needed everyone to come over so they could make a plan. A wave of anxiety shook her insides. Jax was vulnerable like her. Right now, he was as much of a target as she was. "I should put locators on all of them. Didn't you call Ramon a few days ago? I thought he was coming to Phoenix."

Bruce had told her that Ramon was recently working in Palm Springs.

"Might take another day. He was all the way up north in Wisconsin when I talked to him the day before yesterday." Jax sighed. "That whole conversation with the Santinos was crazy. Those guys think you're just going to drop everything and look for that woman? Gregorio Santino, the guy who snaps his fingers and people jump to do whatever he wants?"

She was still stuck on the Wisconsin thing. "We don't have any cases up there." Ramon's sister had been killed in that area. Maybe he'd wanted to finally say goodbye. But right now? "The only other thing I can think of is—"

"Forrest Crosby."

She stared at her husband. "Do you know something I don't?"

"I know I thought he was in love with you."

Kenna winced. The one time Ramon had kissed her was out of relief because they'd nearly died, and neither of them had ever mentioned it afterward. He knew she loved Jax, and he'd never made a real move on her to try and persuade her otherwise. She hadn't been aware that Jax knew about Ramon's feelings when she wasn't even certain.

Jax continued, "He told me he and Forrest hit it off at our wedding. So, he went up there to spend some time with her."

"She lost her husband years ago. She always seemed lonely, and he's... I guess in his own way Ramon is a good guy." It wasn't a case that had brought Kenna to Forrest's house, just a place to stay with her RV. In the end, they'd remained friends. She just hadn't anticipated this twist to their friendship. "I should have loaned him the RV. There's less chance he'd get into trouble if he has his own living space."

Jax kissed her forehead. "As if he's gonna give up a vintage Charger to borrow your house."

"Fine, I guess not." She slid onto a bar stool at the counter. "Okay, the doctor is missing. We're presuming that Buzard has Nicola, right? Same kidnappers, same outfits. Who else would it be? Now the Mafia wants us to find her because they think we're their connection to Buzard."

"Maybe they're afraid of him, and they need you in the mix to take the heat."

"Seems like they shouldn't be afraid of anything, but you might be right." She tried to get her thoughts straight. "We still need to check everything we own and every inch of this house—and our cars—for bugs. We also need to find those two kids and make sure they're good so that I can sleep at night. Then, we need to find that cop who is one of the doctor's minions." She shook her head. "Earnest. If that's even his real name."

She reiterated to Jax how that cop and his partner had shown up at the medical center and agreed to take the kids to get checked out and then settled with social services. He'd been the man drawing her blood, wearing a mask until she'd pulled it off.

Jax said, "That might be how Doctor Santorini got on Buzard's radar. When the cop reported back that you'd seen her for something, they decided to act after that."

"If those kids are alive, then I don't care about the rest of it." She bit her lip. "I'm sorry about Nicola if she is in danger, but it isn't like I can account for everything. We need to find those children."

"You'd ditch the whole idea of taking down *Dominatus*

just for the sake of two kids?" He'd asked, but it wasn't a question. Not really. Because Jax already knew the answer.

"Yes."

There were actually a lot of things she would ditch that case for. She stared him down. Almost daring him to ask her to list all the things she would give up her life and her goals for.

Jax said, "They're bad people. Nicola could be in serious danger."

"I could argue I'm as much of a victim of theirs as she is. And why is it my job to take them down? There's a world full of billions of people. Governments. Police forces. Military. Someone else can do it." She lifted her chin. "I've got too much to lose."

Jax kissed her gently. Before he could say anything, the front door opened.

"It's just me." Bruce wandered in and spotted them. "Again?"

Jax smirked. "I'm making coffee." He wandered around the end of the breakfast bar.

She turned to Bruce. "It's been a long day."

"I'll say. Kidnapped?" He actually looked like he might be worried about her. His usual Hawaiian-style shirt had a sheen of sweat the material had absorbed.

She could say they were fine, but that wasn't the truth. "Jax has a big bruise."

"This isn't show-and-tell." Jax took the carafe to the fridge to fill it with filtered water.

Bruce said, "Good, 'cause I ain't a nurse."

"We need to know if this house is bugged."

He frowned. "Of course, it's bugged. And you just said that out loud, so now they know that you *know* that it's bugged."

"So find them for me and get rid of them."

"Already did, three times. They put more in."

Jax turned from the coffeepot. He'd loaded it all in but hadn't hit the button. She pointed to it to remind him to turn it on, but all of his attention was on Bruce. "You found bugs in my house?"

Bruce nodded, folding his arms and leaning one shoulder against the fridge. "The day you guys went hiking at Camelback Mountain. Then another day when you were doing background on that Fleming woman." He looked at Kenna. "Plus the day after you first realized they had been in your house."

She lifted her chin. "How did you get in and out with the security system?"

"Maizie spoofed it. She said she wanted the practice."

Jax got a mug down, and it slammed on the counter. "I'm guessing I need an upgrade. Seems like anyone can get in and out of this house without me knowing." Maybe he didn't mean to slam it that hard because the second and third mugs landed more quietly.

"I'm a super spy. And the doctor and his people have been kidnaping victims for years with no one discovering what they've done until now. Of course, they can get in and out with no one knowing."

"I know that's supposed to make me feel better, Bruce." Jax stood on the other side of the breakfast bar, across from her. "But it doesn't."

"These people have resources." Bruce didn't back down. "It's not like we're going to beat them at their own game. They've been doing this for too long."

Kenna asked, "So how do we take them down?"

"We need a whole new way of going after them." Jax

didn't move. "We need to change the playing field so we're on the offensive, and *they* get knocked back a step."

That still left the question of how. The only thing she could think of was if they could get someone on the inside.

Jax said, "Might be time to brainstorm."

"That, or we get Maizie to backtrace their surveillance and find out who is watching us."

Bruce said, "We tried that. No go." He looked at Jax. "That's how I know you don't need to feel bad. These people are beyond pros. The pros don't even know how to do some of the stuff they do."

Kenna said, "So you found a group of lawyers itching to take down the doctor and sent them my way?"

He shrugged. "Outside the box, right?"

"I guess I always need a shot at representation if something happens and I wind up in jail." She'd been interviewed by the police at the lawyers' office, but not by the same men who had driven away in a black-and-white police car, wearing cop uniforms, with the kids in the back seat. "I need to call that sergeant."

"Your new best friend?"

She gave Jax a smirk. "I bet he'd love to hear from me."

"Especially when you tell him that one of his guys is responsible for kidnapping and potentially murder."

"He stuck a needle in me."

Bruce said, "You saw his face?"

"I pulled his mask off. It was one of the cops from the medical center."

Bruce's jaw hardened. In fact, his whole body tensed. "Which one?"

"Find the bugs—again. I'll get his name and address, and we'll go talk to him."

"You talk. I'll be explaining some things in...other

ways." Bruce left the room before she got a chance to correct his assumptions on how this was going to go.

She sent a message to Maizie with what she had on the cop, hoping her tech genius could find the information she needed. If they were real cops, not two guys just pretending, there would be a department record of them responding to the callout at the medical center.

When she was done, she flipped her phone face down. "Everything feels like a collection of odd threads right now. Like there's a million different things going on, and I can't get a handle on how it all weaves together. Usually, I have more questions than answers, but it's like all I have is answers, and I'm not seeing the questions."

"You'll figure it out." He reached over and squeezed her hand. "Don't you always?"

"Okay, but a team of eager FBI analysts wouldn't be a horrible idea, right?"

He smiled. "I think someone might notice if I suddenly tasked a group of my staff to help you."

"What? I can be subtle. We'll say I'm a consultant."

"If anyone asks, you *are* a consultant. I signed the paperwork weeks ago just so we didn't have to deal with questions if you started helping. Or"—he cleared his throat—"suddenly find yourself in the middle of one of my cases."

"I would never." She tried to sound aghast. Or, at least, kind of surprised.

Jax just chuckled.

Bruce wandered in and dumped a load of miniature electronic devices on the breakfast bar. "Some of those...you don't want to know where they were."

"No, I don't."

Though, Jax looked like maybe he did. Like he wanted to smash them all with the heel of his shoe. He scooped them up. "These are going on the grill." He headed for the slider that led out to the back.

"Anything on your cop?"

Kenna checked her phone for messages while saying to him, "You and I were both planning to check on those kids. Far as I can see, both of us dropped the ball. I hope we don't regret it any more than I do right now."

Bruce searched the kitchen, then leaned his hips back against the counter and folded his arms. "I found the social worker who was assigned their case."

"So they really were taken to the hospital and then turned over to child welfare?" She'd seriously failed those kids. Sure, she'd been dealing with a lot, but that didn't excuse the fact she'd made far too many assumptions about them being taken care of.

"The hospital wouldn't give me information on them, so I gave it a day and hit up the social worker. I tracked her down at her office, but all she did was give me the runaround."

"Okay. That's at least someone we can follow up with."

He lifted his brows. "After we work over this cop. Find out why he's working with that psycho doctor guy."

Jax came in a moment later. Her phone had pinged with the information.

She asked, "You up for a field trip?"

Her husband said, "I'll pour the coffee into hot cups so we can take it with us." He even poured one for Bruce, who'd already crossed the street to his pickup truck so he could follow them.

"He's a good guy." Kenna buckled her seat belt and took a sip of her drink before they even pulled out.

Jax returned from taking Bruce his coffee. "He had a

flask. He slipped a swig of whatever was in there into his coffee."

She twisted in the seat to see out the back window through the open garage door. "I'll talk to him."

"I called Stairns about it a few days ago, and he said Bruce told him the wound in his chest has healed. At least, according to the doctor. But Bruce didn't seem to be convinced that's true."

"So, he's still in pain and self-medicating?" She'd been so wrapped up in her own medical situation, and everyone on her team letting Jax and her have time as newlyweds, that she hadn't checked in. She'd just figured things were good.

Jax said, "I can talk to him if you want. I mean, I know what he's going through."

He had told her shortly after they met that he had a pain pill addiction problem in high school after an ankle injury. She thanked him and squeezed his knee.

"As long as I don't have to arrest him for something, we'll be good."

Kenna grinned. She confirmed on her phone that it was the correct cop that Maizie had found. He wasn't working tonight, and they had his home address. "Time to get some answers."

If she was lucky, she'd figure out what the right questions were.

The neighborhood was an apartment complex. As soon as Jax pulled up, she spotted the light on in the front window, between the blinds.

"He might be home." A swell of anger rose up in her at the prospect of seeing him again. She was still freezing, and on top of that, she now had a bruise on the inside of her elbow from where he'd dragged that needle out of her arm.

She pushed out of the car and walked to the front door with Jax, spotting Bruce as he pulled into the parking lot and stopped on the far side of a berm. Hanging back, just in case. If he had a problem with pain management, they needed to address it. This team wasn't going to work if people were keeping things to themselves. Like recovery that wasn't going as planned. Or having a relationship with her friend.

Jax hammered his fist on the front door. "Earnest Albertson! Open up, this is the FBI!"

Something shattered inside the house. Was it from surprise, or had something else caused Earnest to drop whatever he had?

Jax pounded again. "Open the door."

"Maybe he's calling his union rep before he does that." She shrugged. But her nerve endings were lighting up. "Back up from the door."

"I'm out of the way."

"Okay, but—" Kenna reached for his arm, all her instincts flaring to life.

The door exploded in a shower of splintered wood and the sound of a shotgun blast.

Chapter Seventeen

The door had exploded outward, creating a giant hole in the reinforced door. Bent metal from the inner frame. Dust everywhere. Kenna had crouched to the right of the door, getting low out of instinct. Protecting her vital organs, one knee bent in front of her and the other tucked under so she could launch up at the first sign of someone making a run for it.

She smiled. It would feel good to release some tension with a physical altercation. All the frustration she'd been feeling lately. She could channel it into her limbs and take down a bad guy. Except, given what the doctor had done to her, that would likely result in her doing more damage to the person than she expected—maybe even killing them.

Probably not a good idea.

Jax asked, "Why do you look like you're having fun?"

Another shot hammered the door, this one going through the hole to hit the neighboring door on the far side. She glanced back at her husband. "Tell me you don't relish a good old-fashioned shoot-out."

He shifted his gun to his nondominant hand and drew

his phone from his pocket to call 911 and ask for police backup.

But the cops might not be a help here. "Isn't this guy a cop? They'll probably show up and defend him."

"You don't know"—another shot hit the door but didn't bust another hole in it—"that." Jax flinched. "Officer Albertson! This is the FBI. Put down your weapon and come out with your hands up!"

From inside the house, Earnest screamed obscenities at them.

"Lovely." Kenna frowned, pulling out her phone so she could see what all the vibrating was about.

Another shot exploded through the hole, this time hitting the siding beside the door facing this one.

She thumbed to the notification and hit play on the voice message.

It was Bruce. "...shooting. He's climbing out the window on the east side."

She hit the button. "Who's climbing out?"

He replied a second later. "The cop. He's got the window open, and he's pushing the screen out, making a run for it."

Another shot rang out, cracking like a firework. She flinched every time the noise was so loud. But if the suspect was climbing out the window, then who was firing through the door. "There are two of them?"

"I'll wait here for backup," Jax said. "You go help Bruce."

Bruce probably didn't need help, but she didn't plan to argue with her husband. "Got it." She stood up out of her crouch, then hesitated. She couldn't get to him to say something or squeeze his hand without crossing in front of the door.

"Go." The look on his face was enough.

She returned that look, hoping he saw what she wanted to say—what she felt for him—in her expression. "Be careful." She turned and ran for the back corner of the building.

"You, too," drifted after her.

She squared up on the corner, then peered around. Bruce was out of sight. A man climbed out of the window, one leg over the sill. Then an arm.

She waited until he was halfway before she moved. Steady pace, gun at a forty-five—which with the bandage didn't feel great. "Hands on your head." Kenna employed all that "command presence" the FBI had taught her, not giving this guy any room to disagree or fight back. "Easy."

He wasn't Earnest Albertson. This guy had stringy hair, jeans, and a dirty T-shirt. He wore Birkenstocks with no socks. One fell off his leading foot.

"Climb out." She held her gun ready. "Any weapons on you?"

Bruce came over, covering her just in case. From inside the residence, another shot went off. Bruce said, "Earnest is in there, firing at us?"

"Firing at Jax."

"I've got this." Bruce let her cover him, moving toward this guy so he could secure his hands behind his back with plastic ties.

"The police will want to talk with him when they get here."

The guy slumped to the grass, his hands behind him, and groaned. "I'm helping the police! I don't need to get in trouble again."

Kenna asked, "If you're helping the police, then why would you be in trouble?"

She heard a shotgun ratchet through the open window

and looked but didn't see the shooter. This guy had been climbing out of the bedroom window. Jax was still pinned down outside the front door, and the cops weren't here yet.

She looked at Bruce. "Stay here?"

"Got it. Go help your boy."

"Don't leave this guy." She grabbed the frame and climbed in the window, moving quietly across the carpeted bedroom. Mattress on the floor, the sheet coming off one corner. Blanket dumped in a pile and a pillow that looked like a bowling ball had rested in the middle.

She eased the door open slowly and looked out into the hall.

Earnest had his back to her. Dark hair with a balding circle at the crown that she hadn't noticed before. He wore a checkered shirt and black jeans a few sizes too big. On his feet were boots that were smudging dirt on the hall carpet.

He lowered the shotgun and reached to a box by his foot for more shells.

"Put the gun down, Earnest!" She shouted loudly enough that Jax was sure to hear her while keeping her body covered by the bedroom door frame. It wouldn't keep her from getting hurt if he shot at her, but it was better than nothing. "Drop it on the carpet and put your hands up."

Jax kicked the front door open, all the way at the end of the hall, and looked before he stepped in. He'd wasted no time coming to her aid as backup. "Earnest Albertson! Gun down. Hands up." His expression remained hard and his tone flat. "Do as the lady says."

She almost smiled.

Earnest set the gun on the carpet. She strode forward, stowing her gun and pulling out more plastic ties while Jax covered her. "We make a pretty good team." She pulled one hand down from Earnest's head, then the other. She could have tightened the plastic down farther but didn't.

No crescent moon scar.

She turned Earnest by his shoulder, which put his back to the wall. His hands were bound and out of sight. It looked like Earnest Albertson. She turned him again. "No scar."

"What?" Jax didn't move, still covering her.

She locked eyes with the man. "Who are you?"

"Isn't this the guy you saw with Doctor Buzard?" Jax asked.

The man smirked. "Who?"

She could ask if he'd ever seen her before, but was he really going to tell the truth? What she needed was evidence. "There's a guy on the back lawn. Your buddy didn't get away. How are you going to explain him being in here with you and making a run for it while you opened fire on the FBI?"

"You ain't FBI."

"I'm not." She thumbed over her shoulder. "But he is." This guy might be in over his head in a major way. "Which means you're in big trouble, *Officer Albertson*." She took a half step toward him. "Where are those kids you took from the medical center?"

His muscles shifted, but she didn't expect what happened next.

His head came down faster than she could react, and he slammed his skull against her forehead, causing her own head to whip back. But she didn't lose her balance.

Kenna worked her jaw side to side. "Ouch."

The man's eyes widened, and his knees collapsed.

"He's going down." Jax took a step closer, kicking the shotgun out of the way. "Guess you have a hard head."

Her head throbbed, pounding where he'd slammed his against it. "That hurt a lot."

"Getting headbutted usually does."

The man blinked, dazed.

She said, "I need to check something. I don't think this is Earnest, but I want to be sure."

"Cops are here." He looked from the open front door back to the man sitting on his behind in his hallway. Shotgun. Shells. Why would a police officer open fire on someone showing up at his house?

Unless he knew for sure he'd been outed and wanted to resolve the situation with as much trouble as possible. She didn't understand it. Only this man could explain why he'd done what he had done.

She headed for the living room but found nothing personal, just the usual couch and TV. He didn't even have a magazine lying around. The remote was tucked away in a console in the couch arm.

The bedroom she'd been in already.

Second room in the hall was more of an office setup. Computer. File cabinet, mostly empty. She found a few old paper bills from years ago in hanging file folders in one of the drawers.

Kenna rifled back far enough to find a birth certificate—along with a second one. Really the only explanation, apart from *Dominatus* was that Earnest had an identical twin. The organization might have had something to do with that, but it could also be unrelated to her enemy.

Maybe Doctor Buzard had wanted a set of twins, one a cop and the other one of his minions. Or they were both in his employ. Maybe the kind of twins who switched out for each other, assuming one persona between the two of them. It would only work for so long.

The name on this birth certificate was Regis Albertson.

She found one for Earnest Albertson right behind it. Time of birth and the date were near exact matches. She took both papers with her back to Jax. "Twins. I'm guessing they're identical."

The man scowled up at her from the floor.

"Which one are you?"

"The one who's gonna kill you." He laughed.

Two police officers announced their presence and came in. "Albertson, why are you on the floor?"

Kenna glanced at the cops. "Are you talking about Earnest or Regis? Because your Officer Albertson is a twin." She looked at the guy on the carpet. "And both of them need to explain what happened to those two kids escorted away from the medical center."

Near as she could figure, Earnest was the doctor's minion, but the cop also used the same name. Either one twin was both, or Regis worked as an officer under his brother's name. An interesting thought.

The cop with graying hair cut high and tight looked at Albertson. "You have any idea what she's talking about?"

Kenna explained about the medical center and the cops agreeing to take care of the kids. She shrugged. "Now where are they?"

High and Tight said, "You couldn't just call the precinct and ask."

"Why didn't Earnest here just answer the door? Why did he shoot at the FBI with a shotgun?" She added an explanation about the other guy who'd climbed out the window.

High and Tight's partner went to the front door, striding out. Probably looking for her "associate" and the man they'd secured on the grass outside.

Jax introduced himself. "This man shot at us through the door. I'd like him to answer questions, but we can do that at your precinct so he can have representation if he so desires."

Why did her mind immediately conjure images of the lawyers she'd met? It wasn't like they'd represent a piece of dirt like this. Unless that was part of how they went after Doctor Buzard, inadvertently gaining intel on him by representing people who knew him or worked for him.

"Kenna, do you need to get checked out by medics?"

She wanted to shake her head, but it was still pounding. "I'll make a statement and file charges because this police officer assaulted me."

"After you broke into his home, forcing him to defend himself?" High and Tight's eyebrows rose.

She focused on his nameplate, pinned to the front of his uniform shirt. *Sandring.* She could remember that name, in case she needed it later. "I'm sure Earnest will explain what happened, along with his reasoning for shooting at his front door. He could have shot an innocent person with all that wild firing."

Jax hauled Earnest—or his twin—to his feet. "Sounds like there's lots to talk about."

The other cop came in, tugging the window climber with him. The suspect muttered, causing the cop to respond, "Shut it."

High and Tight said, "Sounds like we're headed to the station."

The other cop looked back at the door. "There was another guy. He was supposed to follow." He groaned and pinned Kenna with a stare. "Was he with you?"

"I'll see if I can find him." She started toward the door.

High and Tight held out an arm, so she had to stop

rather than walk into it. "No one leaves. You can call your friend. They will show up at the station and answer questions." He glanced at Jax. "Let's load up and roll out."

The two cops went to the door first with the guy who'd climbed out the window. He might be some kind of confidential informant...something like that. The kind of guy who did favors for the cops and stayed out of jail. It looked like his luck had run out, and he knew it.

He grumbled all the way to the front door.

High and Tight stepped to the side, glancing once at the gunshot impact on the neighbor's door and the wall beside it.

"Your buddy did that." She motioned at Earnest—or Regis—with a tip of her head. "And he blew a hole in his door."

"Uptain, you put him in the car, then stay here and wait for the sarge. CSU needs to collect evidence and secure the residence. Make sure we have what we need to confirm the statements."

Kenna figured he meant that they wanted proof whether she and Jax were telling the truth. But the shooter was a cop, and they had a blue code, so she didn't begrudge his loyalty.

Even if it was misplaced.

Her phone buzzed in her pocket. She figured it was Bruce but didn't pull it out. The guy was morally opposed to talking with the police. Even if it meant that several departments across the country had warrants out for his arrest.

"Copy that, Sandring." The officer led Earnest's buddy to their black-and-white patrol car.

"What do you want us to do with Albertson?" Jax

asked. "We can escort him to the police station. We'll follow you there."

"I'll call another car for him."

Jax nodded as if that wasn't a slight. "Very well."

"I'm not going in." He had shaken out of his daze from headbutting her. "I'm not going to the station, and I'm not talking to no one."

Sandring had him cornered against the wall. "So you have a good explanation for firing at an FBI Special Agent in Charge?"

He whipped around to Jax, his eyes narrow. "I feared for my life."

"I wasn't even in your house." Jax didn't back down. "You shot through the door at me."

Sandring grabbed the radio on his shoulder, but before he squeezed the button, he said, "Save it for the interview room."

Yeah, Kenna's head was pounding enough she chose to forego listening to reason. She stepped behind Jax and around him so she could stand in front of the twin. "My head feels great. Thanks for smacking it with yours."

He sneered at her.

"Where are the two kids you took from the medical center? Or should I ask your partner about that? Does he work for Buzard also?" She was on a roll now, no stopping her. "Or is it your twin I should be talking to, *Regis*?"

The sneer dissipated from his face.

Probably because she'd figured out more than he wanted her too. He wasn't the man who had taken her blood at that appointment. Maybe he didn't even know it had happened.

Kenna continued, "I'm guessing he's the straightlaced one. A better cop than you. You're the screwup—the hothead who shoots at FBI agents and doesn't think things through." She pointed at the patrol car. "Your brother got himself a confidential informant. Some junkie looking for a way out, but you'd rather party with the guy, right? More fun that way."

He backed up and slammed into the wall but rallied and launched himself at her on a rebound. Jax got in front of her and faced off with him. "Don't even think about it."

Sandring said, "You have more witnesses this time. If you want any credence with internal affairs, you need to keep your mouth shut." He turned to them. "There's another car here. Let's go."

Chapter Eighteen

Kenna stared at the officer. "That's everything. No matter how many times you ask me." She lifted the cold soda can they'd brought her—the one she hadn't even opened—and pressed it to the spot on her forehead where Earnest...Reggie...whichever twin, had smacked her head with his. "Ah."

It wasn't really cold anymore since she'd been in this room so long.

Her head was still pounding.

"Perhaps you should see a doctor." The detective shifted her chair back from the table.

"A doctor isn't going to find those kids."

"I'll go see if your husband is done and check with Officer Albertson's partner about the children."

"Thanks." Kenna didn't need to make friends with every good cop in every big city—or small town, for that matter. It did help, though. She couldn't remember this detective's name. The woman was heavyset and had a pixie cut that had been shaved on the side. Kenna would guess military background, maybe years ago before marriage and kids.

Her thoughts started to swim in her head. "I need ibuprofen."

"I'll see what I can do." The detective walked out, leaving the door open.

Kenna stayed where she was. Better to sit and think this through, not just because she might keel over if she tried to stand. She slid out her phone and laid it on the table.

Bruce's message had said he was good. Maizie had given him access to the GPS from Earnest's phone—at least the one legally registered to him. He was out there on the hunt for the man who'd taken her blood.

The detective hadn't told her anything about the conversation with Regis or the confidential informant guy who'd jumped out the window. But surely, the police department had made some progress. More than just figuring out if the guy they'd brought in wasn't their officer. Or was. She couldn't seem to think straight.

She held her thumb on the lower half of the phone, then called Maizie.

"You're done with the police?"

Kenna put the phone to her ear, thumbing down the volume so it didn't make her head hurt more. "Not exactly."

"What do you need?"

"A million pain pills. My head is *throbbing*."

"That's not good."

"But aside from that, run a search. According to county records"—just in case the cops were listening in on her conversation—"who owns the doctor's office where I had that bone density appointment?"

She heard Maizie start typing. "What are you thinking?"

"Doctor Buzard had staff. I mean, did he tell the usual people to take the day off, or did he knock them all out and shove them in a closet while he came in?"

"Or he paid them off."

"Or it's *his* office."

"Hmm." Maizie went quiet for a second.

Kenna looked at herself in the mirror. Maybe she did need to see a doctor. The lump on her forehead was darker than the rest of her face. It wasn't bleeding, but she didn't want to have a bigger issue because she ignored the fact something might be seriously wrong.

Who was she kidding? Of course, something was wrong.

She could get checked out, but that might be dangerous with the other things going wrong in her body. Or going right.

Too soon to tell which it was.

Doctor Buzard certainly thought he'd done her a favor. But ask him for help? It wasn't like she was going to call him up and tell him she needed medical attention. Unless she absolutely had to—after she found his number.

Kenna bit her lip. No way would she ask that madman for help. What about the retirement home guys? They might have a good resource for unreported medical services. A private doctor.

But the last time she'd done that, the doctor and Earnest showed up. Before that, a woman and two children had been kidnapped. Another woman had been killed. The guys from the retirement home had admitted, though not in exact terms, that they were responsible for the mother's death. All to keep what Kenna had done from becoming public knowledge. If she told them her current issue—even if she was the one with the injury—would they kill her too?

Her injury didn't matter at the moment. Finding those two children definitely took precedence.

"This is interesting."

If only Kenna could bury her face in her hand, but it wasn't going to make her feel better. It would probably hurt more. "What did you find?"

Maizie said, "I'm texting Jax. You don't sound okay." Before Kenna could ask what she'd actually been about to say, Maizie continued, "The company that owns the doctor's office where you went is a corporation that owns several properties across that part of Arizona. They've actually done some business with the company owned by Marshal Hapsworth and Terri Fleming."

"What happened to her?"

"She was released on bail," Maizie said. "And the Hapsworth Fleming team actually built that doctor's office and the daycare beside it. Which apparently has a slide inside to go from upstairs to downstairs in the toddler area."

Kenna smiled. "Thinking about kids?"

"Yeah, yours."

Her smile dropped. "I think my life and my health need to calm down first. Don't distract me. We need to finish our conversation. What else?"

"The other officer who responded to the callout at the medical center, the one who is Earnest Albertson's partner?"

"What about him?"

"He was found dead in his house a few minutes ago, thanks to an anonymous tip from a concerned private citizen."

Bruce, or so she assumed. "Was he murdered?"

"That has yet to be determined. Police have only just arrived on scene."

Kenna figured Bruce could update her by text. Unless he hadn't actually broken into the house, and he'd only seen the guy was dead through a window. "Anything else?"

"I was looking through the designs Terri Fleming did, because she's an architect, right? She had another website that isn't part of her business with Marshal Hapsworth. More like personal work and custom stuff. She had a few things buried on the site behind a portal you have to log in to."

Which, of course, Maizie had managed to breach.

"One is a missile silo that could be converted into a medical research lab. Like in the event of a deadly contagion sweeping across the population. Ebola virus, or an outbreak of MRSA—you know, the bacteria that causes necrotizing fasciitis. That one is fun to say."

It was, but flesh-eating diseases would be less fun to experience. "Zombies?"

"I watched a movie last night." Maizie cleared her throat. "Because I was done with my homework."

Kenna smiled to herself.

"Anyway, the silo can house two hundred patients, including space for the labs to work on a cure. It can keep everyone quarantined in there with sealed doors and whatnot for months or even years."

"A secret lab."

"Yeah, weird, right?"

Kenna said, "Maybe she just drew up something off the wall that she thought of."

"Or maybe it was a custom job."

Not good, if she was right. "How are we supposed to find a...?" She didn't want to say it out loud. "I actually know someone with a secret hideout." She let out a long sigh. Her head seemed better, or she was just kidding herself. "Please find this doctor guy. I need to know where to find him."

For all she knew, he could be kidnapping people and trapping them in this secret silo so he could do...whatever. Prepare for the apocalypse. After all, he was a crazy person who thought he could do whatever he wanted.

Because the *Dominatus* had given him license to do that.

Maizie said, "There's a little more, but you're not going to like it. I asked Bruce about what I found, but he's gone radio silent. Like finding that dead cop was a favor, and now he doesn't owe us anything."

"Maybe he doesn't."

He'd handed her over to their enemy in order to solve a problem, just not in a way that made sense to her in the moment. He'd also been shot for it. But that was months ago, and they'd talked it through. They were good now, right? Hopefully, not back to keeping secrets from each other.

"What am I not going to like?" Kenna tried to move her head, but it just pounded more.

"The law firm that took on Terri Fleming's case? None other than our friends."

"Hann, Anthony, and Associates."

"Bingo," Maizie said. "They arrived at the hospital on the night she was admitted and argued she wasn't a flight risk at her bail hearing. She was released from jail, pending the prosecutor's assessment of her case since she accused her partner of stealing her work. They need to work through the whole embezzlement and the he said, she said part of the entire thing."

The lawyers at that office had said they didn't know anything about Terri when Kenna had mentioned it.

Which meant they'd lied to her.

"What about Marshal Hapsworth?" There was a solid chance he'd either disappeared of his own volition or was currently missing.

Maizie said, "The cops talked to him at his Scottsdale mansion two days ago. He was cooperative. The DA is deciding whether to file charges."

"They just knocked on his door and informed him he might be going to jail?" Kenna frowned, which, of course, hurt.

"It was reported as an interview on behalf of the prosecutor working Fleming's case."

"And he's healthy, alive, and currently findable right now?"

Maizie chuckled. "You need to rest. But yes. I'll keep an eye on him."

"Good plan." Best to be cautious and stay safe. Sometimes, people even loosely connected to her tended to have a bad time. To get caught up in the case. So far, Jax had come through everything unscathed, but maybe this was only the beginning.

They hadn't even tried to take down *Dominatus* yet. If she went after them at full throttle, she could lose everything. Again.

"Jax is coming down the hall to you."

Kenna said, "Thanks."

"Bye." Maizie hung up the phone.

Kenna turned to the door, but another couple of FBI agents came in, not her husband. One frowned at her.

"What?"

He said, "You don't look so hot."

"Because you know how I normally look?"

"It's an expression." He turned and leaned out the door. "Boss, she needs a hospital."

Kenna called out, "No, I don't!"

The other agent was a woman with gorgeous dark skin and brown hair that framed her face. Her lips curled up at the corners, but then she clocked the state of Kenna's face and winced. "I'm Special Agent Andrette Herron."

"Nice to meet you." They shook hands.

"You really don't look so good." Special Agent Herron came over and touched the sides of Kenna's face, then gently palpated her forehead.

"Ouch."

Special Agent Herron strode out the door so fast Kenna had to blink. Then she was gone.

Jax came in then with his phone to his ear. "Yes, sir, I will." He came close and looked at her forehead.

She grasped a handful of his shirt on the side of his ribs. Absorbing some of that steadiness so she would be able to stand. In a sec.

"Yes, sir." He listened some more. She could sort of hear whoever was on the other end of the line. "Understood, thank you." He tapped the screen and stowed his phone in his pocket. "He really slammed your head good, didn't he?"

She closed her eyes in lieu of a nod. "Buzard has some things to answer for."

Herron frowned, standing behind Jax. "Who?"

"Long story." Kenna held onto her husband, and he helped her stand. "I'm so glad I need more medical tests. That's fun."

His thumb swiped across the inside of her elbow where she still had that needle mark.

"I need my gun back. The police took it."

Jax nodded. "Yes, you do. But not if you're getting an MRI."

"If Buzard put a tracker in me, maybe it'll wipe the thing. Like an EMP."

Jax scrunched up his nose. "Let me worry about that, and I'll make sure you're taken care of."

"Can these nice agents work my cases? Someone needs to be looking for those kids and Nicola Santorini while I'm at the hospital."

"We'll work something out." He took her hand, leading her to the door. Looking back at her. Probably to check she could actually walk.

Kenna had been knocked down too many times to be fine with it happening again, and all because some ingrate smacked her in the head. But if she went down into the pit of negativity, her mind could come up with all kinds of crazy theories about brain damage and skull fractures. Or even having a permanent dent in her forehead.

I don't want this to be my life, Lord.

And if it was? She would have to accept the fact that a surrendered life meant she wouldn't be in control of what happened to her. God was the one who had the final say. She had to trust Him that it would all be for her good and for His glory.

Someone shouted behind them down the hall. They were almost to the lobby where cops brought arrested people into the building and booked them in, not the public entrance, which needed to be a safe space for anyone to come in off the street.

A uniformed officer ran past them so that Herron had to tuck in close to the rest of them. The officer's belt creaked as he ran.

Two other officers ran by them as well.

In the lobby, those running cops pushed through a side door that read Holding. The sergeant behind the desk yelled into his phone. "We need an ambulance! We have a prisoner in distress!"

Kenna tucked closer to Jax, who stopped where they'd be out of the way. He asked, "What's going on?"

When the sergeant looked over, all three agents flashed their FBI badges.

The cop behind the desk said, "Guy down in holding. He quit breathing. They're trying to revive him."

"Who?" Herron asked.

"No idea who he is, but he looks like one of our officers. I guess they're twins?"

Kenna hissed out a breath. "Reggie is dead."

"Someone killed him." Jax looked at her. "And Regis's partner."

"We need to find Earnest. Because he either did it, or he's next."

"You're going to the hospital."

She said, "Call Bruce. He can help your agents look for Earnest. He's already on it."

"You sure you want our lives to intersect like that?"

He was probably worried Bruce wouldn't want to work with agents. Not that they would ever find out he was formerly a spy—unless he wanted them to know it.

"I'm done soft-stepping. It's time to hit back at Buzard and get this thing figured out."

Chapter Nineteen

"Ow."

The doctor chuckled. "Got yourself a doozy right here."

She eyed him, entirely too smart not to be suspicious. Then again, he'd given her something good, and the floaty feeling she was experiencing right now probably made her more...pliable. As long as Jax was here.

"I'm not crazy."

The doctor frowned but didn't quit his examination of her. "Did a medical professional say you were?"

Hmm. "Not exactly."

"Then it's not official. It would never hold up in court."

"I'm not really worried about court."

His lips twitched, but the frown was still there. "Your tests showed a cranial fracture, but what I'm finding doesn't really line up with that."

She bit her lip. "Is it better than it was?"

He looked at her. "You think it should be? Like bones magically start to heal at an accelerated rate?"

"Don't worry about it." She waved his hands away and

sat up. Everything rotated around her. "I'm not the subject for your next paper."

"Whoa." The doctor held onto her shoulders. "No walking until tomorrow. No running for a month."

She started to argue.

"You won't change my mind." He let go of her and backed up, standing beside the hospital bed. "I'm sensing you're the kind of patient who takes advice and then does whatever she wants. Would I be right about that?"

She wasn't going to admit to anything. Not if it ever did go to court.

"Yes." Jax had entered the room while she wasn't paying attention and now stood at the end of the bed. He looked at her and didn't manage to hide the wince. "She'll be resting plenty, thank you, Doctor."

Kenna pressed her lips together as soon as the doctor had left the room, saying something about paperwork for release. "It's not like I can lay in bed and also find those kids and Nicola."

"You have people for that now."

She didn't like this idea at all. "You're going to derail your career for the sake of helping me?"

"I will if I think it's necessary." He folded his arms across his chest.

Arguing wasn't going to get her far. "Where is Bruce? And Ramon? I need to call Maizie and check in."

"We're going back to the house so you can get some sleep."

"It's already healing. The doctor said so."

"We'll see." His brow was set. He wasn't going to budge on this. "Remember when you were hurt in Salt Lake City, and I was taking you home? We were in line for food or something like that. You said you were going to the bathroom while I was in line, and you split out the back and went to see the victim's husband."

She bit the inside of her lip.

"I'm not saying you have *zero* credibility. I'm saying I have reasonable expectations for what you may or may not do based on what you think needs to be done. I'm *asking* you to delegate to your team so you can focus on healing."

Kenna's head might not be pounding anymore, but it also didn't feel great. She didn't have the energy to think of an argument, much less use it and actually succeed.

"You have people to help you now. You don't need to do everything by yourself, even just to keep people safe." He came over, moving slowly so he could sit on the side of the hospital bed.

"I don't like it here."

"That's why I'm taking you home."

"I don't like people being in danger when I can do something about it, but I'm stuck like this." That doctor guy had a lot to answer for, thinking he was doing her a favor but arguably making her more breakable. Nothing had happened to the man who headbutted her, while Kenna ended up with a fractured skull. This sucked.

Jax smiled gently. "I know. That's why everyone is on board to help you. Bruce and Ramon are going to meet us at the house."

She said nothing.

"I need you to agree."

He was going to make her promise, knowing she wouldn't go back on her word. She ground her teeth.

"Kenna."

"Fine," she said. "They can do all the work, and I'll rest."

He leaned down and kissed her. "It's the smart play. Rest. Heal. Later, we'll find the bad guys and kick butt."

It took a couple of hours to get released from the hospital, hit the pharmacy for some prescriptions she wasn't going to take, and get back to the house. Kenna pushed open the door from the garage to the house, realizing she hadn't driven her own car in days. "Jolene, we're home!"

"Are you talking to a cat?" Bruce stepped into view, holding one of Jax's beer bottles. He took a sip, then said, "You don't look so good."

"This conversation is quick, then you're going out looking for those kids. You can have one beer and no more because you're driving."

Bruce eyed her for a second, then gave her a short nod.

"Where's Ramon?"

"Making coffee!" her friend called out from the kitchen. "And talking to Maizie."

Jax slid his arm around Kenna from behind and held onto her waist. "Couch?"

She wouldn't have to keep herself upright like on a bar stool. "Sure."

He led her to the sofa and helped her sit. Ramon came in with a cup of coffee and handed it to her. "You look terrible."

"There are two kids who need finding." But still... "How is Forrest?"

Her friend in Wisconsin was an author, a widow, and a solitary person. In a lot of ways, she fit Ramon, but there were also ways they might not mesh. Kenna would need to see them together for real to assess if she thought they could go the distance. Which, most likely, both of them would consider none of her business.

"Don't ask me about my love life, and I won't ask you about yours." He stood over by the TV unit, looking tired, as if he'd driven for hours. Maybe even a whole day. Racing down here to help her.

"Thanks for coming."

He shot her a look, like he wanted to roll his eyes. "You should've called me days ago."

"I wasn't going to interrupt...whatever you were doing."

"I work for you. Isn't that the deal? You call me, and I come."

"We're all supposed to have a healthy work-life balance."

Ramon stared at her. "Sure seems like you have that." He looked at Jax. "That's why we're having a meeting when you're injured rather than having you rest."

She shifted on the sofa and leaned against Jax, winding her arm around his elbow. He put his hand on her leg, so she tucked her knees up on his lap. "I'm resting."

Jax chuckled under her cheek.

She glanced at Bruce. "You worked Terri Fleming's case with me. Did you know the law firm Hann, Anthony, and Associates represented her after the police took her in? They were also connected to her business prior to us taking her case."

Bruce lowered his beer bottle before taking another sip. "The intel I got was that the law firm is connected to a lot of businesses in town, but if they're about taking down Buzard and his operation, then they aren't our enemy. They're our friends."

"I wouldn't go that far." Kenna needed to think for a second.

Jax said, "How did you find out about the law firm in the first place?"

She would much rather be talking about the kids and how to find them, but the two officers who had removed them from the medical center were both dead. No one else had seen the kids after they left. Even so, she was going to send Bruce or Ramon after any kind of lead they could get if Maizie didn't come up with anything from scrubbing local traffic cams—a long shot, and it could take days to find something, but the alternative was having no leads at all.

Bruce said, "Amara sent me their information."

"You talk to her?"

He shrugged one shoulder. "She's been busy with Zeyla, helping her recover from what was done to her."

Kenna's cousin—or sister, depending on how she wanted to look at it—had suffered when *Dominatus* removed several of her organs to illegally transplant them into their people who needed the healthy tissue. Amara had texted her a few times. They hadn't exactly had a happy reunion, and Kenna had seen Zeyla before she was transferred to the secure rehab facility, but Kenna hadn't ever spoken to her as she'd been unconscious at the time.

"Amara knows I would help them, right?"

Bruce said, "She knows you just got married."

So she'd left Kenna alone rather than asking for help? Ramon had taken off as well, leaving her to enjoy her newlywed phase. Bruce had stuck around as a bodyguard of sorts.

She had zero problem with spending as much time with Jax as possible, but it also felt like her team had deserted her. And it felt as if her mother didn't really want Kenna in her life. Amara was technically her aunt, but that probably didn't have anything to do with it. Kenna being targeted by

Doctor Buzard might be the real issue. Maybe Amara simply didn't want Zeyla anywhere near anyone connected to *Dominatus*. Even if it was only that Kenna had found herself on their radar.

Jax asked, "Who is taking Nicola Santorini, and who is finding those kids?"

Ramon lifted one hand. "Kids."

"Fine." Bruce glanced at him. "I'll go after the doctor. Even though she kicked you out of the office, and she's connected to a Mafia family."

"Why do you think I'm taking the kids? I'm not tangling with the Mafia." Ramon shook his head.

"Those kids have no one else. The Mafia just don't want to get their hands dirty with the police and the FBI watching. They'd rather have Kenna do it because they think Jax will give her a pass for whatever she does since they're married."

That might not be true, but it was a nice idea. If it didn't mean she was breaking the law.

"Thanks for that." Kenna shot Ramon a look. "The Santorini family wants me to find Nicola for them because she's part of their family, and I'm connected to them from a guy I knew in Vegas. It's a whole thing."

And it felt a lot like being shoved up against a wall. They'd blame her if she didn't succeed or give her zero credit for finding Nicola if she did. Either way, she got nothing, and they walked away with no responsibility.

"She pulled away from the family, didn't she?" Ramon shrugged. "Either they want her back in the fold, or they want to punish her for pulling away."

"Maybe they just care about her." She shifted a little so she could talk only to Jax. "What about Dana?"

"You're worried about her? She's in a secure facility."

Jax spoke softly, his face close to hers. "I'll make some calls. Send a couple of agents to reinterview her under the guise of possibly opening a federal case into kidnappings like Nicola's and make sure she's all right."

"Thanks." Kenna shifted back to lean her head on his shoulder. Which hurt, but she didn't care. She wanted to sit close to him. They had each other, so why not make the most of it? "If we believe she was taken for Doctor Buzard, for whatever reason, then we could find him in order to find her. That might be easier than trying to track who took her and where they went."

She needed her thoughts to work themselves out faster than this. And fatigue was creeping up on her. The guys would get to their tasks if she fell asleep, but that didn't mean she appreciated being sidelined with an injury.

Probably, God was getting her to learn something about not being so independent. Trusting Him and trusting the people He had put in her life. But who in the world actually *liked* the lesson they were learning in the middle of it?

"So, how do we find this doctor?" Ramon asked.

Bruce said, "Aside from him kidnapping Kenna again?"

"She already has a tracker from Maizie on her, right?"

Kenna lifted her head. "I don't know where it is. The whole house was bugged, our cars and probably our phones have GPS trackers in them. The ones in the cars were planted. They probably hacked our phones." Her rambling might not make much sense, but they would get the point. "If you want to LoJack me, I'm all for it. I don't want to get lost again."

In fact, that was a regular part of her nightmares lately. After they'd visited Dana in that recovery facility and Kenna had been at Buzard's mercy, she couldn't help thinking about being trapped in a facility.

"None of us wants that." Jax sounded like he had a lump in his throat.

Kenna had always held her own autonomy in the highest regard. Her freedom and her ability to think for herself and make her own choices had been targeted at times. By friends. By colleagues. By bad guys she had faced. With an organization like the *Dominatus*—who could take it all away and there would be nothing she could do about it—all the fear she'd always stuffed down had resurfaced.

Almost as if she had some kind of repressed trauma. Or this might be just a natural reaction to the life she'd lived. But she didn't need a psychologist to dig out things her mind didn't want to remember. Why face the nightmare if she didn't have to? She'd rather think of it as a completely rational fear of being trapped somewhere or being locked up and declared mentally unfit to be free.

"Either that headbutt scrambled my brains, or whatever Buzard did to me, he's messed with my brain chemistry. Or something."

Jax turned his head slightly but didn't kiss the injury on her forehead. "Everything is going to be fine. Just get some rest."

"I haven't even finished my coffee."

She felt him chuckle under her cheek again, and he said, "There will still be coffee when you wake up."

"And breakfast fries?"

"Sure."

She let out a long sigh, her eyelids refusing to open. They almost felt like they were stuck down. She sank into the warmth of her husband next to her, knowing he and her friends would take care of her. She'd never had that before in her life. Not the way she had it now.

None of it had turned out like she'd thought it would. But it was still good.

She didn't want to lose any of it.

Even with everything going on, Kenna needed to keep hold of her purpose. The reason God had ensured she had the skills she did. Despite the threat, she was going to find those kids. And Nicola. Because that was what she'd been born to do.

Her brand of justice.

Then, she'd be coming for *Dominatus*.

Chapter Twenty

"It's been sixteen hours." She pushed open her car door and climbed out.

Jax did the same on the other side. "You needed the sleep, and we didn't sit around doing nothing while you were resting."

"I don't like it." Her head felt a whole lot better, but that didn't make much sense. How she could already be almost pain-free less than a day later? Whatever Buzard had done to her might have gone beyond replacing her marrow with more bone so that they were nearly solid. A process which destroyed her body's ability to produce more red blood cells. His fix for that issue had also apparently given her the ability to repair injuries faster than she should be able to.

"I don't want to be a mutant. I dreamed about nanites in my bloodstream last night. You know, like those tiny robots?"

He shot her a look like he thought she was cute.

"Let's shake some trees." She caught the hand he held out, and they walked together to the front entrance of the main building of the retirement home. "If I'm going to be a robot, at least I can use my powers for good. Solve some more cases."

"Whatever it is, I'm not sure you're a robot, but we will figure it out. And we'll deal, just like we deal with everything."

"Together."

He nodded.

"And if I get pregnant? What if the baby is a robot as well?"

He looked like he didn't know whether to laugh or be concerned. "Now that we know you're not pregnant, maybe birth control is a good idea. Just in case."

"I don't want to have a robot instead of a baby."

He shrugged. "Whatever happens."

They would face it together. Kenna sighed. "Thanks."

Her life was so crazy right now she needed his steadiness to help her keep her footing. All the way over, they'd listened to her app that had the Bible in audio, resting in the Psalms and listening to David's prayers for help. It seemed fitting to ask God for help when the enemy seemed to be all around them, and there was nothing they could do to stop the attacks.

Right now, she couldn't trust anyone outside the circle of the team she had built.

Kenna felt better with Ramon here, as well as Bruce, but none of it was a guarantee of success. Or that they would all get through this and still be alive at the end of it.

The door opened before they even reached it, swinging back wide. But it wasn't the receptionist guy who'd shown them around last time.

The lobby was empty of people. The only residents in sight were the men they'd shared that basement table with.

One sat behind the reception desk. Four and Five flanked them on opposite sides of the room. Three was the one who'd opened the door.

It seemed desolate, but the place was clean and tidy. Just void of people except these men.

"Expecting us?" Kenna asked.

Three shrugged, closing the door behind them. He wore jeans and an oversized dark gray shirt. Clothes that could probably use replacing, but he didn't seem like the type to worry a whole lot about shopping. "We figured you would be back sooner or later."

Jax asked, "Where are the staff and the residents?"

One didn't get up from his chair behind reception. "Surprise field trip."

"Are we supposed to believe that?" This might not be a real care facility. "We need to ask you questions, but if you're just going to lie and give us the runaround, then maybe there's no point in trusting you for anything."

None of them responded, not for several empty seconds that seemed to echo in the expansive lobby with the chandelier hanging from the high ceiling. Finally, One said, "You haven't found the doctor yet."

Three glanced over at his associate.

Interesting. She caught something in his body language but couldn't put her finger on what it was. "Have you?" she challenged. "Because if we joined forces, we might actually have a better chance of tracking her down."

Instead, it seemed like they were here waiting around, content to do nothing. Not waiting for her to fix their problems. Maybe it was more like they expected her to ruin their lives. But not so they could jump into action and avenge themselves. They came across as...tired.

As if they might, to an extent, at least, be looking for an end to it all.

A way out through no fault of their own.

They way they acted almost seemed like a quieter version of Terri Fleming on that rooftop. But she'd been desperate and determined to take the future into her own hands. These men seemed...resigned to what happened but also fully prepared to act as if they intended to try and stop it.

One leaned back in his chair, making it creak. "You think we know where she is?"

Kenna asked, "How do you contact Doctor Buzard? When you need something, how do you reach him?"

"What makes you think we need to reach him?" One's expression didn't change.

"Come on. You need him protected so you can continue to receive your treatments."

"So do you." One lifted his chin. "Are you going to kill him and sign your own death warrant?"

"I want those two kids from the medical center safe, and I want Nicola free to live her life."

"Not good enough. The first chance you get, you'll kill Buzard."

Jax said, "There has to be someone else in the world who can help all of you. Otherwise, you're living your life under the thumb of that madman."

One shrugged. "Hasn't been all that bad so far."

"Because you've been trapped so long you learned how to accept it." Jax let go of her hand and crossed to the reception desk. "You want change, but you also don't."

Kenna squeezed his hand because he'd realized the same thing she had. It was a blessing that they were on the same page a whole lot.

Four and Five closed in a little, but she didn't see any weapons. Jax had taken another day off to help her, but he should probably be at work. Instead, his life was likely in danger, and he was opting to spend the day with her. At the potential cost of his career.

He was fine with that trade-off. Or, at least, he said he was.

Kenna wasn't sure she felt the same.

He had chosen to become an FBI agent, put the work in, and passed all their qualifying tests. Now she was going to let him throw it all away? Sure, it would be great to work together. But this wasn't the kind of relationship where one of them had to change everything about themselves just to make it work.

She couldn't completely hear what Jax and One were saying, and that was fine. Kenna moved next to Three, who looked almost...sad. She kept her voice low. "Are you okay?"

Four glanced over at them, but she ignored it.

"Three?" She wanted to nudge him but kept her hands to herself.

He worked his jaw around and swallowed. "It doesn't matter."

"I think it does. If it's worrying you, maybe I can help."

Four glanced over at them again. "He said it doesn't matter."

Jax stopped talking to One and looked back at her. Not because she'd interrupted his conversation, but because he wanted to know if she needed help.

She wasn't the one with the problem. At least, not right now. And not this particular conversation. Fine, she had a ton of problems.

Kenna looked at Three. "I'd like to help."

"Yesterday, you were half dead."

"And today, I feel much better." She tried to be reassuring with a smile, but it probably didn't work.

"I'd be careful if I were you."

She eased closer to him, wondering at his tone when he said that. She'd only been trying to help. "I should be careful? Is that a threat?"

Three smirked. "I am a threat to you. But I'm not threatening you."

Even if he was an older man, he was certainly not harmless. She wasn't going to take the risk of going toe to toe with him, so long as she could use that to prove a point. He was probably right about her being less than a hundred percent, even if she disagreed with his "half dead" comment.

Jax stepped to the side, so she could see One was still in his seat. "You guys need to start talking. You know more than anyone about this guy. Maybe you don't want him out of the picture, but we do. Buzard isn't our target. At least, not today. This is about protecting innocent people who are caught up in what he's doing."

Of course, he was referring to the kids and the doctor, but he might also be talking about her in a way. No one else would be able to see the little bit of tension that bled through his features, but she knew him well enough now to spot it.

One said, "No one protected us."

"Me either," Kenna pointed out. "But that doesn't mean we have to let it happen to anyone else. These people are dangerous, and now we let them have two little kids? No. Not if I can do anything about it."

Before she was even finished, the door behind her swung open, and several men in suits strode in. Kenna spun to face them, backing up at the sight of Gregorio and his guys entering the lobby.

Three actually shifted and tugged her behind him. "Greg."

The Mafia don glared at him. "I should have killed you when I had the chance."

Three shook his head. "You never had the chance. And you won't get it."

Perhaps it wasn't so smart to challenge a Mafia don to his face, in front of men who would kill to protect him, but it seemed like they knew each other.

Gregorio looked at her. "Your time is running out."

"I don't answer to you." She lifted her chin. "Nicola is your family, not mine."

"You put her on someone's radar."

"I'm not rehashing this entire conversation again when we already established you don't want to put the work in. You want someone to blame."

Three shifted his weight from one foot to the other, keeping his body loose in case he needed to fight.

But Gregorio's guys no doubt had guns, just like Kenna and Jax.

If this situation turned into a shoot-out, none of them were bulletproof.

She lifted her hands. "My husband and I came here about Nicola. So we can find where she was taken or where we should start looking for her. We need help because these people have dirty cops on their payroll."

For all she knew, Doctor Buzard had been regularly snatching people from their lives for years.

Gregorio looked at the older men. "You know where she is?"

Three said, "I told you I'd keep tabs on her."

"But you let her get kidnapped."

"You're the one who drove her away. She left Vegas in

the first place because she couldn't stomach being around you."

Gregorio shifted closer to Three. "So you swept in like her savior, along with that junkie daughter of yours."

"Better than—"

"Guys." Kenna got between them, pushing Three back a little. Trying to get them both to stand down. She could've let them keep talking, and she might have learned even more information. Like how Dana was evidently Three's daughter. Did she know her father was here, in Phoenix, keeping an eye on Nicola—and probably Dana as well? But they were escalating, and she needed them to focus. "We aren't going to find Nicola this way."

Kenna turned to Three. "Have you talked to Dana? Is she safe?"

"She's good where she is." Three didn't look at her. He kept his focus on Gregorio.

"If we work together, we'll have a better chance of finding Nicola." They probably wouldn't agree easily, but maybe they'd listen to her idea if she divided up tasks to work toward the same goal by doing different things. "And anyone else Buzard has taken."

"He's a Santino, and I don't care. You think we're going to do this for altruistic reasons?" Three scoffed. "Buzard ruined my life. What do I care if he's doing the same to anyone else? Far as I can see, it's not my problem."

"You wanna go talk to Dana? Ask her if she thinks you should help find Nicola."

He flinched.

"Does she even know that her friend was taken because of you, and she was traumatized witnessing it?"

"I had nothing to do with that!"

She refused to flinch. "He's operating because you haven't stopped it. It happened because you sat around and did nothing."

"You have no idea what my life is like."

She folded her arms. He needed to learn the same about her. "I don't let evil continue if it's within my power to stop it. Even if doing so could cost me my life."

"Guess you're a better person than we are."

Gregorio huffed, making Kenna glad he didn't feel the need to respond to Three's comment. None of them would have appreciated whatever he might've shared.

Kenna said, "That means you need to listen to me. Because what I'm saying is right."

Three turned and looked at One, Four, and Five, who still stood sentry. Jax watched it all go down with part of his attention on Gregorio's men. She shared his fears. This whole situation was a heartbeat from ending up in a bloodbath.

One pushed his chair back and stood. "We'll take you to the place where we go for treatments. It's usually deserted when we're not there, so it isn't a base of operations. But maybe the doc left something behind we can use to track down where he is."

"You'd all better pray I find her." Gregorio pointed a finger, sweeping it across all of them.

She had a feeling, in due course, he was going to find an FBI investigation launched into every business he had for saying that to an FBI agent. She'd done more as payback for a whole lot less.

One came over to her. "I want some assurances."

She said, "You can be sure I'm going to find those children and get them to a situation that's safe."

"And Buzard?"

"I guess you'd better find him before I do if you want to keep him safe." But between her, the FBI, and the Santino crime family...

He probably didn't have a great life expectancy.

Kenna said, "Let's go."

Chapter Twenty-One

"What's that saying?" Gregorio watched the four from the retirement home approach as a pack. "Misery acquaints a man—"

Kenna finished for him. "—with strange bedfellows."

Gregorio eyed her. In the dim light of two in the morning, between streetlights, she couldn't exactly make out the look on his face. Maybe she'd impressed him by knowing that Shakespeare quote, but she wouldn't count on it. His head tipped to the side. "Bulletproof vests?"

Jax shifted beside her, his shoulder against hers like a united front. "We don't take chances."

His vest didn't have FBI on the front because this wasn't precisely a sanctioned operation. They were going to break into this house. No one had said that aloud, but she'd done jobs like this often enough to know what was likely going to happen.

There wasn't much that could surprise her after everything she'd seen. Even here in Scottsdale, though in a different fancy neighborhood. She needed to find out if Jax or Maizie, or even Ramon, had discovered what happened to the little girl the Rosenburgs had been holding in a locked room. A little girl who had the potential to grow up and cause all kinds of serious havoc, but it was only instinct that gave Kenna that impression. The kind of instinct that said Kenna might be hunting her in ten years. There wasn't much she could do until the girl actually committed a crime.

It was the kind of scenario that kept her awake at night.

They'd congregated down the street in front of a house with a For Sale sign on the front lawn. Even the sign was fancy, with a wood frame and everything. The whole neighborhood of houses set back in the hills were mansions, really. The kind of Scottsdale houses lived in by multimillionaires, with a security guard on the front gate and no access for the riffraff. Just the country club dues and a Lexus in the garage beside the BMW.

One didn't stop. "Let's do this." He walked right by her and Jax, Gregorio and his guys, and led his team to the house about a quarter mile down the street. Maizie had caused an internet outage in the area. No matter the network—cellular or local provider—no one in the neighborhood had signal. That should keep them from being caught on camera.

She stuck beside Jax with her weapon holstered in the back of her belt. Hopefully, she didn't have to use it here. The point was to keep these men, these strange bedfellows, from killing each other. A tenuous alliance at best, but they had to maintain the balance until they could go their separate ways. Whatever their history, it didn't mean they had to coexist.

"Good?" Jax glanced over.

She nodded. "Maizie said the same corporation that worked with Fleming and her business partner owns this house and a whole lot of property in the city and out in the middle of nowhere. Those long stretches on either side of the highway where there's just miles and miles of nothing. She's looking at everything."

Jax brushed a strand of hair behind her ear. "As soon as this is figured out, we'll jump in the RV and go find us some nothing."

She smiled. "Thanks."

"You've given up a lot to live with me. I probably don't say thank you enough."

"It's less than you think." She reached over and squeezed his hand. "And the trade-off has been more than worth it."

"I just don't like that this Buzard guy seems to have been living here and operating whatever he's doing for years, maybe even decades."

They walked together, cutting the corner to cross the lawn in front of the house. No lights on. None on the neighbors' houses either, though she saw a couple of flashlights or lanterns in windows. The house had a main structure, two stories, and a wing on the right with four garage doors on the side of the house. No water in the fountain in the middle of the drive. The place reminded her of that resort she'd been to with Jax, where Preston had been shot.

Maybe in the long term, she was going to start to dislike Arizona. It seemed like a lot of things she'd uncovered had been here or near to it. Could be it was the best place for Jax to do his job, though. After all, for the cases they worked, the bureau brought justice and truth where there wouldn't be any without them. Maybe this area could use all the help it could get.

But then, was it really worse than anywhere else?

People pretended they were civilized. Or that neighborhoods were "safe" or that towns had low crime. Sometimes, it seemed like a moral high ground folks lived on to make themselves feel safe. Or better than those who lived in dangerous, high-crime areas.

Nowhere, no person, was immune to the effect of sin in the world.

Jax continued, "It's just making me think about how I got my job here. Seems a little coincidental that you met this doctor guy in Colorado, or Wyoming, and he lives in the same city we do."

Kenna winced. "You think it was orchestrated? That Buzard wanted me, or us, here? Your promotion happened months before we even knew *Dominatus* existed."

One of the retired guys whipped his head around—Three.

"What?" Kenna shrugged. "I'm not afraid to say the name, and you know it. Maybe you should have some courage. Fight back."

"I had a friend who thought the same."

"Good for him."

"Sure, because they killed him. Two doesn't have to worry about any of this anymore. He's free." Three turned to the door, did something she couldn't see, and managed to somehow bump the door open. Or jog the lock loose. Odd, but he stepped aside and held the door open. "Ladies first?" Except for the sneer on his face, that might've been a nice sentiment.

She shook her head. "Not on your life."

One chuckled and started to go in. Gregorio and his guys had gone around the back entrance. The older men from the retirement home—One, Three, Four, and Five—all had no vests and no weapons, but One pulled out a hand-held device.

"What is that?"

"Thermal imaging. So we can see if there's anyone in the house."

They stepped into an expansive dark lobby where her footsteps echoed up to the ceiling. She followed him down the hall with Jax's hand on her shoulder so they could keep track of each other in the dark. When they were deep enough into the house, she flipped on a small flashlight that shouldn't be seen by anyone from outside. She shone it around the dark wood paneling on the walls and the huge canvas paintings. "This is where you came for treatment?"

There probably wouldn't be anyone on that scanner. The house remained quiet, and his screen didn't show any hotspots. The only people he was likely to see were Gregorio and his guys. Maizie had seen an outbuilding, like a pool house, on the listing for the house online, so they were going to check that out before coming inside.

"This is where we always come," Three said. "If he finds out we're here when we weren't asked to..."

"I appreciate you helping me. I told those kids they were safe with the police, but it wasn't true. Wherever they are, they need help."

Three said nothing.

Which made her wonder if that was why they were doing this or if Three's concern for his daughter Dana had him here trying to find her best friend.

"We should check for a basement that isn't obvious. Or hidden rooms." There had been quite a lot of those in her life recently, and most of it had to do with *Dominatus*.

"What about spooky attics?" Three asked. "Is that on your list?"

"If it is, you're going up there."

Jax squeezed her hand, and she heard a quiet chuckle.

"Still nothing on this thing," One said. "Everyone, split up. Go through every room."

Jax said, "Kenna and I will head upstairs."

He led her back to the bottom of the staircase that wrapped around a plant or some kind of tall artwork that stretched from the ground floor up two stories in the small space between flights of stairs. If she touched it, would it clank together, or would she accidentally knock it over?

Three followed them.

She spotted him on the turn between floors, unsure if he was sticking with them to back them up or for another, more nefarious, reason. "In which room did you receive your treatment?"

"Up here." He motioned up the stairs. "I'll show you."

"And his staff?"

"Wearing old-timey medical outfits."

"And creepy white masks?"

His footsteps faltered. "How did you know?"

"Because I've seen them. These people take whoever they want. They do whatever they want." And they were currently ruining her happily ever after.

Jax stopped at the top of the stairs and turned to her, swiveling his head around. Protecting her. Okay, so maybe her life wasn't being *ruined*, but that didn't mean she had to like what was happening.

Three caught up to her and reached the top at the same time as she did. "What do you mean, 'these people'?"

Jax moved them all away from the edge of the stairs.

She said, "*Dominatus.* Buzard works for them, and they're probably the reason he's doing all this. Some part of their master plan means they need people who are souped-up...or whatever he did to us." A lot of that was conjecture, but why make her stronger if he didn't intend to use her for something? "Did he make your bones denser?"

Three headed down the hall, not answering her question. At the end, he spread wide a set of double doors and stepped into the room. "He did a lot of things. Experimenting. Working out the kinks of his genetic research, finding new ways to solve the problems his procedures created."

He stepped into the room, which had a row of empty medical beds. Darkened screens on all the monitors. Big plastic sheets had been set up around the beds so each one could be temperature controlled—the patient zippered in a small plastic room and kept apart from the others.

Three continued, "In the beginning, there were nine of us."

Words sat on the tip of her tongue but never emerged. Would he be on board for taking down the doctor? The lawyers she'd met were all in for it. Their fight was about getting someone to testify to what he'd done. Three might have evidence. The weight of all of them testifying could force a judge to rule against Marcus Buzard. He would be shut down for good.

But those lawyers were also intertwined with other parts of this investigation, in ways she didn't fully understand yet. She'd have said she trusted them before. Right now, she wasn't so sure.

"If we bring down Buzard, he leads us to the larger group—to the people he works for. An organization that thinks they run the world." Kenna probably couldn't fight them alone. "If we work together, we can bring them down."

"Doctor Marcus Buzard doesn't work for anyone."

She frowned, partly aware of Jax circling the room and looking at everything. "What do you mean? The *Dominatus* run the show here, like they run it everywhere. They kidnapped me in Colorado just a few months ago, and Buzard was there. He was working for them."

"He doesn't work for them here."

"The whole reason I'm on his radar is because of them. Because my family dedicated their lives to taking them all down." And doing so had nearly cost them everything. "Buzard knows about me because of them. It has to be why he did this to me."

Three shrugged. "I only know what I know. He might be scared of them, but they don't have a say in what he does here. This place—the whole operation in Arizona—is about what he wants."

"And what is that?"

"I wish I knew. But not knowing is probably why I'm still alive." Three turned away and walked to a wall, sliding back a panel that revealed a window. He stared out.

She needed him to keep explaining this to her. "Three—"

Jax cut her off. "I heard something. Stay quiet for a second."

A moment later, she heard it as well. "Sounds like a footstep."

Three didn't turn from the window.

Jax asked, "Are there any other rooms off this one or passageways?"

He didn't answer.

Kenna strode to him, tugging around his shoulder. "This is the world you want Dana to live in? Or do you want to do some good, make it a whole lot safer for her because you took down this evil?"

"If he dies, I die."

"Because of some kind of failsafe device he put in you

both, or because you won't get your treatments? Assuming you aren't just being esoteric?"

Three said, "We need the treatments, or we die. And so do you."

She sucked in a breath.

"Both of you need to put that aside for a second and help me figure out who else is here." Jax's steady tone birthed a steadiness in her.

She latched onto it, thanking God for providing this man to be in her life. Praying they would get through this. "Come on." She tugged Three over to Jax.

"There's someone behind this wall." Jax shone his flashlight through the dark, cutting it with a beam that chased away the shadows.

"It's a storage closet." Three pushed on the wall, his fingers splayed. He stepped to the side and pushed again. A latch was released, and the panel slid to the side. He shoved it more, pushing it into the wall so the opening revealed the closet inside. Rows of shelves stacked with medical supplies.

In the center, a man sat on a chair.

Jax moved the beam from his canvas shoes, up the man's scrub pants to a scrub shirt. Gooseflesh rose on the man's bare arms below the sleeves, wrinkled with age and pale as if he hadn't seen the sun in a long time.

He shifted the flashlight up to the man's face. Gaunt from malnutrition, his eye sockets seemed sunk into his face. Where his eyes should have been, scar tissue covered the space—as if his eyes had been removed or the lids were sewn shut.

His mouth opened, and he sucked in air.

Three pulled his gun and leveled it at the man.

Kenna shoved him to the side. "Don't!"

The gun went off, the shot going wild. It hit a gallon container of liquid, which started to pour out onto the floor. The man in the chair screamed.

She didn't let go of Three. "Don't shoot him!"

"I recognize him." Jax took a step into the room.

Kenna shoved Three's gun down. "Holster that weapon."

Jax stopped in front of the man. "Special Agent Walter Collins?"

Kenna gasped. The missing FBI agent from the cold case?

He was here.

Chapter Twenty-Two

"Let go." Three struggled against her.

Kenna didn't back off. "Are you gonna kill him?"

"I should. Freak like that."

The man in the chair was breathing hard and listening to the conversation.

She said, "You don't know anything about him or what he's been through."

"I'm not gonna let him kill me. I'll kill him first."

She dragged Three out of the room, giving him no choice but to come with her. "That man in there can hear you."

"So?"

Kenna let out an exasperated breath. "Don't get me started. Go back to your other friends or something. Jax and I don't need you here."

He lifted his chin, a defiant expression barely visible on his face. "I'll go tell them you know this guy." He practically shoved her away, then ate up the distance to the door with long strides.

Alone in the master bedroom, filled with medical bays,

she let out a long breath. Turned to the open closet door and Jax...

Heard something.

"Who's there?" Kenna froze, listening for movement in the room. No one had come in the door. Was there another panel?

She breathed in, almost silently. Stretching out with her awareness, ready to notice some kind of anomaly. Just the slightest disturbance.

Someone trying to hide.

"We aren't here to hurt you. We want to help."

She'd told that to the kids at the medical center. The protective older brother and the little girl with the broken arm. She'd reassured them that the police were there to help.

Lie.

She hadn't known it at the time. She'd been naïve, and those kids would never trust her now. They would never believe anything she said.

"Kenna."

She turned to Jax, and the man still seated on the chair inside the closet.

Jax crouched. "Special Agent Collins?"

"Don't call me that." His voice sounded rusty, as if he hadn't used it in decades.

"I can call you Walter?" Jax kept his tone easy and soft. "I'm Oliver Jaxton. I'm the Special Agent in Charge of the Phoenix office. My wife is with me. Her name is Kenna. My job is how I know who you are, Walter, and why I know you've been missing for decades."

"I'm not missing. I'm right here."

Kenna set her hand on Jax's shoulder, then leaned down

and touched Walter's hand. "Mr. Collins, would you like to leave this closet?"

"Is that where I am?" His fingers shifted under hers. Papery skin, loose with age.

Why wouldn't he know he was in a closet? "Can you stand?"

"I'm not an invalid, girl."

She ignored that. "I can help you up. We all have rough days, don't we?"

Jax held the guy under his elbows.

He straightened, bones cracking and creaking. She turned to Jax and mouthed, *How long has he been sitting here?*

He shook his head, a considerable amount of disbelief on his face when he mouthed back, *Who knows?*

"Enough talking."

Kenna whipped her head around to Walter. "We can help you if that's what you want." No reason to overwhelm a captive with freedom he wasn't ready for, but he had to understand what was possible. "Do you have any injuries we need to know about?"

She should ask if he had weapons in his scrub pants pockets but doubted he did. If he had, it was more likely he'd have used them already.

Jax held one elbow, and she held the other, but Walter seemed to walk okay. His shoes were almost silent on the floor. That might be on purpose so he could move unnoticed through the house.

"Are there any more people like you in this house?"

Walter said, "I'm sure he'll come out soon enough."

Kenna winced. That didn't sound good. She wasn't helping this guy just because he could provide them valuable intel they might not get otherwise, but that was a big bonus. They had to convince him to talk to them. If an ambulance picked him up and took him to a hospital to be assessed, it could be hours or days before they were allowed access to him.

What they needed was for him to talk to them before any of that happened. Calmly and of his own free will. They had to convince Walter to tell them everything he knew.

Jax said, "Let's go find the others. See what they have."

She took the first step toward the doors, and at the same time, the doors swung shut and closed. A man stood in the corner, shadowed from view, but dressed in the same clothes as Walter.

"Hey—"

Before she could finish, he smacked his palm on a button on the wall. An alarm rang through the room, maybe through the whole house, stopping only for a robotic-sounding female voice to say, "Containment protocol initiated."

"Lorin, what have you done?" Walter sighed.

Jax asked, "Lorin Barone?"

"Congratulations, you know who we are." Walter's tone remained flat.

"You aren't keeping us here." Kenna strode over to Lorin but didn't get too close. "Open this door and let us leave."

The man didn't emerge from the corner, his face in shadow.

"I mean it, you can't keep us here." Kenna could contact Maizie, even though there was no phone or internet signal, and they could get help. But if Jax called it in, the full force of the FBI would show up. These guys had no chance against the FBI's SWAT team.

She tried the handle, but it didn't budge. "Open this door."

He said nothing and didn't move. She grabbed the guy by his shirt and turned him, slamming him back against the door. She gasped, about to launch in with another demand to be set free, when she noticed his mouth.

It looked like Lorin's eyes.

No lips.

No opening.

Just scar tissue.

Under her hands, she could feel something beneath his shirt. His fingers wrapped around her wrist. No mouth. What she felt under his shirt must be some kind of feeding tube, a way for him to get calories without eating.

He pushed her away.

"Don't expect an answer from him," Walter said. "He's a man of few words."

Deep in the house, she could hear banging and yelling but couldn't tell who it was or what they were saying. Kenna slid out her phone, one hand against the mute man's chest. She dialed Maizie and said to Lorin, "Don't move."

He lifted one hand and drew a cross on his chest.

Cross my heart.

Kenna's breath shuddered out of her. The phone rang once, then cut off. She looked at the screen and saw she had no connection. "I should be able to get through."

Walter said, "I guess you're stuck with us."

Jax shook his head. "If we are, then you can explain what's going on, why you're here, and why you're insisting we remain with you."

She kept an eye on Lorin, wondering how a mute man and a blind man communicated. They seemed to know each other. Was it because they had been taken together and have since forged a bond in their captivity? "The two of you have been here a long time. More than fifty years."

Lorin stared at nothing.

"We need to know what you know about Marcus Buzard."

A gunshot exploded somewhere in the house. A fight, or someone trying to get out of a locked room they had been shut in. Had the alarm and the contamination protocol locked everyone in whatever space they occupied at the time? They could be spread across the house with no way out.

Kenna kept trying. "We need to know what he's doing here and what he wants."

Lorin looked at Walter for a long silent moment, then turned and touched a keypad beside the door. Just a flat panel. He pressed his thumb to the pad, and the lock on the door clicked.

"No sudden movements." Kenna still had her gun within reach.

He looked at her, opened the door, and stepped out.

Jax led Walter by the elbow. As they left the bedroom and headed down the stairs, the sounds grew louder. Someone—or a few people—were trying to get out.

"You are going to set us all free, aren't you?" Kenna addressed Lorin, not altogether sure why since he couldn't answer verbally.

Walter said, "We aren't the captors."

"If you're trapped here in this house, why not figure a way out?"

"You think we haven't tried?" Walter said. "It's why I'm blind and why the doc took away Lorin's mouth. Earnest's ears."

Kenna's stomach clenched. She'd seen something on the

sides of Earnest's head, but not what it was. She would certainly never have guessed that it was this. "I'm sorry that happened to you." She turned back to Walter at the bottom of the stairs. "We can help you, if you let us."

"No help for us."

Jax said, "That's not true. You just need to believe us. Trust that we can get you free of this doctor. He's ruined too many lives already. Stopping him from hurting anyone else is the reason why we're here."

As with Three, it seemed altruism didn't really ring true as a reason for any of them. Maybe Walter, like the men from the retirement home, didn't care about other people. He saw no way out for himself. Why would he bother helping others when it wouldn't do him any favors?

"You take him down," Walter said. "But it doesn't have anything to do with us."

Kenna frowned, wondering how that could be when these guys were here, as part of his operation. Or were they simply a pair of forgotten caretakers of the house? She needed a whole lot more information from them in order to figure this out.

"I'm going to call in the bureau," Jax said, while they all followed Lorin into another room. A library with a sitting area of a leather couch and armchair and shelves of books on the walls. Above a fireplace at the end was a framed image that looked like it had come from a Victorian-era medical book.

"Then you can be certain that it will have to do with you."

"We are as much his victims as you are." The voice was robotic and full of static. Lorin turned from a sideboard, a small device in his hands. He typed on it with his thumbs, and the same voice spoke again. "But we will tell you what you want to know."

Kenna said, "As much as I want to hear everything you have to say, I don't want you to stay here. We can leave the house and go somewhere else. The hospital. A police station. Even a house or a park. You don't need to remain in this place. You can leave."

Lorin's device said, "We can't leave."

"He's right." Walter tugged his arm from Jax's hold, bent, and lifted his pant leg. What had been secured to his ankle looked like a monitor, the kind put on parolees to track their movements and ensure they didn't leave a specific area.

This one had a test tube of green liquid in it.

"Break the tube so it can't go into your bloodstream," Kenna suggested. "You don't have to live like this."

"It's not glass," Lorin's device said. "It is unbreakable."

Walter let go of his pant leg and straightened. "We cannot leave."

Jax shook his head. "I refuse to believe that. We can find a way to get those off you."

She picked up where he left off. "I have a friend who knows about devices like that. We can get you free of them." She pulled out her phone again, looking for a connection. The app Maizie had designed worked whether the phone had signal or not and whether there was internet nearby or not—even though she had no idea how that could be, other than some kind of Bluetooth connection. She opened it and sent a ping, asking for Ramon and Bruce to back them up.

"There's nothing you can do to help us." Walter moved past Jax, padding slowly on those canvas shoes. He reached out and touched the back of his hand to the bookshelf on the left, following it all the way almost to the end, where he crossed to the fireplace. When his feet hit the tile in front of the empty grate, he reached up and found the mantel.

Walter hooked two fingers around the corner of the framed image of a human body—with labeled parts—and swung it out.

Behind it was a safe.

Jax said, "I don't suppose you know the combination."

"Lorin can open it for you."

The device parroted out, "Are you certain, old friend?"

Walter tipped his head to the side, in the direction of where Lorin stood. "It's been a long time. But it's over now. We've been discovered, and you know why we can't be free. Why we will never be free—except in one way."

She flinched. "I'm not going to let you kill yourselves."

"It isn't up to you, Kenna." Walter turned to her with those unseeing scars. "We all make our own choices, and this is mine. Lorin can choose his own way."

"I'm not leaving you," the device said.

Information shouldn't have to come at the cost of two men's lives. This macabre scene was enough to give her additional nightmares to accompany the ones she had. But living with the knowledge that she could have set these men free and hadn't been able to convince them to choose life would haunt her more than their disfigurement.

"We aren't leaving." Jax folded his arms across his chest. "Not unless the two of you agree to come with us."

"We're not coming with you," Walter countered. "Take what you came here for and leave. Take the others with you."

And then what would happen to these men?

Kenna took a step closer to Walter. "We can take down Doctor Buzard. We can stop him, but we can't do it without your help."

"My help comes in the way I choose to give it. I choose my last act of defiance." Walter motioned to Lorin. "Open the safe so these people can leave."

Jax moved to Walter, while Kenna shadowed Lorin and watched him open the safe.

Jax said, "There are people who will want to know what happened to you. They want to see you."

"My family can continue with the memories they have of the man they remember. Not this man you see before you."

"You're FBI. You need to make a statement and tell the bureau what happened so we can investigate. Arrest the person responsible."

Walter replied, "And if that person is me?"

Lorin reached into the safe and slid out a hard drive and a single envelope.

Walter said, "Now, the two of you leave."

"Please listen to me," Jax said, trying one more time.

She could honestly say she understood wanting to live life on your own terms. They didn't seem to be under duress now. They knew they couldn't leave, not without disabling the devices on their ankles. But it was like they didn't want to live.

They didn't even want to try.

"Don't give up." Her voice sounded thick. "Please."

"We can help you. Both of you." Jax's arms were tight by his sides. "Please."

Lorin walked to a panel on the wall that lit up like a tablet screen, which he tapped several times. Selecting something. The lights in the house flicked on, glowing red, and the alarm came back on. The overhead speakers broke off the low chime long enough for the voice to say, "Thirty seconds."

"Thirty seconds to what?" She looked at Lorin, realized they didn't have time for him to type an answer, and said, "Walter! What are you doing?"

"Leave. Now."

Jax tugged on her arm. "We have to get the others."

"The doors will unlock," Walter said. "When the time runs out, don't be inside the house."

"Come with us!"

Jax tugged her to the hall, then in the direction of the front door. Tears streamed down Kenna's face.

Doors opened on either side, and the men they'd come with stumbled out. The older men from the retirement home, Gregorio and all his guys—one of whom had a wet red spot on the side of his shirt.

"What happened?" She swiped at her face, tugged along by Jax.

They started to slow as a group. Gregorio said, "Some of us let their frustration get the better of them."

Overhead, the voice from the speakers said, "Fifteen seconds."

"What's going on?" One asked. His nose was bent, and blood dripped from his nostrils.

Four went over, lifting his hands so his thumbs were on either side of One's nose.

"We don't have time for that," Jax called out. He dragged the front door open. "We have to get out of here."

The voice on the speakers began a countdown from ten.

"Come on!" Jax drew her outside ahead of the rest of them. One of Gregorio's guys stumbled off the porch step and landed on the gravel on one knee.

Four shoved him aside and started running down the drive.

One, Three, and Five ran after him.

Gregorio helped up his friend, and another of his associates helped the injured man.

Jax set the pace, moving swiftly away from the house. She had to almost run to keep up with him.

Gregorio called out, "What did you find?" He was eyeing the stuff in her hands.

"Hopefully, a way to find Nicola."

They had just reached the end of the drive when the house erupted into a fireball that blew out all the windows. But none of the glass shattered. Windows blew out in one piece, landing on the ground around it. She saw the frame of the house bow out with the force of the blast.

The roof lifted off the house, and a massive smoky fireball was tossed up into the sky.

Chapter Twenty-Three

"Where are we going?"

Jax let go of the steering wheel with one hand, reached over, and held hers. "The FBI office. Everyone else split, but we need to make this official. Cops and FD are going to show up and take care of the house."

"We need Maizie." That was the only way they were going to get information off this hard drive in her hands. So why was she still shaking? They were more than a mile from the wreckage of that house. The others had all run off, jumped in their cars and split, leaving Jax and Kenna to deal with the fallout.

But they couldn't exactly do that and continue to be free citizens. They'd broken into the house. They either had to face the truth or figure out how to spin this.

Either way, they'd found themselves caught up in something huge. Maybe even in over their heads.

Maybe that's why she felt a bit like she was drowning.

"Do you have something to plug that drive into?"

She frowned, holding onto his hand for dear life. "I have my laptop."

"We need FBI analysts with the tech to read it. The whole thing could be corrupted or password protected, and we have no way of getting into it."

"Or the scope of what's on it presents a threat." Her voice broke on the last word.

"We should use the resources of the FBI." He squeezed her hand. "This definitely presents a considerable threat. More than what we knew. He kept those guys for years."

He needed to read the letter, the one that was in the envelope labeled FBI. Then the bureau would finally have an answer on their cold case.

She inhaled a breath that shuddered through her.

When she closed her eyes, all she could see were those two men, one with no mouth and one with no eyes. Like a macabre representation of the old Japanese saying. *See no evil, hear no evil, speak no evil.* Had there ever been a third man? That saying was supposed to be about mindfulness and avoiding evil by not even participating in it.

As with so many things she'd encountered, it seemed that Doctor Buzard warped the world around him to suit his aim.

"Don't let him do that to me." She opened her eyes, her breath coming fast. "Don't let them take me."

Jax swerved across a lane of traffic and bumped up into a parking lot, stopping across two spaces. He put the car in Park and turned to her, sliding his hands across her cheeks so that his fingers threaded into her hair. "He's not gonna touch you."

She held onto his arms, needing his steadiness to keep her straight. Otherwise, she'd be falling apart. "Say it again."

"I'm not gonna let him touch you."

She managed to nod.

Jax pressed his forehead to hers, hanging onto her as

much as she was hanging onto him. The doctor had targeted her. He'd touched her. They'd messed with her genetics and altered her physically. And yet, not to the extent that Lorin and Walter had been detained as prisoners for years.

Why did some things happen to others versus what had happened to her? People made choices, took actions, and God was sovereign. She probably wasn't supposed to understand it, but that didn't mean her mind wasn't going to wrestle with the idea.

The road some walked was much harder. She'd had a taste of what chronic illness felt like, but it had been an anomaly for her to feel that way. She couldn't imagine a lifetime of fighting the kind of daily fatigue she'd had just weeks ago.

Jax's strong fingers massaged the stress from the back of her neck. "I want to go to the FBI office, but if you want to go home—"

She shook her head, cutting him off. "Let's go to your office."

"I trust my people. We can keep this tight."

She nodded. "I trust you. The rest of the world, not so much."

He chuckled. "Not Maizie or Ramon?"

"It's not the same." She drew back, and he let go of her. "Not that I think they're going to betray me."

"I know what you're saying. And I trust the FBI, but the faith I have in you?" He stared at her. "The rest of the world, not so much."

She held on to that idea all the way to his office, through the extensive security procedures—*oh, did I leave that knife in my boot? I forgot all about it*—and up to the floor where he worked. Jax was still chuckling about all the weapons she'd had on her when they stepped off the elevator.

An agent she'd met before at the police department, Special Agent Herron, glanced over. She was standing behind a desk in an ocean of pairs of desks that faced each other, spanning a wide room with a wall of windows. TV screens on the wall displayed most of the major news networks, national and some local.

"This is fancy."

Jax glanced over, blushing slightly. "It's too fancy. I'm still reading the manual on how the wall screen works."

"You're the boss. You have people for that."

"Come on." He lifted his chin to Special Agent Herron and walked Kenna down the hall to another room that was more like a computer lab.

A woman in khakis and an FBI polo shirt hopped off a stool. "You have it?"

Jax glanced at Kenna, then handed over the hard drive.

"You never planned on going anywhere else?" She was about to put her hands on her hips when he drew the letter from his pocket.

"Want to read this with me?"

"You're trying to distract me. It's your letter." She wandered to the technician and sat on her stool. "I want to know what's on the hard drive."

The tech, whose name badge above the emblem said, *Melissa Glor*, looked at Kenna with wide eyes. "It could take some time to—"

The computer chimed.

"Huh." She had inserted the hard drive into a port, and the screen now populated with files. "It's loading everything." The technician clicked her mouse, moving through the file directory. "No viruses, no encryption. Looks like all the information is right here."

"Great." All Kenna needed now was a cup of coffee.

Melissa glanced between them. "I'll get started logging and indexing everything."

Jax eyed Kenna, all suspicious. As if she was the one who'd withheld information from him. In fact, the opposite was true. He'd planned all along to come here, no matter what she said. He was determined to care for her. But at the same time, the boss of this office needed his personnel on the job.

She wasn't going to resent him or begrudge what he felt like he had to do. Why be petty about it? That would only put a wedge between them because she'd be using the weight she had as his wife to make his life more difficult than it needed to be.

"Does your office have a coffeepot?"

Jax cracked a smile, wandered to her, and kissed her right in front of the technician. "I'll be back in a second. Try not to cause too much trouble."

She gaped.

He walked away, laughing.

"Okay, so *that* has never happened before."

Kenna glanced over at Melissa, who was around five feet tall. Blue eyes and neat brown hair secured at the back of her head. "What's never happened before?"

Melissa leaned toward Kenna and sniffed slightly. "The boss, laughing. He's usually a pretty serious guy. Professional and respectful. It's...nice to see a different side of him."

"And sniffing me just now?"

"You smell like smoke."

"The house exploded."

Melissa let out a tiny noise, high-pitched. "Your house?"

"No." She probably shouldn't explain much since

knowledge could be construed as Melissa being an accomplice. "The place where we got that drive."

Kenna dragged her phone out of her pocket and pulled up the app for local emergency service calls. They were going to find those two men, and who knew what else, in the wreckage. Once they put the fire out, the police would begin the lengthy process of investigating.

The whole thing would no doubt drag on for weeks, if not months, before they tied it to Marcus Buzard and whatever he had going on nearby.

Several fire trucks, a chief's unit, an ambulance, and a police car had been dispatched to the house that exploded. It was being taken care of.

Kenna asked, "Do you have a legal pad?"

"Sure." Melissa went to a desk and came back with a new one and a pen.

"Thanks." Kenna wrote down her statement. Everything she had to say about the house, the two men inside, and who they were. She kept the others who'd entered out of it. She also didn't mention breaking in. The part where she wrote that the men had initiated some kind of self-destruct to blow the house after a short countdown sounded like science fiction. The investigators would find evidence that corroborated the truth, and then her statement wouldn't seem so outlandish.

Jax came back with coffee halfway through, and she went to refill it herself after she was finished writing everything down. He walked with her to get more from the break room.

When they were walking back to the technician's lab, she asked, "Did you read the letter?"

"I had a colleague come in and be a witness. We documented everything with photos, dusted the envelope for prints, and then reviewed the contents of the letter. Given it was addressed to the bureau and not just to me, I figured sticking to procedure was a good idea. Just in case it was contaminated with something."

"Like Anthrax?"

He shrugged. "It isn't worth the risk."

"And the letter?"

"The agent is making you a copy so you can read it for yourself, but essentially, it is Walter's manifesto. He was investigating the doctor and a group of men who went missing. The men were former military, thought to be abducted by the doctor."

"The retirement home guys."

"That tracks." Jax nodded. "Lorin was also the subject of an investigation, but the two weren't related. Walter must've gotten too close to Buzard. He was staking out Lorin in a bar one night, and the doctor captured both of them out back and took the gold. The letter says Buzard used the gold to fund the building of his 'silo.'"

"Like the plans on Terri Fleming's website."

"Yep." She went first into the lab. "Melissa, is there anything on the drive about a silo?"

The technician glanced over. "Actually, yes. Why do you ask?"

"Call it a hunch."

Jax chuckled.

Kenna continued, "Anything on that drive about where it is?"

"Not yet." Melissa dragged over her stool and sat, opening files from the drive. "Most of these look like schematics. This one is for a water filtration system." She tapped the mouse. "I don't see any maps, but there are a lot of invoices."

"Delivery address?" Kenna went to look over her shoulder.

"This is a storage facility. My dad uses it to keep his boat." Melissa opened another file. "I'll keep looking for anything with a location on it."

"Thanks." Kenna sipped her coffee, walking around but not quite pacing. She needed to move so she could think. Her phone started to ring in her pocket. She slid her finger across the screen and put it to her ear, knowing exactly who was calling. "Banbury Investigations."

Jax glanced over, and she mouthed, *Ramon.*

Her associate on the other end of the phone said, "So you aren't somewhere you can speak freely."

Kenna answered, "It's possible we can do that, but I'll need more information from you on the incident."

Ramon said, "On store security footage, we found a van that met the cop car. The two cops handed the kids off to a couple of guys in overalls. We followed the van to a parking garage. They went in and never came out."

Kenna set her mug down on a metal counter that stretched along one side of the room. "Did you find it?"

The kids had to have been transferred to another vehicle. That, or they were still in the parking garage.

"Another bait and switch. The van is here, but it's empty. I doubt we'll find any evidence inside. These people are pros."

"Got it."

"You guys are good?"

"Almost got blown up, but we're all right. Sifting through evidence now."

"I'll want the whole story later. Specifically, why Jax let you get into a situation like that in the first place."

Let her? That was an interesting way to put it. "Maybe it was my idea."

"I know it was your idea. That's not the point."

Kenna rolled her eyes because Ramon wouldn't be able to see it. "I have work to do."

"Apparently, so do I." Ramon hung up.

She lowered the phone and emailed the law office of Hann, Anthony, and Associates. If anyone would know the address of this silo, it was likely the person who had designed it—whose company had probably been involved with building the place.

A screen on the wall flickered to life. Melissa said, "There's your silo."

Kenna turned to the technician. "Please tell me that hard drive says where it is."

Chapter Twenty-Four

"It might," Melissa said. "But I'm still working on putting it all together."

"I want to know as soon as you do. We need a location and whatever else is on there," Jax said, sounding very much like the boss of the office.

Kenna slid off the stool so she could pace out the waiting, ignoring how her head hurt. "I should call Maizie."

Jax held up his hands. "Hold on. Let the bureau do this."

She couldn't really argue with that, even though she wanted to. What if Maizie could get the information faster? "I'll get Ramon and Bruce there to scout out the locations we know, places that coincide with what Terri Fleming told us about land with nothing on it and areas owned by the company who commissioned the drawing. If they can get us intel, we'll have a better idea of what we're walking into."

"What if you get the FBI a better idea of what *we're* walking into?" His expression remained impassive, but if he felt as if he needed to take care of this rather than Kenna going in...

"I'm not going to argue with you about doing your job. Justice happens either way, but sure. Your way means it's official." In a way that no judge could argue with. FBI agents would log evidence and concern themselves with correct procedure. Otherwise, there was a chance that a criminal could walk free. "Why would I argue with that?"

If Buzard had been kidnapping people for years, doing research. Experimenting on innocent folks...

She had to stop him. Doing it on her own was far different than accepting that there was a better way. But how could the FBI move in until they had a location to move on and proof that the doctor was there? He or some of the missing people. "Bruce and Ramon can take a look."

Jax kissed her quickly. "Waiting until the analysts and techs here are done isn't a bad thing. We rest up. We move when there's a warrant in hand."

She nodded, watching him stride out of the room. She grabbed her phone from the tabletop and thumbed through to call Bruce.

He answered before the first ring even finished. "You're on speaker with me and Ramon."

"Anything new?" She turned to Melissa and her screens, scanning the images for a location, but it looked like more schematics. Plans for ventilation and invoices for steel.

Ramon said, "Maizie has been asking the lawyers to get info from Terri Fleming, but they aren't responding to our requests."

"I wondered if they were hiding something. I guess this is it."

"You think they're with *Dominatus*?" Bruce asked.

Kenna scrunched up her nose, but that only reminded her that her head hurt. "I didn't, and you know them better than I do. I thought they were with the resistance, but maybe their allegiances are a little more dubious."

"Want us to go ask?" Ramon suggested. "We can find out what they know."

"I'm sure you could." She tried not to smile. "But we need to know where the silo is more than we need to chase those lawyers. Get addresses from Maizie for the properties the corporation owns and then head there and do some recon."

"You got it, boss." Bruce sounded energized now. "We'll go scout it out."

His voice had shifted on that last word. Kenna frowned, wondering if it was worth calling him on what exactly he meant by recon. In the end, she simply said, "The FBI needs intel so they can plan an effective takedown. Ideally, that means you get photos of missing people who are being held captive. Or some other kind of irrefutable proof that Doctor Buzard, or whoever is in charge down there, is breaking the law. Got it?"

"Probable cause," Ramon said. "We're on it."

"It's a long shot."

Ramon said, "Isn't that what you're all about?"

That made her feel better. As a former FBI agent himself—even if it had been a long time ago—Ramon knew what she meant. He understood the gravity of the situation and the fact the FBI couldn't go in without a warrant. They couldn't throw their federal law enforcement weight around without a good reason. Otherwise, there would be entirely too much fallout.

The feds didn't need any more bad press. They needed to give the public as many reasons as they could to continue trusting them.

Men like Earnest Albertson gave every cop a bad name.

Her phone started vibrating against her ear. "I'm getting another call."

"Later." Ramon hung up.

She clicked over to the other line, a number that wasn't saved in her contacts. "Banbury."

"I suppose you have all kinds of people calling you with information." The voice belonged to Gregorio Santino. "But this isn't hearsay."

She sank back onto the stool while Melissa tapped away, clicking and swiping through the information the way Maizie did. Absorbing data at high speed.

Kenna asked, "What do you have?"

He said, "We're keeping an eye on your friends."

"My friends?"

"Those old coots and their secrets. We can't let them disappear, not if they're protecting that doctor. He's got my Nicola, and he needs to answer for it." Gregorio barely took a breath. "For all we know, they're the ones who kidnapped her, and they probably blew that house so we wouldn't find anything."

So, he had no idea what she'd found. He'd never seen those two men inside, Lorin and Walter. He had no clue that the FBI now had a hard drive and a letter explaining how the two of them had been caught, which solved a decades old cold case.

Kenna asked, "Any idea where they are?"

"Like I said, we're keeping an eye on them."

"And?"

Gregorio hedged. "Are you gonna bring your FBI friend?"

"My husband?"

"I guess it's better than your associates. Any of the other ones—those lawyers or the two who work with you."

"Gregorio, are you actually going to tell me what you want or what's going on?" She blew out a breath, not meaning to sound irritated. "If you need help, just ask."

He snorted. "These guys are your problem. I just want Nicola."

"Where are they?"

It figured that if the men from the retirement home wanted to protect Buzard so they could continue to get their treatments, then they could be going to him to warn him. But Gregorio was continuing to act as if he didn't know who they were. At the house, it had been clear that the men knew each other. Which made sense if Nicola and Dana had been close for years and Dana was, in fact, Three's daughter.

Gregorio said, "They drove like their car was on fire and headed out into the middle of nowhere. Parked at the base of a hill, got out, and hiked up. Probably going to meet him."

"Where is it?"

"I'll send you my location."

That was good. She'd be sure where he was and that this wasn't some kind of ruse. "Any way to see what they're doing or if they're meeting someone?"

"That's more your deal than mine."

Kenna said, "I'll take a look at the area and talk to Jax about FBI assistance."

"Just you and your husband."

"That's not your decision."

"Then don't bother. These guys will inform the doc you're coming for him, and he'll disappear. You'll never catch the guy." Gregorio scoffed. "You think this guy doesn't have a fed in his pocket?"

He was probably right about the bureau. After all, Buzard had a cop on his payroll.

Gregorio said, "They could lead you right to him if you hurry. Guess you should get a move on if you want to take this guy down. 'Cause if they're here to warn him, then the guy is gonna show up sooner or later. Don't you want to be here when that happens?"

Kenna blew out a breath. Of course, he was going to manipulate her into being the one who finished this. He would swoop in and rescue Nicola, not caring whether justice was done or not and what the collateral damage might be.

She had a wider perspective than that, but her focus was those two children. Jax could take care of the official part, where Buzard went before a judge.

"Send me the location." Kenna hung up on him and texted Jax rather than trying to find him in this maze of offices.

Her phone pinged, and she copied Maizie in. She'd just finished articulating the request in a text when Jax pushed the door open.

"What do you have?" He strode over.

She explained Gregorio and his orders. Not a request. Jax made a face before she was even done but waited until she was finished before he said, "I don't like it."

"Either way…"

He nodded. "We should go check it out."

She slid off the stool. He checked in with his people who were doing their operation planning, and she had Melissa send her a rundown of what she'd discovered so far. But delaying either of them would only make this take longer. If she and Jax could find the old men and get a handle on what they were doing—especially if Buzard showed up—then it would help everyone.

. . .

Twenty minutes later, Jax turned off the highway into the parking lot for a state park. Her phone pinged with another text, a steady stream of updates she'd been getting from Gregorio.

"This seem weird to you?" Jax parked by the trailhead, turning off the car before he glanced over. "I mean, why would those guys come out here? There's nothing out here."

She had mapped it. "Maybe they're purposely keeping their distance from that place. I figure they know more than they've said through all this, and if they need to keep Buzard's secrets, it's because they'll die without his treatment." Her throat clogged at the end.

Jax reached over and squeezed her hand. "Let's go find out."

They would get a resolution one way or another. The doctor had to be taken down, but when it could potentially cost her life, it certainly put extra weight on the whole thing. Would she lose her life in horrible or painful ways just because what the doctor did to her wasn't being maintained? Or would she go back to normal, for good or ill? Right now, she couldn't worry about herself. Otherwise, she might second-guess a decision that could mean the difference between justice and Buzard getting away—or life and death for one of his victims.

She messaged Gregorio that they were here and walked with Jax toward the location the Mafia boss had given her. "Looks like it's up the trail, then off to the side. Maybe over that ridge."

"Good thing I wore my hiking shoes."

She snagged his hand, grinning at the rubber-soled dress shoes he had on. "We've already been nearly blown up today. What else could go wrong?"

"You had to say that." Jax's phone rang.

She walked beside him, listening to his responses. Unable to discern from his side of the conversation who he was talking to, though it was definitely a work call. Not personal. Had he spoken to his dad recently? It had been clear in Colorado, shortly before their wedding, that his father had been connected somehow to *Dominatus*. Jax's mother and his sister had been kidnapped around the same time as Kenna. They'd been used as leverage to get her to cooperate when she'd been the target. She hadn't heard if his father had ever explained what his connection was to the whole thing.

Maybe Jax knew but didn't want her to think less of him for his father's actions. As if she would. He certainly didn't think less of who she was due to her own connections to the enemy she was trying to figure out how to fight.

Huge bushes flanked both sides of the path, just a wide stretch of sandy red dirt. All of it was so dry that it was brittle. Up ahead, hills covered in scrub brush rose from the horizon. Hopefully, they didn't have to walk that far.

"Thanks, bye." Jax slipped his phone back into his pocket. "They got to some marked maps, so they've got longitude and latitude. They're cross-referencing who owns those areas to see if there's a connection to the house that exploded."

She still wanted to have it out with the lawyers, though, and now was as good a time as any to get all the loose ends tied up. Kenna called the number for their office. It rang a few times, the line clicked, and then it rang once more. "This is Lisa Romeo."

Transferred before she'd even told them who she was? Kenna guessed they had her number on file. "And you know who this is, or so I figure."

"What can I help you with, Mrs. Jaxton?"

Kenna said, "You've been representing Terri Fleming all along despite acting as if you had no idea who she was and saying you'd 'look into' her case."

The only response she got was, "And?"

Kenna rolled her eyes. The air was cooler the farther they walked, and a breeze kicked up, ruffling her hair across her face. She tucked it behind her ear and nearly stopped. Nah, that wasn't a bad guy. Probably just some kind of critter out here, more disturbed by them than they were by it.

Kenna asked, "What else aren't you telling me?"

"We were honest about needing you to testify."

"You really think you're going to get Marcus Buzard in court?" Given how long he'd been operating and what was about to go down at the silo, she figured it was unlikely he would survive, even if that was the plan.

"We're not talking about criminal charges," Ms. Romeo said. "We're talking about at Tribunal."

Kenna glanced at Jax, who looked at her. "And what is that?"

"It's the way things have always been done."

"You work for *Dominatus*."

Jax's brows rose. He stopped on the trail, and she shifted closer to his warmth.

"It's the way things have always been done," she repeated. "The doctor and his research present a threat to our mission. He's a loose cannon who is only out for himself and has outlived his usefulness."

"So, you only used him, and now you're done." Were all the lawyers with her enemy? There was no way to tell. Even if one or more were with the resistance, they wouldn't be able to admit it over a compromised phone line. And bringing down Buzard served both aims, so the resistance would likely be on board with ending his reign of terror.

"We all serve the will of *Dominatus*."

Kenna said, "That's a real shame. I almost respected you guys."

"The doctor will go before the Tribunal."

The call ended.

Kenna lowered the phone and said to Jax, "She hung up on me. Can you believe that?"

"Pretty rude."

She chuckled, blowing out a long sigh before she explained what Ms. Romeo had said. "Guess we're going up against *Dominatus* whether we like it or not."

"Before we get to that, we have another problem." His attention shifted to the area around them.

She hadn't noticed, but he'd been in protective mode. Making sure she was safe to do her job. She would've kissed him if, just then, Gregorio's men hadn't approached them from every angle.

Guns drawn.

Jax moved closer but slightly to her right with his weapon drawn.

She glanced around. "What's going on, guys?"

Gregorio stepped into view up ahead on the trail.

"We had a deal." As soon as those words came out of her mouth, the reality of what this was hit her full force.

A double cross.

She squeezed the buttons on both sides of her phone and sent Maizie an emergency alert.

Chapter Twenty-Five

"Did we have a deal?" Gregorio stopped a short distance back from two of his men. Keeping himself protected. "I don't remember."

"Where is One and the rest of his buddies?" Jax asked.

Gregorio shrugged. "How should I know?"

Kenna scanned the others, trying to figure out which one might have an itchy trigger finger. None of them had their guns higher than waist height, but in a fraction of a second, they could raise their aim and squeeze off a shot.

Either she or Jax could be left bleeding out in the Arizona dirt.

She asked, "What is this? What's going on?"

He'd lied to her. Drawn them here under false pretenses. She clenched her jaw, refusing to let on how angry she was. This was a waste of time.

"Both of you, lay your weapons on the ground," Gregorio said. "All of them."

After a standoff lasting a few seconds, Jax started to lower into a crouch. He touched his gun to the ground.

One of the men took a step toward Kenna. "All your weapons on the ground."

He came forward a little more.

Kenna shoved his hands out of the way, twisting his body to the left. She slammed into him, and they both hit the ground. She heard a grunt behind her but had to trust Jax could deal with his side alone. They were two against one, but only if Gregorio stayed out of it.

She reached for the guy under her, planning to slam his head on the ground. He hit her shoulder with both hands.

Someone else grabbed her around the waist and hauled her off him, her legs flailing. She yelled and kicked out. Trying to dislodge his hold on her.

"Enough!" Gregorio yelled, the sound hollow across the open space.

The man holding her spun her so she could see one man pinning Jax's arms behind his back and the other holding a gun to his head.

She gasped, the sound sticking in her throat so that it came out choked and desperate. "Let him go!" She screamed the words but didn't kick and struggle. She had frozen, everything in her cold at the thought of losing Jax.

"Now you understand what I will do to get my Nicola back."

The man holding her set her down. She tore her gaze from Jax and looked at Gregorio. "Let him go."

After a second of silence, he shook his head and said, "I don't think so."

The guy she'd tackled to the ground stood up. He patted her down more thoroughly than necessary and found most of her weapons. The ones he missed were hard for her to reach and weren't going to give her the upper hand in this situation.

He tossed all her things on the ground, along with her phone.

The others did the same to Jax.

She pushed out a quick breath. "You want me to find her, and you're taking the tools I need to do that?"

Gregorio said, "I'm not taking anything except the collateral I need to ensure your cooperation." He lifted his hand and flicked his finger to the men holding Jax.

They shoved him toward Gregorio and then walked him in that direction.

Kenna moved to go with him. Purely a reflex.

Hands grasped her upper arms. She tried to get free, but the doctor and his useless modifications didn't give her anything that would help her right now. Why couldn't she be super strong? Who wanted to be dense and more breakable?

Kenna cried out in frustration, and a hand clapped over her mouth.

Jax glanced back and looked at her, the gun still pointed at his head. One move and a bullet would take him out. She read the desperation on his face. If only she could say something. All she'd be able to do was bite this man's hand. She didn't want that taste in her mouth, and what would it solve?

They walked him away, and she heard a helicopter in the distance.

Gregorio headed toward her, and the other two held her arms. Kenna couldn't do anything but glare at him. She swung out a leg and tried to kick Gregorio, but they dragged her back.

He only laughed at her.

At least, all her struggling caused the one man to release her mouth. "You aren't taking him."

"I'm doing what I need to do. You do as you're told."

She gritted her teeth. *Jax.* "Don't take him." Tears rolled down her cheeks, and she couldn't even brush them away. They pulled her hands so far behind her back that her shoulders were white hot with pain, all the muscles stretched to their limit.

"It's already done, Kenna." Gregorio's voice sounded dead. "Bring me Nicola and Doctor Buzard."

"What?" She gasped.

"I want them both."

"He's going to be arrested by the FBI." At some point. Not imminently. "They will deal with him."

"I have my own way of doing things. My own…" The words seemed to escape him.

But she knew what he meant. "Your brand of justice."

His white teeth flashed in the dark. A predator about to sink his teeth into prey. "Exactly."

"I'm not handing him over to you."

"In that case, I'll contact your office at a later date with the location where you can find the *pieces* of what is *left* of your *husband*." He punctuated each word in a loud voice. "That's the outcome you have chosen."

Kenna shook her head.

Up ahead on the path, the helicopter landed, far enough away that it wasn't overly loud and there wasn't too much dust swirling up in the air. She couldn't see him anymore. Couldn't see the men holding him or where they had gone. Were they loading him into the helicopter?

Gregorio ran his fingers down her cheek.

She jerked her head away from him.

He laughed, but it was short-lived. "You will bring me Nicola and the doctor, and only then will I release your husband."

"Unharmed." She wasn't going to accept any other outcome. If they had to come to an agreement, then fine. But she wasn't leaving without the assurance that Jax was going to be alive at the end of this. And unhurt.

He said nothing.

"If you hurt him in any way..." What would she do? Burn the world down? Gregorio probably didn't want to know what she was capable of when it came to her family.

She saw his teeth again.

He said, "An eye for an eye. Isn't that how it goes?"

Kidnapping or revenge wasn't what the verse meant, but she wouldn't get distracted expounding on a Bible verse right now. "You want two people, and I get one back? That's what you call fair?"

"Seems fair to me." He took a step back. "And it's what will happen. Or you have nothing."

"You'll have nothing as well. I'll still have a shot at justice."

"I've killed people for a lot less." Gregorio lifted his chin to one of his friends.

A meaty hand grabbed the side of her neck, squeezing. Cutting off the blood flow to...

She struggled to get away.

Everything went black.

"Kenna."

Someone shook her shoulder.

"Kenna."

"Is she breathing?"

A heavy hand landed high on her chest, staying there while she drew in air and blew it out. She bided her time for a second, remaining still until she had gathered her wherewithal and could come out swinging.

"Whoa." Hands grabbed her wrists, gently.

That was what got her to think twice.

"Easy."

She blinked her eyes open and saw stars. On the ground. On the same trail. "Where did they go?" She shoved Ramon's hands off and sat up, nearly falling over. "Where's the helicopter?"

Bruce turned back from something and came over. "There was a chopper? Or can you hear it? If they hit you hard enough, you can probably still hear something that sounds like a helicopter, but it isn't."

"There's nothing out here. It's quiet." Ramon still held onto her.

She squeezed the outside of his arm, and he let go of her. She explained what had just happened. From them being drawn out here with a ruse to him having a gun to his head.

Gregorio's dark bargain.

All of it.

"Help me up."

"In a second." Ramon looked at Bruce, who shone a flashlight on the ground. "Found it?"

"Phone. The screen is shattered, but it still works. Set of car keys. Jax's wallet. Knives, pepper spray, and three guns."

Kenna said, "Grab it all. We need to move."

Bruce and Ramon pocketed most of it. She'd have taken Jax's wallet, but it didn't fit in any of her pockets. All the weapons that were hers, she put back where they went. "We need to call it in."

Bruce whipped his head around to look at her. "You want cops out here?"

Ramon said, "We can be gone before they get here."

"That's not what I mean." She shook her head, and it kept swimming when she stopped. She blew out a long breath, trying not to throw up or fall over. "The FBI needs to know their Special Agent in Charge was just kidnapped. Especially when the kidnappers are demanding a ransom for his safe return. They didn't promise to return him unharmed, which means they could do anything."

More tears rolled down her face.

She scrubbed them away, probably smearing dirt from the ground on her cheeks. Her skin felt gritty, and so did her fingers.

"You want his people looking for him," Ramon said, his tone quieter than usual.

"We're going after the doctor. Just like we were planning before. We need to rescue those kids that no one else seems to care about!"

Bruce stared her down. "And your husband?"

"I have to at least make it look like I'm doing what Gregorio wants. The only way to get Jax back is to find the doctor. And if we find him, we find the kids and Nicola."

"Okay." Ramon nodded. "I'll use Jax's phone to contact the Phoenix FBI office. They can come out here and find it in the dirt all shattered, and I'll make up a story about how I saw some guys in suits..."

He looked at her, a question in his gaze.

She nodded.

Ramon continued, "They shoved him into a helicopter. I saw the whole thing, but there was nothing I could do."

Kenna didn't like him lying, but she had to get moving. They all did. If the feds found out she'd been here, they would want to interview her for hours. She was pretty sure Jax didn't have that long.

Gregorio had gotten impatient, enacted this plan, and upped the ante on her finding Nicola. He was going to use whatever means necessary to get her back.

"Do it. Leave the leather wallet with his credentials in it next to the phone. That way, they'll know for sure it's him who is missing." She took her own cell phone and turned back in the direction she figured the car would be.

Bruce jogged to catch up and walked alongside her.

She heard Ramon start talking into Jax's phone, yelling as if he was terrified of what he'd just seen. Reiterating everything at max volume and putting on quite the performance.

Bruce held out his elbow.

She slid her arm through it and held on, walking beside him. "Thanks."

"Anytime, kiddo. You know that."

Hard to believe she had more tears in her, but it seemed she did. She glanced back, trying to focus behind her. Not on Ramon. She stared at the place where Jax had been—the last place she'd seen him.

Prayers filtered through her head. Disjointed snatches of things that probably didn't make sense, but God would know. He'd understand her heart in this and hear her meaning, rather than the nonsense she was saying in her head.

They needed help.

She needed a plan, a place to look, and the strength to do it. She needed a guarantee that Gregorio wasn't going to renege on the arrangement and kill Jax anyway.

Like a child throwing a tantrum, justified or not, she cried out in her head that it wasn't fair. That after everything she'd been through, she didn't deserve to have to go through this as well. That losing Jax would be too much.

But even in the middle of the despair, she felt the peace

of God flow through her. He had this all in His hands, and she had to trust Him. Jax had put his life in God's hands as well. Kenna only needed to rest in the fact that He wouldn't allow Jax to reach the point of despair.

Ramon caught up. "Okay, they'll probably be here soon, so we'd better get out of here."

Kenna nodded, and Bruce asked, "You okay? Any injuries we need to get looked at?"

"What do you think?" she said.

"Then we need a plan." Ramon glanced sideways at her, holding a flashlight so it illuminated the wide path in front of them. "Because if we need to give the Santinos Nicola and the doctor, we need to know where to find them."

"It's the only way I'm going to get Jax back alive."

She hoped.

Chapter Twenty-Six

Kenna walked into the conference room first. Lisa Romeo was nowhere to be seen. Instead, the younger one who'd shown up to the park that day rose from her chair.

"Where is she?" Kenna opened her hands, looking around even though there was no one else in here other than this woman.

She cleared her throat. "In case you don't remember, I'm Beth Potter."

"Right. Ms. Potter." Kenna nodded. "I thought Terri Fleming was going to be here?"

She heard a commotion in the hall behind her. Ramon strode into the room, muttering. Kenna asked, "Where's Bruce?"

"Right behind me." Ramon dragged out a chair and slumped into it.

"Problem?"

Ramon said, "Nothing an apology won't fix."

Ms. Potter seemed a little flustered at Ramon's appearance. Because she was only five-one, and he was a much taller, broad-shouldered Hispanic man who looked like he'd worked for a cartel for years—because he had—and still had that edge to him.

"Oh," she said. "Well, I'm sure whatever happened, there's been some kind of misunderstanding." She looked at Kenna. "Ms. Fleming should be here shortly."

"We don't have time to waste," Kenna said.

She had people to save and no idea where to start looking. A wild-goose chase wasn't a good use of her time. Nor was lying on the bathroom floor and crying.

Her head was pounding. She refused to even think about Jax and what kind of situation he was in right now.

She couldn't do anything to change it, so wallowing wasn't going to help.

Actually, she could change it by finding Doctor Santorini, Marcus Buzard, and any of the other missing people.

Her phone rang. The screen said *Special Agent Herron*. Kenna didn't pick up. She had already sent the woman an explanation text and mentioned that she had nothing more to say until she'd figured out how to get Jax back. Probably, the FBI wanted to help her, but the risk they wanted to hold her responsible was far too high.

Ramon huffed. He probably thought she was referring to him and whatever had happened on the way over, but she wasn't. Just these lawyers, giving her half answers and constantly leading her where they wanted her to be.

Because they all worked for *Dominatus*.

She pulled out a chair and slumped into it, sitting next to Ramon. She reached over and squeezed his forearm.

"Ow."

She frowned at him.

"Don't worry about it." He ran his hands down his face.

"I'm supposed to be reassuring you, not the other way around." He paused for a second, like it made his point more effectively, then said, "We're gonna get him back."

"I know we are." If she said more than that, she'd start thinking about Jax again. Thinking would lead to crying, and then where would she be?

This was a case to solve.

She could try and think of it like any other, but that wasn't ever going to be true, so she didn't bother.

She looked at Ms. Potter, who had sat at the table again. Ruffling papers while they all waited.

Kenna asked, "How many of them do you think are resistance?" She spoke loudly enough Beth would've heard her, but it still sounded like she might be talking only to Ramon. Trying to have a private conversation.

The young lawyer stiffened.

"I figure at least one. Otherwise, I'd be dead by now. All of us, probably." She leaned toward Ramon a little more. "They can't have been working on this for long because Doctor Buzard hasn't been found yet."

"Maybe they want you to find him just like the Santinos," Ramon said. "Get you to do their dirty work for them. If we're lucky, they'll keep Bruce until we're done."

She glanced at him, wondering if that was for real or if he was being sarcastic, and she spotted a gleam of humor in his gaze. She hadn't seen that in a long time. Not that their lives were conducive to much laughter, especially lately. She was happy. Kenna wasn't going to say otherwise since she finally had the life she'd been after for a long time.

But the kind of carefree laughter that came with no worries?

Not so much a part of her life.

Ms. Potter got up and left the room, leaving the door open.

"You think she left anything good in those papers over there?" Ramon asked.

Bruce strode in. "What are you two doing?"

"I could ask you the same thing," Kenna said.

Bruce shook his head. "If there are any resistance fighters in this organization, you just put it in the head of a true believer that it's a possibility."

"Ms. Potter?" Kenna didn't figure her for a *Dominatus* operative, following orders even if that meant giving her life.

Bruce said, "Scared her to death, the two of you did."

"I'm the one who gets an apology." Ramon shifted in his seat. "They asked for my middle name."

Before Kenna had time to ask what on earth he was talking about, more people came in. A couple of operatives, er, lawyers that she'd already met and then Terri Fleming.

Considering that the last time Kenna had seen her, Terri had been trying to jump off a downtown high-rise building, she looked good. But definitely less bright than when she'd hired Kenna to investigate her business partner.

Terri took a seat on the opposite side of the table, and Lisa Romeo sat beside her. The lawyer said, "We've apprised our client as to the situation and have advised her that if she answers your questions, it's possible you could have the FBI pass on a good word to the district attorney to explain how she aided you."

Ramon reached over and squeezed her knee, probably harder than necessary. She bit the inside of her lip and said nothing.

Bruce leaned against the wall to Kenna's right, where she could see him, and he could see everyone in the room. He folded his arms. "Ms. Fleming, we're aware you are the architect of a decommissioned missile silo that has been refurbished into a medical research facility. We would like to know where it was built."

Fleming stared at the table.

What was with this woman who had hired her to investigate her business partner, Marshal Hapsworth, when she'd been embezzling herself the whole time? She'd put Kenna in the middle of a grab for whatever face they could save. One or both of them would go to prison soon.

This woman clearly knew her future wasn't too bright. Otherwise, she wouldn't be so downcast. She'd been exposed, ruined, and arrested. After trying to commit suicide, she was going to have to find reasons to live.

Reasons to keep on fighting.

"A group of men took my husband," Kenna said. The words tumbled out without thought. But she'd played this wrong. She should've started talking about this woman's business partner and then talked her around to doing this out of spite or even for revenge.

Sympathy didn't work as well as sticking it to the other guy usually did. But it was too late now.

"They are going to kill him if I don't find a woman, a doctor who was kidnapped, and the man who took her. The same man who hired you to design that silo. Or maybe he purchased the plan from you?" Kenna let that hang in the air for a second. "I need your help, Terri." She leaned forward and put her elbows on the table, lacing her fingers together in front of her.

All of them would be able to see the ugly scars on her forearms.

She was also covered in dirt.

Kenna had reconciled how she felt about her scars. She followed a Savior whose scars were evidence that He had set the whole world free. She had, in a very small and very individual way, found a way to *fellowship in His sufferings* as the Bible said to do. Because she understood what it meant to give of yourself so that someone else could live.

Bradley had done it for her years ago. She hadn't realized what it truly meant then.

God had paid the ultimate price for her eternal destiny.

Now Jax might shadow that in this life. But if Kenna had any ability at all to create the future she wanted—needed—then she was going to move heaven and earth if God allowed it. She was going to get him back.

She stared across the table. "Terri, I need to know where that silo is."

Even Ms. Romeo looked moved. One of the lawyers standing to the left, almost like guards in the room in the same way Bruce was standing, wiped under her eye.

Ms. Romeo held her pen poised over a notepad. "We're all after the same goal here. I'm sure we can come to some kind of arrangement."

Kenna shook her head. "We're not on the same side, and you know it."

"My company would like to speak with this Doctor Marcus Buzard." She read the name from the pad as if she'd never heard it before.

Kenna didn't buy it one bit. "For what purpose? He's a kidnapper, and he uses his medical knowledge to experiment on people." She looked at Terri. "These are the kind of people you want to represent you?"

Maybe this law firm was the reason Terri Fleming was in trouble in the first place. What if they'd arranged for her to work with Buzard because she had already designed the silo, or they knew she could? Their firm could have made the professional connection.

Terri cleared her throat.

Ms. Romeo said, "Please limit your questions to the matter at hand."

"Because you don't want her to realize she's been played?" Kenna shifted her gaze from Romeo to Fleming. "Sooner or later, Terri is going to realize she's just a patsy for *Dominatus*. A group that doesn't care when people get caught in the crossfire. Especially abused children who fall through the cracks and go missing."

Terri gasped. "Children?"

Kenna said, "I'm trying to find a brother and sister. The police officers, who were supposed to take them to the hospital, handed them over to someone else. The officers are both dead. The children are gone."

Ms. Romeo shifted in her chair.

"Hard to hear, isn't it? That a man you worked with does things like that." Kenna sat back in her chair. "It can be hard when you realize you're party to that kind of evil. You sit up here in your fancy offices, and you believe you're not fully a part of it. Or you convince yourselves you're doing what you can to fight it."

The lawyer stared at her with a hard expression, all of her discomfort gone. "You have no idea what we're doing."

"You're not giving me what I need to put an end to this. Which is why it's gone on so long. Because you haven't done what's necessary to finish it," Kenna said. "And now my husband has been kidnapped, and you're still hedging."

The client looked at her lawyer, but neither said anything.

Until finally, Ms. Romeo set her pen down. "In my experience, finesse is far more effective in the long run. If it hadn't worked, then none of my sisters would be alive, and neither would I."

"I'm going to take them all down. But first, I'm going to do what it takes to get Jax back."

"You're part of the program he built. Doctor Buzard designed the modifications made to in vitro babies and the treatment that allows for successful birthrates."

Kenna asked, "Are you...?"

Ms. Romeo said, "Some of us."

"He really created it?"

"The *Dominatus* hired him for that purpose, for his groundbreaking research."

Ramon leaned over to Kenna and said, "And his lack of morals."

The lawyer's lips pressed together into a thin line. "He needs to be shut down. Once and for all."

"Agreed." Kenna wasn't going to trust any of them as far as she could throw them. Not that it would be impressive or anything.

This was a Banbury Investigations case. If anyone was going to help them, it would be the FBI.

Kenna said, "We need to know where the silo is."

The client across the table started to hedge. "I'm not sure—"

"Don't bother," Ramon said. "No one is going to believe you."

"I don't have much to offer. Just what I know," Fleming said, but she wouldn't meet Kenna's gaze.

"Just answer the questions." Bruce shifted off the wall but didn't move closer. "Because it's the decent thing to do."

Her face scrunched up, but Fleming fought through whatever it was. "I thought... I mean, he was handsome. He asked me to come to his house, and I wore my nicest dress."

Kenna winced inwardly where this woman wouldn't see it. "A house?"

"When I got there, it was just dirt. There was a tiny hut in the middle of nowhere, like a shed. I knocked. I thought I was going to get murdered by some stranger, but the door opened, and he was there. He led me through the whole place, giving me the tour so I could see what I'd designed. He seemed...giddy. The place was empty. I remember our footsteps echoed on the floor. There weren't any missing children or other doctors. It was just him." She lifted her chin.

Kenna asked, "When was this?"

"Six years ago."

Bruce said, "When the disappearances started. The ones where people saw men and women in old-timey medical outfits with scary white masks. He takes them and doesn't care who might witness it and have to live with the nightmares for the rest of their lives."

"I didn't know!" Terri wailed.

Kenna looked at Ms. Romeo and saw zero empathy on the woman's face. "I guess you can explain to her how she got caught up in this."

"Representing her will be sufficient." She turned to the woman beside her and said, "I spoke with the DA. They're going to offer you ninety days in a minimum-security prison, and then you'll have community service hours to complete. It's a very generous offer."

Bruce said, "Some of those prisons are like resorts. Golf. TV. Hobnobbing with rich people who are in there for insider trading."

Kenna leaned forward. "Terri, where is the silo?"

"I'm sorry. I'm really sorry for everything." She looked at Kenna and nodded. "I'll give you the address."

Chapter Twenty-Seven

Ramon stopped at the driver's door and turned to her, his face shadowed by the streetlights around the law office parking lot. "We have the address. Let's just go."

She shook her head, moving to the passenger's side. "If we go in with guns blazing, we could get killed or captured."

"I mean..." He shrugged. "Captured is fine. We'll just fight our way out and rescue everyone as we go."

She didn't share his same certainty. In fact, she was barely holding it together right now. Thinking any second that her phone was going to ring or beep with a text. Gregorio might contact her with information about Jax—a photo or another threat. Or the FBI could call to say they'd found his body somewhere, mangled and cold.

Bruce wandered over to where his car was parked, alongside hers. He stopped in the space between her door and his without crowding her. "What are you thinking?"

She shifted her weight, too amped up to be still. "Gregorio lied to get Jax and I to that state park area. He said he was following the retirement home guys, but if he wasn't, then we can contact them. Use the number they gave us."

Ramon asked, "Didn't Maizie say that was for a pay phone in New York?"

"We have to try," she said, half aware that the law office towered over them to one side. Were the lawyers up there, watching them have this conversation? For all she knew, they could have surveillance in the parking lot that allowed them to listen in to everything she and her associates were saying.

"We can find out if they know about security at the silo or if there's another way in."

Bruce said, "You really think they're going to help us get in and take down that doctor guy?"

Kenna worked her mouth side to side. "I have an idea about that. Let's go."

She climbed into the passenger's seat of Ramon's car, not wanting to make this call where there was a chance the lawyers might hear it. If only she was in Jax's car with her husband. Leaving it where they had, back where he had disappeared, made a whole lot more sense. It was proof he'd been there. Proof he hadn't left to go somewhere else.

Because he'd been taken.

Ramon hit the gas and peeled out of the spot. She checked the side mirror and saw Bruce behind them.

Kenna glanced over at Ramon. "Thanks for helping me."

"Just make your call."

She figured that meant, "You're welcome," but ignored the fact his gruff response sounded curt. Jax was missing, and Ramon was all in for helping her do what it took to get him back. Despite how he might've felt about her.

Any romantic feelings for her had probably dissipated a while ago, and if he did still have some, it really wasn't her problem. He wasn't making it her issue to deal with, that was for sure. Hopefully, he'd find someone—the person God had planned for him. Not just a whim or a way to self-destruct. He seemed to live his life on a knife-edge, but that was his business. All she was able to do for him was pray.

So she did that.

The peace of God was something she would always need, for herself and for the people she considered family.

After a minute or so, she found the number where she'd saved it and made the call. While it rang, she said to Ramon, "We need to check in with Maizie."

"Pretty sure Bruce is doing that. He's getting good at looping the kid in."

Before she could respond, the call was answered. "Yes?"

"This is Kenna Banbury-Jaxton." She wanted to add that last part. The two sides of who she was, personal and professional. "Who is this?"

"Depends on what you want."

She figured One, considering the tone, so she explained what Gregorio had done.

They hadn't seen these guys since the house explosion. For all she knew, they could've found the doctor and convinced him to go to ground and disappear. A huge operation couldn't be erased in just a few hours, but if the doctor thought he was secure in his bunker—the silo Terri had designed—then it was entirely possible he had enough hubris to think it was impenetrable.

"We need your help to get in." She wasn't going to sugarcoat it.

"Get in where?"

She said, "The silo," then gave him the location Terri had given them. "We're going to save those people."

"And you think I'll stop you?"

"I think you want to, but you know it's not the right

thing. We have to know if we're going to get killed by some security system he has set up before we even reach the door. I need you to be straight with me. People's lives are on the line."

"Yeah, mine."

She gritted her teeth, the phone hot against her ear. Ramon was driving eighty-five down the freeway. "Mine, too. Right?"

"So why are you all fired up to get yourself killed?"

Kenna said, "Because it will save other people's lives, and it will stop him from doing this again."

Of course, there was still the problem of how to get Jax back when she wouldn't give Buzard to the Santino crime family. No matter what she'd promised, that wasn't justice. Maybe Nicola could convince Gregorio to let justice take its course.

But was that justice going to come in the form of a *Dominatus* Tribunal?

All she cared about was saving those people. And getting Jax home. She would do whatever it took to make that happen.

The rest of it, she was going to leave in God's hands.

"Very well."

Kenna frowned. "You're going to help me?"

One was silent for a moment, then said, "Three, Four, and Five aren't going to like it. If I can find something to help them afterward, then I'm going to do that."

"He can't be left to continue."

One said, "I'll give you Buzard. Whatever happens to me... Well, in the grand scheme of human history, it's not really relevant, is it?"

That was probably a rhetorical question. "Thank you."

"I'm not doing this to be appreciated."

Kenna bit her lip. "The architect told me where to find the silo. I need to know how to get in—"

Noise over the line cut her off at the end.

"One?"

He said, "What are you...?"

He might have been talking to her or someone else. "One?"

A crackle burst against her ear. She winced.

One said, "No, you're not going to—don't. Don't!"

One gurgled. He cried out.

Kenna lowered the phone and said to Ramon, "Call Maizie. I need to know where he is." She listened to the call but heard nothing more. "One? One!"

Ramon had his cell to his ear, driving with the other hand. He tucked it between his shoulder and his chin, grasped the steering wheel with both hands, and changed lanes fast. He got off the freeway at the next exit, pulling into a gas station parking lot. Bruce pulled up behind them.

Ramon and Bruce got out, talking between them while Ramon made the call.

She checked the call with One was still open on her phone, but she still couldn't hear anything. "One?"

He would be dead before they got there. But she had to try.

Ramon slid back into the driver's seat. "Okay, got it. Thanks, kid." He dropped his phone in the cup holder and hit the gas.

Kenna grabbed the door handle, holding on while he swung out of the parking lot. Ten minutes later, they pulled off the main street into the parking lot for a flooring store. He drove around the back, unlocking his phone with his thumb. He handed it to her.

She still had her phone connected to the call with One,

but she laid it in her lap. On Ramon's screen, a dot blinked. "Up a little farther, almost to the next building."

"Never mind," Ramon said. "I see him."

He pulled off to the side by a chain-link fence behind the big warehouse building. It looked almost new in front, with gleaming windows and a fancy sign. Back here, cardboard and Styrofoam overflowed the garbage.

What she wouldn't give for a nice cooling breeze.

It wasn't going to fix the gritty, hot feeling and the dirt all over her. She needed a shower after being left on that trail, but who cared when there was a job to do. Going home would feel so wrong without Jax there. She might be able to wash herself and snuggle Jolene for a second, but that wasn't what would get her husband back.

She shoved her door open and ran over to the dark lump in the shape of a man lying in the road. "One!" Kenna collapsed beside him and rolled him to his back. She gasped. Blood coated the front of his shirt. "One."

He inhaled a rattling breath that sounded like some of the blood was in his lungs. "You."

"I'm so sorry." Of course, he had been killed because of her.

Because he'd been about to betray his friends and the doctor to help her. They had to have known somehow—heard him on the phone with her—and understood his intent.

"I'm so sorry," she repeated.

That rattling sound felt like it moved through her. Maybe it was the sound of her heart, unable to handle all the pain of what was going on. Too much grief. Even though she knew what loss felt like, it surprised her all over again with how much it hurt every time.

"Silo," One croaked out.

She winced, her hand on his shoulder. "Don't try to talk. We'll get an ambulance."

Ramon had a knife out. He cut One's shirt open, pulling back the sides to reveal his chest. A number of stab wounds leaked blood in steady streams. Ramon leaned down with his head turned so he could listen. He knocked in different places on One's chest and then shook his head.

"Hold on." She leaned close to One, refusing to admit defeat. "We aren't going to let you go."

"Silo." He coughed and blood bubbled up from his lips. "Door."

"We'll figure out how to get in. Don't worry about it." She swiped a tear from her face, probably smearing blood across her cheek, but she didn't care. "Don't worry."

His hand found hers. One turned hers over so her palm was up. He traced something on her hand, wincing. Pain in his expression and more blood leaking from him. He wasn't going to last much longer.

He tapped her palm with his index finger.

"What is it?" She looked at her hand.

He drew a number three on her skin with the tip of his finger.

"Three." He repeated the gesture, and she said, "Three." He tapped a dot on her hand. "Period. Four. Four..." He kept going.

Ramon typed on his phone, entering everything she said. He muttered, "Those are latitude and longitude numbers."

When the numbers stopped, Ramon said, "Got it."

One's hands slid from hers, falling to the ground by his sides. He inhaled another rattling breath, but it caught far too soon. A second later, his head lolled to the side.

"There's nothing more we can do for him."

She looked at Ramon but couldn't say anything.

"It's not the location Fleming gave us. Maybe it's another way in."

She should nod, but she hung her head instead. She didn't have the energy to do anything just then. A man was dead, and she should've been able to protect him, but in the end, there hadn't been anything she could do.

I'm powerless. She squeezed her eyes shut. *God help us.*

Bruce hauled her up. "Come on, girlie. Time to go." He walked her back to the car and put her in Ramon's passenger's seat. When he reached over with the seat belt, she grabbed it and clicked it in.

"Thanks."

He squeezed her shoulder and shut the door.

Kenna ran her hands down her face, praying some more. Trying to figure out a way they could do this, but her mind couldn't come up with any answers. She needed God to step in like He did. In a major way.

Ramon started the car. "They knew he was talking to you, and they took him out. That means they'll be headed to the doctor to inform him that we're on our way. We don't have much time."

She managed to nod. "What did Maizie say?"

"Those coordinates are for property owned by the same corporation. It's about a half mile from the shed that Fleming said was the entrance, so...a back door? Another way in?"

"I hope so." She had so much riding on this that part of her had to admit she couldn't do it. In a way, that made her want to curl up and quit. But God could bring them through this. He could do it all. "Let's go."

Ramon squeezed her knee.

Her phone buzzed. She lifted it from the cup holder

and hit the power button on the side. The number Gregorio had used flashed on the screen with a notification for a message. An image sent by text.

"Jax." She fumbled to unlock it.

"What is it? What did Santino send you?"

The text thread loaded. Her stomach flipped over at seeing Jax tied to a chair with sweat across his hairline. His face was set hard, anger infusing his features. It wasn't directed at her, but it still hurt to see it there on his face.

"Kenna, what does it say?"

She pushed out a breath. "Gregorio wants an update on where we're at. He's giving us four hours to bring Nicola and Doctor Buzard to him, or he'll leave Jax in the desert in pieces."

Bile rose in her throat, and she swallowed it back down.

"It might be time to call in the FBI. Tell them what we know." Ramon glanced over, then focused back on the road. "If we tell them where the front door is, maybe they can distract the doctor while we sneak in the back. That could work, right?"

"That's a pretty good idea."

"That's why you keep me around. For my *pretty good* ideas." Ramon gently shoved her knee. "Make the call."

He wasn't giving her much choice except to do as he said, but that was exactly what she needed. A team who had her back. People she cared for, who cared for her, and who were here to help her get her husband back.

"Okay, I'll call them."

Chapter Twenty-Eight

Ramon cinched up the straps of her bulletproof vest—the one Jax had her wear when they went into the house that blew. "You'll be no good to anyone if you get yourself killed."

She stared up at him. "Are you really going to let that happen?"

"Then I guess we'll both be fine." His eager-to-go expression turned a bit wistful.

Bruce came around the hood of his car. "You two are watching each other's backs. I guess that means I'm on my own."

"Sure," Kenna said. "That's how this works."

She grabbed the rifle from the back seat and put the strap over her head so she didn't have to hold it. An old tactic to save the strength of her arms. She didn't exactly need it right now, but old habits and all that.

"Let's go." She slammed the rear door and led the way through the trees toward the spot that One had told them about.

The FBI was going to storm the front door, most likely

because she might have inferred but not explicitly stated that Jax was being held in the silo. They'd drawn their own conclusions and needed to be part of this entire case and the takedown. After all, they had the hard drive of evidence and the letter written to resolve the cold case.

Kenna was simply going to enter—hopefully, by the rear door—do what she needed to do and stay out of the FBI's way.

Her phone vibrated with a call from Maizie. She answered it with, "Ready?"

"The program is finished. It'll calculate how you move in space and time and overlay that on a three-dimensional rendering of the schematic."

"You're a genius, Maze."

"It's downloading to your phone now. And by the way, this place is huge. It could take you hours to search."

Kenna stopped where she'd be able to see...whatever was here. She crouched behind a dry bush of mostly branches but with some green to it, getting poked because she needed to see far enough. Stars stretched overhead. Something skittered in the dirt, moving past her.

"That better not be a snake."

Maizie laughed. "What?"

"Arizona is great, by the way. I love the desert."

Beside her, Ramon said, "*Mentirosa.*"

"Liar." Maizie laughed some more.

"You guys are just trying to distract me."

Bruce squatted over on the other side of the bush. "Seems like you distract yourself just fine."

Kenna needed to get this night over with, but she also couldn't rush into any of it. Doing that would only mean she missed something that could be important, and perhaps that would put someone's life in danger.

"Ramon, go see if it's a door." She nudged him.

He said, "Ask Maizie what's on that satellite view map. Does it show a door?"

"Maizie?"

"I heard, and there's nothing."

Kenna said, "Let's go. One wouldn't have given us this location if there's nothing here."

She rose out of her crouch and started into the clearing. No structure. Not even a small shed.

When she got near enough, she spotted something on the ground. "Looks like a manhole cover."

"Or some kind of hatch." Ramon grabbed the edges and pulled, but it didn't move.

"What did they even teach you in that cartel?" Bruce pushed him out of the way, grabbed the manhole cover like it was a steering wheel, and rotated it a quarter turn. Inside, the mechanism clanked. "Here we go." He lifted it open and eased down inside first.

A whole lot different from the men at that house, offering for her to go first. Even if it had been a joke, her colleagues treated her nothing like that. They were all willing to take the risk for each other.

Bruce flicked on a flashlight down below them, at the bottom of a short ladder. He looked up from an alcove or at the end of a hallway. "It's clear."

Ramon patted her shoulder. She climbed down the ladder and, at the bottom, shifted the rifle in front of her. Ready to defend themselves just in case the worst happened.

She held aim down the long corridor. Lights were spaced out every twenty feet or so, leaving shadows between.

"Let's go." Bruce went in front of her.

She followed him down the long hall, which had to span the distance between the hatch and the silo that Fleming had designed. "Are we going down?" she whispered. The hall seemed to be descending, though it wasn't steep.

"I bet it's a ventilation shaft." Bruce lifted his watch and looked at the screen. "Maizie wants access to the internal computers as soon as we find a terminal."

"Copy that," Kenna said. "You guys worry about that. I'll worry about getting the people out."

Her phone buzzed.

"Hold."

They all sidestepped, stopping with one shoulder to the wall. They crouched together, and she slid out her phone. "The FBI wants to know where I am. Special Agent Herron wants us to go with her to the front gate. They're about to approach."

Ramon nudged her from behind. "Tell her we got lost."

She replied to the agent what Ramon had said. It could be construed as the truth, but only as a stretch. The FBI didn't need to worry about Kenna. They only needed to worry about doing what was necessary to rescue the people here and save Jax.

Bruce flipped off his flashlight and whispered, "Someone is coming."

She turned the brightness all the way down and huddled behind Bruce's back, praying whoever was in the hallway with them didn't come this far down. She looked at the program Maizie had created from the architectural designs and saw they were still several hundred yards from the structure. Maybe even half a mile.

One level had rooms that Fleming had labeled "residences." That was likely where she would find people, if they weren't spread out through the facility.

"Okay," Bruce whispered, rising slowly to stand.

She followed him, and Ramon came up behind her. The three of them headed down the hall until they reached another alcove and a hatch that looked like it belonged on a submarine. Whoever had been in the hall with them must have come through it, or it was only some small kind of animal they hadn't noticed underfoot, like a rat. Better not to know.

Ramon did the honors with the door, similar to the hatch they had descended into but this one faced them like a giant safe door. They stepped into the decommissioned silo.

She looked at her phone. "Left, and we need to find stairs to go down four floors."

"Room-by-room search?" Bruce asked.

"No, we're going straight to the residences. Those rooms are big enough for groups of people."

Neither of them argued. Ramon found the stairs, and they hurried down the floors, emerging with him leading the way into a brightly lit hallway four floors below where they'd entered. The light made her head pound, so glaring she had to blink against it.

"Go." Bruce patted her shoulder, and they hurried down the hall in a line.

Overhead, a speaker system resounded with a loud alarm, a series of steady beeps. The lights flashed red, pulsating for a few seconds, before they turned back to the glaring white. Then, the alarm shut off.

"Incoming."

Ramon had barely said that when someone stepped out of a room ahead of them and yelled. The man ran toward them, visibly unarmed. Young and wearing plain white clothes. Scrub pants and a Henley-type cream shirt with the sleeves rolled up. Hair in need of cutting and skin with a sheen of sweat.

Ramon shifted, so his weapon was out of the way when the man slammed into him. They went down just as several more people came out into the hall.

One of them yelled, "They're down here already."

They thought she and her friends were FBI. "We're here to help you!"

The one who'd yelled had red hair and a lot of freckles on his face and arms. He was dressed similarly, with shoes that made barely any sound.

Ramon punched the guy on him in the head and shoved him off, standing up in time to cut off the one who ran at her. He slammed the guy against a wall so that his head bounced off. Ramon bent to go through the guy's pockets.

Kenna turned back and saw Bruce grappling with two people, and she got in the middle of it. All the worry about what damage she might do to someone else—innocent or not —rolled through her head, and she pulled her punch.

The guy dropped to the floor anyway.

"I see computers." Ramon ducked into a side room while sticking something in his pocket.

She and Bruce followed.

Bruce said, "I'll barricade the door and get all this connected to Maizie. You guys do what you need to do."

"Sure?"

He nodded. "I'll be here until the feds come. Unless that doctor shows up."

"And when I can't find you later because you disappeared?"

"I'll try not to get shot again."

Not exactly what Kenna meant. Ramon grabbed her arm, though. "Come on." They went to the door.

Kenna said, "Barricade the door."

Bruce nodded.

"I'm counting on you to stay alive."

He had his phone out already, held to his ear. "Yeah, Trouble. It's me."

She and Ramon stepped out into the hall, and he said, "Where now?"

Kenna checked her phone. "Turn left at the end, and the rooms are on the right." They'd have to fight their way through if they encountered any more resistance from people who lived here. "Hopefully, after that alarm, they're all drawn to the front door up on the surface."

"Then who is guarding the people that are held down here?"

Sure, they were making assumptions about what went on down here. Maybe everyone was here of their own free will, captured to make it look like they were victims, but in the end, they believed in what Buzard was doing.

But then, those two children...

Kenna couldn't let go of the fact she had told them they were safe. That nothing would happen to them. That they'd done the right thing and could trust the police.

She had to help them.

"This is it." Ramon stared down the hall, then shook his head. "Looks like a cellblock."

"No, it doesn't." She knew what this was. "It looks like patient rooms at a facility." She went to the first door and peered into the tiny window with wire crisscrossed in the glass. An older man lay on a bed inside the room. His clothing was the same color as the sheets and walls.

"This guy has a thing about white." Ramon checked a window. "No one here."

She looked in another few rooms but didn't see the kids.

Each one had a single patient, and all of them seemed to be asleep. At the end of the hall, she spotted a familiar face. "Nicola."

Kenna tried the handle.

"Here." Ramon handed over a keycard.

"Where'd you get that?"

"Off the guy I downed. Figured it might be handy."

"I guess we'll find out." She swiped the card into a card reader beside the door. It clicked, and the light turned green. "Hold the door."

If they both went in and the door shut, they'd be trapped inside.

Talk about the stuff of nightmares.

"Got it." Ramon stayed on lookout, standing where he could hold the door open.

Kenna shifted the rifle across her body to behind her back and went to Nicola. She shook the doctor's shoulder. "Nicola, can you hear me?" She shook her shoulder harder. "Doctor Santorini!"

The doctor blinked but said nothing. She stared at the wall beyond Kenna's shoulder with a vacant expression. Drool slid from the corner of her mouth.

Kenna gasped. "Nicola, what did they do to you?"

"Someone is coming." Ramon stepped into the room and let the door click shut.

Kenna rushed to the other side of the door and put her back to the wall to stay out of sight.

Out in the hall, someone walked by the room. "I saw them come this way."

Chapter Twenty-Nine

Whoever was outside passed the door and continued on down the hall. Kenna's phone buzzed. She put it on speaker, then tucked the phone in the front pocket of her vest. "What's up, Maze?"

"Hang on." A second later, the teen said, "Yeah, Bruce. Click that."

Nicola seemed like she'd had some kind of procedure or been given a drug that made her compliant. Someone's sick idea of compliance from the people who were being held here. Likely, all so they could be experimented on.

"Okay, I'm back." Maizie's voice rang through much clearer now. "I'm opening all the doors. There are sixteen patients, or whatever there are, on that floor, and they're going to go free."

Kenna looked at Ramon.

"It's the right thing to do," the teen said.

"No one is going to argue with you," Kenna said. With Maizie living for years as a captive, it probably meant a lot to her to be able to give others the same chance at freedom she'd had.

Nicola continued to lay on the bed, staring at the far wall. The room was little bigger than a prison cell, but with a small dresser beside the bed. No artwork. Nothing personal. Not even a book.

"They all should be free," Kenna said. "But they also need care and probably medical help. We can't just let them be out into the world without having doctors look them over."

The doors buzzed and clanged and swung open all down the hall.

Ramon darted out into the hall, and she heard running footsteps, followed by a quick double shot from his gun.

She went to the door, but Nicola shuffled in front of her out into the hallway.

The hall had filled with patients in their white scrubs, all shuffling along in the same direction. What had Buzard done to them to make them like this? A lobotomy was a terrifying idea. No one was allowed to perform that procedure on another person, right? Not anymore.

But it wouldn't produce this kind of uniform behavior, would it?

Kenna joined the stream of patients, keeping an eye on the older man behind her as she made her way to Ramon.

He stood up with blood on the front leg of his pants. A man lay dead by his feet. "What now?"

"We're seeing where they go." She tugged his shirt-sleeve, and he moved with her. Down endless halls, through a wide room with long metal tables and scientific equipment. One wall held cabinets with environmental controls, rows and rows of test tubes in little racks inside. Beakers with lids containing liquid in all colors. Containers with hazard signs on them.

"Maizie?" Kenna said, low into her phone. "Any idea what he's doing here?"

"I have his whole computer system up. It's all his research going back decades, and there's a lot of it."

Ramon leaned over. "Just dump it on the internet. Let the people see what's going on here."

The patients all turned another corner and walked through a set of doors into an open expanse. It looked like a school gym with paneled wood flooring. They stopped in the center, huddled together in a group.

Dominatus wasn't going to like it if the world suddenly found out what was happening here.

"Here it is," Maizie said. "I found the security system." She paused for a second. "I can see you. There have to be cameras all throughout. Even in the private rooms. I can see all of it."

Kenna looked up at the rafters in this ceiling but didn't see any cameras.

"Smile," Maizie said. "You're now live on Banbury Investigations social media accounts. All of them. I also sent a link to Special Agent Herron, so she can get to the feeds. They'll have all the intel they need if they can see in every room in the entire facility."

Ramon lifted his hood, covering his face. Trying to shield himself from view?

She rolled her eyes, lifted her hand and waved. "Everyone, say hi."

The group of patients around her all lifted one hand and waved. "Hi," murmured across the group.

"Whoa." Ramon turned one way, then the other. "I think we should get out of here before—"

Doors opened at the far end.

"Everyone, down!" Kenna yelled the command.

The crowd around her ducked simultaneously, and she swung the rifle up, squeezed the trigger, and slammed the three men who entered with a volley of bullets. They had guns of their own, and at least a few shots whizzed across the air above her. One knocked out a light fixture, spraying glass on the group.

Nicola screamed.

Kenna fired at the man, who ducked back into the hallway. The other two men were now lying on the ground where they'd fallen. She looked at Nicola, who stared at her hand. Blood coated the doctor's fingers.

She looked up at Kenna. "What's happening?"

"You tell me." But that wasn't their most pressing issue. "We need a way out of here." Was the woman lucid enough to understand that? Or was this only a temporary stay in her situation? Just a moment where she was jogged out of the stupor and able to talk for a second. Any moment now she could descend back into that walking automaton way of being.

It certainly didn't count as living.

Nicola straightened and her gaze settled on Kenna. "I know you." She shook her head. "I can't think from where."

"What do you know? Like your name, or what this place is?" Kenna looked around. It felt too much like they were waiting for something.

She grasped the elbow of a man near to her, lifting gently. "Come on. Please. We have to go, everyone."

The group straightened.

"Head for the door."

No one moved.

"Why is this so creepy?" Nicola looked down at her clothes. "Why am I dressed like them?" Her voice rose in pitch.

"Hey, Doctor?" Ramon got in front of her. "We need to get these people out. You can freak out after."

The young woman looked up at Ramon. "Oh, um. Okay. I'm okay."

"Good." He glanced around. "Let's move, people."

Kenna said, "Everyone, to the door."

The group started to shuffle toward the men Kenna had killed.

"Maybe not that way." She winced, going with the group. "But I think the word 'everyone' is the trigger."

Nicola shook her head and shivered with the movement. "I don't want to be here. I don't want to be doing this."

"That's why we're leaving," Kenna said. "Is this the way?"

"Check your map." Ramon motioned to her phone.

"Maizie."

She'd just been remembering aloud that the girl was still on the phone, but Maizie asked, "Yes? What do you need?"

"You're dumping everything on the internet?"

"Working on it," Maizie said, sounding distracted. "I'm compiling it all, but there's a whole lot of raw data. I've got to make it look like exposé articles. No one is going to read terabytes of raw data without a reason to look at it."

"And the live feed?"

"It's catching you in the hallway in three, two—"

"Hang on, everyone." The group slowed but didn't stop moving. "Maizie is there anyone out there?"

"Nope. Hallway is clear."

Ramon pushed through the group to go ahead.

Nicola followed him, rushing between people to catch up to the tall man. Kenna didn't really blame her, but she'd rather have Jax here any day.

"I need to find the doctor." Then she'd have a shot at convincing Nicola the best course of action here was to go back to her family so that Jax would be set free. Not that she would hand over Buzard to the Santinos, if they could even get him past the FBI. That would be condemning him to a slow death by torture at the hands of a crime family when he needed to face the right kind of justice—the kind that gave him a chance to repent and rehabilitate.

"Maizie, where do I find the doctor? These people need a safe way out, and I need to get what I came for."

Nicola glanced back.

Kenna sent her a reassuring smile she didn't feel.

"This way," Nicola said, darting ahead and turning a corner. Ramon snagged her arm and pulled her back, but it was too late.

The shot slammed into her left shoulder before she could get out of the line of fire.

"Everyone, against the wall!"

A gunman emerged from the end of the hall. Ramon fired off two shots while swinging Nicola behind him and saying, "Put pressure on it!"

She hit the wall, gasping as she slid down to sit. Leaving blood smeared on the paint behind her as she cried and held her bleeding arm.

The group huddled around her, all of them trying to stand against the wall.

More shots smacked into the wall, and Ramon crept over to it. He looked around the corner and fired two shots, then two more. "Clear."

"Okay, everyone. Let's go." Kenna helped Nicola up and ushered them all along. If she got them to an exit or to the bureau agents, they'd have help. She could double back for Buzard.

He had to be here somewhere.

One of the men turned to Kenna. "I know how to use that." He motioned to her rifle.

She was about to object when she spotted the Marine Corps tattoo on the inside of his forearm. She pulled the pistol from the back of her belt, where she'd slid the holster. "How about this?"

He took it and immediately ejected the magazine, then slid it back home and racked the slide back. "Ready."

"Ready." She was going to keep a close eye on him but prayed that whatever instinct had been trained into him would win out, and he would help her protect these people. "Keep any eye out. Shoot anyone that's not us and doesn't have an FBI badge."

She didn't trust cops right now but wasn't going to tell him to shoot any. She'd let that be his judgment. "Maizie, update?"

"Two men headed your way, coming up behind you."

The marine swung around, and she spotted blood on the back of his neck. From the glass that sprayed down on them when the light was shot out? He fired a single shot, then two together. "Okay, that feels good."

Kenna spotted the deceased men behind them, dressed in old-timey medical clothing. "If everyone is wearing white, it's going to be difficult to figure out who is who."

They passed a corkboard with papers pinned to it.

Kenna had a crazy idea and snatched a pushpin off the wall. She grabbed the arm of a young man in front of her and stuck the pin in the fleshy underside of his forearm. He flinched, flailing his arms before she could get out of reach. She ducked. "Easy. You with me?"

"I-I think so." He looked around, still walking with the rest. Falling out of step.

"What's your name?"

"Sean."

"Okay, Sean. You know where the exit is?"

He said, "Maybe. I think so."

Nicola dropped back to walk with them. "I can help Sean find the exit. I remember some things." She looked at Sean. "The yellow fire extinguisher."

"Right. And the door with the light."

"We need to get there."

"Okay," Kenna said. "Sounds like we've got the beginning of a plan."

"No go." Maizie didn't sound happy.

The marine asked, "Who's that?"

"I'm your guardian angel, Axel."

"Are you hacking military files, Maze?" Kenna walked with the crowd, following Ramon.

Maizie said, "Facial recognition."

"Now tell me what the problem is with the plan."

"It isn't bad," Maizie said. "It's just not going to work. There are too many captors, and they're making their way to you. They all have guns. They're between you all and the front door."

Kenna said, "Maizie, let the FBI in. Open all the doors and let them in."

"They aren't quite through the inner doors. I'm unlocking them now." Maizie paused. "I think I have a roundabout route for you. I can lock the people coming for you in a hallway, seal it, and leave them there."

"Do it. Get the bureau down here," Kenna said. "What about the doctor? Is he here?"

Axel whipped his head around, watching their six but also interested. "What doctor? Wait, there was a doctor." He shook himself. "Why does he terrify me?"

"I need to find him. But I don't want him dead. I need him alive so he can face justice."

"I'd rather put a bullet in his head, thanks for offering, though." He leaned down to the phone, getting in Kenna's space. "Where is he? I'm gonna kill this guy."

"I'm in favor of this plan," Sean said. "In case anyone is interested."

Kenna figured she should stick her pushpin in everyone walking with them, but she would have to get them all convinced to help. "We need somewhere to hole up. What have you got, Maze?"

"Sean Reed. Nineteen, double major in biology and chemistry." Maizie sounded like she was in awe.

"Let's focus, shall we?"

"Somewhere to hole up, got it." Maizie went quiet again.

"No offense," Axel said. "But I'm not stopping until I'm out of here. Got it?"

"I understand. If you could get the rest of these people out, I can finish this."

Up ahead, Ramon said, "You're recruiting?"

"Everyone, keep an eye out for assailants, okay? We don't need anyone else getting shot." She made her way to Nicola. "Can you tell me, did you see any kids while you were here? I still need to find the two who came to your medical center that day. They were taken as well."

Nicola frowned. "Maybe. There was a ward. I went there once because he—the doctor—needed me to look at patient files. I don't know who it was for."

"Can you show me where it was on a map?" Kenna slid the phone from her vest, thumbed to Maizie's map, and handed it to Nicola.

Sean glanced behind them. "Where did that guy go?"

Ramon stopped up ahead, bunching everyone together. "What is it?"

Kenna looked for Axel, but he wasn't behind them. Down the hall, out of sight, gunshots rang out. "He's going after the doctor." She turned back to Nicola. "Tell me where, then take Sean and these people and get out of here. Maizie will clear a path to the FBI."

Ramon skirted around them and took the phone. "Let's go get those kids."

Kenna fought the urge to go get the doctor before someone else did, but she knew what Jax's first priority would be.

So, she went to save more lives.

Even if it meant he lost his.

Chapter Thirty

Up ahead of them, somewhere down the hall that seemed to stretch forever, gunshots rang out.

"Axel is going to run out of bullets." Ramon glanced at her. "You okay?"

"My head is swimming, but I'm good." She'd been head-butted, but that felt like forever ago. "I'm good."

"I've got you. And if you're not all right, I've still got you."

"Back atcha."

Ramon chuckled. "Ten-four, good buddy."

"Can we just do this?"

"There's the Kenna we all know and love."

She rolled her eyes. "How was Wisconsin?"

"No go."

"What? That's a shame."

Ramon sighed. "Can we just do this?"

Kenna figured that was the end of their conversation, so she picked up the pace and headed for the source of the sound while keeping her gun up. Her feet moved the way they'd been trained, almost silent on the floor. Everything loose. Aches and pains forgotten. Nothing in her mind but instinct and the need for justice. It was who she was supposed to have been.

An agent.

An investigator.

"Those kids had better be where Nicola said they were," she muttered. "Or I'm going to crack some heads together."

From the phone tucked in her vest, Maizie said, "There are bigger rooms up ahead."

"Copy that." She had to ask, "Are we still broadcasting live online?"

"Yes. And in true social media style, I manipulated what everyone was shown next, so it went out to millions. The views just crossed half a billion, and it's climbing. We also have TV news broadcasts coming in and out as part of their programming."

"Assuming people believe it's real." Kenna figured there were some people watching who didn't think this was live. Probably more like a fabrication or some kind of simulation.

"No one will be able to ignore this."

Kenna said, "That's exactly what I'm afraid of."

She slowed at the end, knowing Ramon would want to go through the door first. He didn't even hesitate. Her friend stepped past her and went first, hooking around the door and going left. She did the same, moving right.

Any analyst who knew what they were looking at would see that as a cop move. They'd look into Kenna, and assuming they could see his face in the footage under his hood, they'd find him. They'd learn that she had been at Quantico with Ramon, giving them more to talk about when they discovered the disgraced and then exonerated former FBI agent was here working with her. He deserved to have people see that he was a good man, who worked to save people now.

"Nicola's group got up two levels so far. They haven't encountered anyone," Maizie said. "And the agents are inside, heading toward them."

"Good."

Ramon looked around. "What is this place?"

She stared at the huge vats of liquid, bubbling behind Plexiglas. "They're warm." She could feel the heat coming off each one. "Eight of them."

More gunshots, this time from all the way at the far end of the room.

She spotted movement through the glass and liquid. There was someone on the other side of this vat. Above them, a raised metal walkway surrounded the room, suspended from the wall.

"I don't think I wanna know what's in these," Ramon said. "Whatever it is, they're mass-producing it."

She tracked the person moving on the other side, watching them try to sneak around behind her. Kenna waited until the last second and swung around, slamming her rifle against the person's shoulder. She caught the edge of the face as well, and the porcelain mask shattered.

Earnest's black eyes stared back at her, and he launched toward her, no mercy in his gaze.

Kenna got the rifle up just before he was too close. The gun jerked between them, and Earnest froze. She pushed him away with one hand and the gun, and he toppled back. The bullet had gone through the right side of his abdomen and exited out the back, hitting the Plexiglas of the vat behind him.

The round hadn't penetrated the glass.

Cracks began to form, and a slight dribble of liquid ran

down from the spot where the bullet had smashed into the exterior.

Kenna said, "Time to go."

She spun around and hurried after where Axel had gone. Ramon was right behind her.

"I should—"

"It's fine." Kenna kept running. "You don't always have to be in front."

He grunted, but she ignored it when she spotted an open door. Axel cried out from inside the room that was full of rows of hospital beds. Tiny bodies lay on each one, hooked up to wires connected to IV bags. Beeping machines. Each patient had a mask on their face.

Ramon dragged her back and went into the room first, saying nothing.

She followed him and shut the door behind her.

Axel lay on the floor, the gun discarded out of reach. Or dropped because the slide was back. He had run out of bullets before he even finished the job.

"Did you kill him?" Kenna asked.

Doctor Marcus Buzard stood over Axel with a hard expression on his face. An interesting change from the usual blank he gave her. Not that Kenna had all that much experience with him.

He wore black shoes, slacks, and a cream shirt under a white lab coat with two pens in the breast pocket. His skin was still clammy, as it had been the last time she saw him. She might wish that was a sign of some kind of end-stage illness, but if he died, she wasn't going to get Jax back.

"I really wanna kill this guy," Ramon muttered.

"Maizie, are we still live?"

Buzard flinched, just a tiny flex of the skin around his eyes.

Maizie said, "Yes. Everyone can hear you."

Kenna rolled her shoulders. "You have eleven children in this ward. You had even more that were in holding cells. You and your staff kidnap people and keep them here, where you do experiments on them. Do you deny that, Doctor Marcus Buzard?"

The doctor stared at her. "How can I? The evidence would appear to be damning."

"What justification can you possibly have for stealing people like this?"

He lifted his chin, just a fraction.

She spotted a tiny amount of movement on the floor. Axel wasn't dead. He'd just been knocked to the ground. "Ramon," she whispered.

"On it." He went over, dragging Axel away from the doctor just in case either one of them decided to end this more decisively.

"Well?" Kenna asked. "Surely, you have a reason for what you're doing. Some kind of master plan or research project no one would sign off on because you're certifiable."

The corner of the doctor's mouth curled up. "Is that a clinical diagnosis?"

"That you're bat crap crazy?" She shrugged. "It might be. You've given me enough justification to believe that with the amount of times you've kidnapped *me*. Experimented on me. Altered me in ways I don't even begin to understand."

"You think I've experimented on you, Kenna?" Buzard looked around. "When I'm so busy in here, working on my master plan?"

"Tell me what it is!"

Buzard said nothing.

"The FBI are on their way down here. You're done. It's

over," she said. "Whatever you're doing down here, you won't get to finish it."

Rage built in her, not just for what he'd done to her but for these children lying helplessly in their beds. If only she could kill him for what he'd done.

Maizie's voice came from her phone speaker. "Bruce and I would like you to know that killing him doesn't get Jax back."

Ramon asked, "How about a citizen's arrest? Are we allowed to do that?"

"You cannot stop me." Buzard didn't move. "You cannot stop any of us."

The look in his eye was unsettling. This felt wrong. Her head was pounding, her thoughts swirling around like a whirlpool in her mind. She looked at Ramon but couldn't figure out what to say or what should happen next.

His eyes were glassy and slightly unfocused.

From her phone, she heard, "They shut the feed down. Someone hacked my system and stopped the broadcast! We're blind."

Buzard's lips curled back, revealing neat rows of white teeth. "I guess it's over."

Ramon lifted his gun, and she had to step in. Kenna shoved his aim to the side, and they both stumbled. Her hands braced against the floor. She needed to get up but couldn't figure out how to do it.

"No." She got up, pushing upright and finding her weapon. Moving on instinct.

She was kneeling, so she aimed the weapon at the fleeing man and squeezed the trigger.

The sound echoed through her head.

Doctor Buzard hit the floor at the end of the room, his

hands pushing the door open. A spray of blood coated the door.

She had to know he was dead.

Kenna grabbed Ramon's arm and tugged. "Come on."

She managed to get up but didn't move. Like she'd forgotten what she was doing. Who didn't sometimes walk into a room and forget what they'd gone in there for?

She turned to Ramon.

"Why do I feel like this?" Ramon crawled over to Axel, shoved him to his back, and pressed two fingers to his neck. "He's alive."

Alive. Dead.

"The doctor." Kenna went to Buzard, doing what Ramon had just done but finding no pulse in the doctor's neck. "He's dead."

Ramon swore loudly.

She shared the sentiment, given the situation, but didn't like hearing those harsh consonants. "Jax." Tears gathered in her eyes.

Maizie said, "I have an update about that."

Kenna frowned. "What is it?"

"As soon as you found the doctor, Bruce made a call. The law office answered."

"Did he betray us?" Kenna had to ask, even if she didn't want to know the answer.

"No. He's giving them a shot to do us a favor. To earn our trust back."

"I don't want to trust them." Kenna needed to focus on finishing this operation so they could get out of here. Get him back.

But how? Nicola was trying to escape, and the doctor was dead.

Ramon came over. "What is he doing, Maizie?"

At least he looked about as happy as Kenna was about this.

Maizie said, "They feel so bad about everything that, as a show of good faith, they're going to go get Jax back for you. Bruce said he should go with them just to make sure it all goes down in a way that means he comes out of it alive."

Kenna winced. "I don't suppose there's any way to stop it?"

"He's already out of the hatch."

Back they way they'd come in? She shook her head. "He told you to tell me after it was too late?"

"I was going to tell you before, but I would've interrupted you getting the doctor to confess live online. And it would have compromised the mission to get Jax because the Santinos might've been listening."

Kenna said, "At least they don't know the doctor is dead."

A move like that could've cost Jax his life if the Santinos found out that she had reneged on the deal. Ramon squeezed her shoulder. Before he could say anything, the doors slammed open and armed federal agents raced in.

Kenna and Ramon both lifted their hands.

"Guns down!"

Ramon crouched to put his weapon on the floor. She held still while an agent lifted hers over her head.

"Are there any other weapons on your person?" the guy pretty much yelled in her face.

She nodded. "I'm not going to use any of them. I'm Kenna Banbury. My husband is—"

"We know." Special Agent Herron strode into the room wearing tactical pants, her vest over a shirt, a pair of black boots, and clear glasses she'd pushed up onto her head.

"You should tell me where you got those pants."

Special Agent Herron's brows rose. "How about you tell me where to find SAC Jaxton? And why these children are here. And all the rest of *what on earth* is going on here."

Uh-oh. "I can explain." But could she jeopardize what was happening to Jax? If she told the FBI and they went after the Santinos, she might compromise the lawyers' attempt to rescue him. "I just want Jax back safe, that's all."

"Then start talking."

Chapter Thirty-One

The tent door flapped back, and Special Agent Herron stepped in. Kenna quit pacing the length of the floor and said, "I need to go."

They'd taken everything. Her vest, all her weapons, and her phone—hanging up on Maizie in the process.

Special Agent Herron stopped several feet away and didn't look at Kenna or Ramon in particular. "Until such time as you can tell me where Special Agent in Charge Jaxton is, you'll remain here to answer further questions."

Ramon sat on the end of a folding table they'd set up along with this white canvas tent, which was outside the front door of the silo, in the middle of nowhere. It might be impressive how quickly they'd erected a mobile command center, but she didn't care. She just wanted Jax back.

The FBI was going through every inch of the facility, processing every single victim, everyone who worked with the doctor, and every single molecule of physical evidence.

This was going to take hours.

"I need you to let me go so I can reconvene with the rest

of my team." Maybe Ramon as well, so she motioned between them with a finger. "Let *us* go."

"It's been brought to my attention that the doctor did medical procedures on you. I'd like to discuss those." She shifted, bringing a notepad and pen to her front. "When I'm satisfied with what I've learned, you'll both be free to go."

Ramon didn't move. Probably because if he did, it would come across as aggressive.

"Are you going to answer any of *my* questions?" Kenna folded her arms. The need to find Jax and know if he was all right was driving her insane. If only she could shove everyone out of the way and just...run. Find him. Hold him, which would probably feel like hanging on for dear life.

"What questions do you have?" Special Agent Herron wandered to the table Ramon sat on, dragged a chair back on the tarp they'd laid on the floor, and sat down. She crossed one leg over the other, calm even though she also had that hyperaware demeanor of an agent waiting for the situation to explode around them.

Kenna took the chair opposite.

Ramon hopped off the table where he'd have had his back to them, grabbed a chair, and straddled it so he could lean against the back. One knee jogged up and down until Kenna wanted to push against it to get him to still.

But she felt the same on the inside.

"What was in those vats?" Kenna crossed one knee over the other, proving to this agent she could be just as calm in the middle of a crazy situation. "We were exposed to it, right? When some of it leaked out."

"Part of the reason you're in here is that you were exposed to a substance we believe is an infectious disease Doctor Buzard was creating."

Kenna bit the inside of her lip. "Are we infected?"

"Limited exposure seems to have little effect compared to direct contact. The preferred method of infection is through an immunization, which is, in fact, a dose of the disease designed to infect everyone in the world with the contagion."

Kenna frowned. "He was going to tout the disease as the cure so he can target *everyone*?"

Ramon said, "As if people don't have enough distrust of medical companies already?"

"What does it do?" Kenna asked. "He isn't just trying to kill everyone, right?"

"According to information contained on the hard drive you kindly turned over to us," Special Agent Herron said, "the disease will kill a third of the world's population. The other two-thirds will recover with stronger immune systems and every function of the body operating at optimum. It's designed to alter the genetics of the person infected, but if it doesn't kill you, it makes you some kind of—"

"Superhuman? I mean, not powers but better. Stronger. Faster. Smarter."

Special Agent Herron nodded.

"I think I might already have been given it."

The agent didn't seem surprised.

"More master race crap?" Ramon shook his head. "Where have I heard this before?"

"In the last hundred years or recently?" Kenna asked him.

"Maybe they're one and the same."

He thought *Dominatus* connected back to Hitler? Or at least the eugenics research that the Nazis based their philosophy on. She wouldn't put it past them, considering how long the organization had been in existence. But it was far more subversive than that.

After all, they had gone this long without being discovered.

Kenna squeezed her eyes shut. Had Jax been rescued? They had taken her phone, so she had no way to contact Maizie or Bruce. She prayed that her associate was only going to make sure the lawyers did the right thing and didn't mess up in a way that cost Jax his life. She had *everything* riding on this, and all the trust she needed to have for Bruce stretched thin. So taut it was about to snap if anything went in any way other than perfect.

I'm still learning how to trust. No matter what.

Maybe that was the point of all this. A test, a way to grow in her reliance on God. Because who knew what was going to happen to her in the future? She might be called to go through things so much worse than anything she'd ever faced before, and she would need a robust foundation of relying on God and the fact that He was in control of everything.

If that meant she had to walk the road ahead of her without Jax? To bury him and have to keep going with her life, keep fighting the good fight?

This time, she would have God. So it wouldn't be like losing everything, even if it certainly felt that way.

"Doctor Marcus Buzard is dead," Special Agent Herron said. "We have recovered his body, and we are in the process of shutting down this operation. All of his people have been arrested, and those he was experimenting on are safe now."

Ramon glanced at Kenna with one eyebrow quirked up.

"What?" she asked.

He shrugged one shoulder. "Maybe he wasn't experimenting on those kids. Maybe he was infecting them, and the ones that lived, he was going to release them back into the world so they could spread the disease."

"Those who didn't catch it would go in for an immunization," Kenna said, terrified of the picture that painted in her mind. "They would get it as a result, and soon enough, the entire world would've been exposed to it."

Special Agent Herron nodded. "There was a manifesto included on the hard drive. We didn't find it right away because it was buried. His master plan was for one person to take over leadership of the whole world."

"Sounds like a warped view of the book of Revelation." Kenna shook her head. "Like trying to usher in the end times."

Ramon asked, "How does that go again?"

Kenna glanced at him. "I'm not going to tell you. Why don't you go read it for yourself?"

That was the only way he was going to be changed—if he sought the truth on his own and realized what he'd found. No matter how much she explained, she couldn't argue him to faith. He had to decide on his own what he believed.

"Maybe I will." Ramon nodded. "For the case."

She nearly smiled but didn't. "Special Agent Herron, I need to leave."

"Sit back down, Ms. Banbury."

"It's Mrs. Jaxton. As in Special Agent in Charge Jaxton, my husband. Your boss."

Herron glanced around. "Is he here? I don't see him."

Ramon asked, "What's going on?"

"Given your company's actions, word came down from the highest ranks of the Department of Justice that you're to remain here to explain why footage of this operation leaked onto the internet along with the information contained on the network that the FBI has only just gained access to."

Kenna's stomach clenched.

Herron continued, "Your staff took matters into their own hands. These persons must surrender themselves to the FBI for questioning while we determine if charges are going to be filed."

Ramon started to argue.

"Subverting justice for your own ends isn't legal, Mr. Santiago."

"It's just Ramon."

Herron said, "I highly doubt you are *just* anything. Any of you. Or the young woman in your employ. Isn't that right, Mrs. Jaxton?"

Maizie.

Kenna lifted her chin. "Any questions you have as to the actions of my employees can be directed to me. I'll be making any statements you require."

"And if I *require* that your employees be interviewed by the US Attorney's office, what happens then? You cut and run, and your company goes underground? That is how you work, isn't it?"

Well, *yeah.*

"Our enemies employ the same tactics." Kenna shrugged. "How else do you expect that we can survive to bring justice when people like Buzard believe they are above the law, that they can kill millions and change things on a global scale?"

"So you consider yourself above the law?" Special Agent Herron asked.

"That's not what I said."

"Your little speech to Buzard is going viral. Many are calling for a psychological evaluation, and perhaps they are right. Maybe you have cracked."

She'd thought for a second that Herron was talking about Buzard needing an evaluation, but he was dead.

"Kenna isn't crazy," Ramon said. "She's the sanest person I know."

"Your credibility hangs on the edge of a precipice, Mr. Santiago. Given your history with the bureau—"

"He was exonerated. The actions of one dirty FBI agent —who was connected to a family whose whole goal was to affect national culture, politics, and policy—don't count against a man who was doing his job. Who stuck to his oath as an FBI agent until he had no choice but to be what everyone believed he was."

Herron said, "Sounds like a self-fulfilling prophecy."

"Like me believing in conspiracies means I find a conspiracy everywhere I turn?"

"You tell me." Herron shrugged.

This wasn't the time to lean forward and bang her head on the table, but it was tempting. "I didn't make up what happened here."

"You're right. This is undeniable." Herron leaned back in her seat. "Now tell me, where is SAC Jaxton?"

Kenna bit the inside of her lip. "Nicola Santorini, one of the doctor's victims, will know where he is. Her family took Jax to force me to get her back so I could exchange her for him. Like a ransom demand. They also wanted the doctor."

"The one you killed?" Herron asked. "Strange way of bargaining for your husband's life."

"Things don't always work out the way we intend."

"That might be the truest thing you've said so far."

Ramon shifted in his seat. "So you're arresting both of us, like we had anything to do with this? On whose orders? I want to talk to that person so they can look me in the eye and tell me what laws I broke here."

That tactic might not work, considering they *had* broken laws. However, it was down to what the prosecution could prove beyond a reasonable doubt. Still, when Kenna's mental health was being called into question, as if she was some kind of cracked conspiracy theorist who had misled everyone on her payroll, that was a scary idea.

As if she was this charismatic leader convincing her followers to give their lives for what she believed. Sounded an awful lot like how *Dominatus* operated if anyone was going to ask her. Not that it seemed like they would.

At least, not without her needing her lawyer present.

"I need my phone so I can find out where Jax is." Kenna pushed out a breath that sounded like she was gasping. Like a pressure cooker releasing a little of the frustration that had bubbled up in her until she was about to explode. "If you want to know whatever it is you're asking, then I need something in return. I need Oliver Jaxton here."

She sat back in her chair and crossed her arms.

Special Agent Herron drew her phone from the inside pocket of her blazer and looked at the screen. "You'll be speaking with my superior next. He just arrived from the San Francisco office. He'll be covering for SAC Jaxton until we can get all this sorted out."

"Great. I'll just tell him the same thing I've been telling you."

Special Agent Herron stood.

The tent flap lifted inward, and an older gentleman stepped inside wearing a suit with a red tie. Hair slicked back.

"Three."

Herron glanced at Kenna, probably wondering what

that was about. Then, she faced her boss. "Sir, I'm Special Agent Andrette Herron."

He nodded, and they shook hands. "I'd like to speak to these two alone."

Two more men stepped into the room, flanking the door.

The "boss" said, "I'll be protected."

Herron didn't appear to like the break in procedure but couldn't argue. "Of course." She skedaddled out of the tent.

Three stood on the other side of the table. Four and Five stayed by the door. All of them were dressed like special agents, like a Secret Service detail. Maybe that was what they planned to do. The president knew about *Dominatus*. Maybe they were going to kill him.

Or her thoughts were all over the place.

Kenna lifted her chin. "You killed One."

"The only answer to betrayal is death." Three's expression was cold, pure ice. "We all know that."

"Whatever you tried, it didn't work. Doctor Marcus Buzard is dead. It's over."

His head tipped to the side, very slightly. "Is it?"

Ramon said, "We're not going to prison, bro."

Three didn't even look at him. Perhaps they didn't have any say at all in what was about to happen. *Dominatus* was cleaning house and using the FBI to do it. This wasn't even close to being over. "At least tell me all those kids are going to be taken care of."

The lawyers, if they were on the right side, were getting Jax free. Bruce would hopefully make sure all that went successfully.

Maizie would be protected by Stairns and Elizabeth, no matter what happened.

"They are infected." Three paused, as if that was a sufficient explanation.

"So they can't be out in public until they're cured. Do *not* tell me you want this virus to spread." Was it contagious enough she and Ramon were infected, or had they been injected? Kenna was about to flip her lid—and maybe flip this table.

Sounded satisfying. But would it really make her feel better?

She knew what would make her feel better.

Three said, "What I want is immaterial. You've signed our death warrants by killing Marcus Buzard, but revenge isn't in my power. There are greater forces at work here."

"*Dominatus.*"

"We serve the future."

Ramon said, "I'm going to kill all of you."

Three whipped something from behind his back and fired it at Ramon. Kenna reached for her friend, but he toppled back off the chair, jerking as electricity raced through his body from the twin electrodes in his chest.

Three set the stun gun, still connected to Ramon and still zapping him, on the table as if nothing had happened. Kenna grabbed it and thumbed it off, stopping the charge. "That's enough."

"Let's go, Kenna."

She refused to stand. Four and Five came over, dragging her by the arms. "Where are we going? You can't just take me somewhere. The FBI will want an explanation."

"We have a warrant from a federal judge to take you to a holding facility."

There was no way that was true. "Where are we *actually* going."

"Don't ask questions you don't want to know the answer to."

Kenna kicked out with one foot, then spun and tried to do the same with her other foot. Her arms were jerked back, nearly separating her shoulders. She screamed at the tearing feeling in her joints, and the whole world swam around her.

She hit the ground, and everything was swallowed up in darkness.

The past. The future.

All of it was gone.

Epilogue

K enna sat with her back to the wall, which was fine because it had padding. White surrounded her, including the white floor. She smoothed her fingers down the leg of a pair of white scrubs. Her white shoes were discarded across the room.

Her hair hung down over her shoulders, lank and unkempt. The ends needed cutting.

That errant thought drifted away, and she couldn't catch it again.

Goose bumps rose on her arms. She needed the blanket but lacked the energy to get up and cross to the cot where she slept to fetch the blanket. What was the point? She'd exhausted herself at first, working out with push-ups and all the Pilates stretches Jax had drilled into her head when she had to recover from an injury. The sit-ups and leg raises he had her do to maintain her muscle mass.

Now, she was wasting away.

Not just because of the constant nagging nausea in her stomach.

The door lock clanged, and a man stepped into the room. His spitting image, down to the way he walked and that sweaty skin. The shiny bald head.

"Doctor Buzard."

"That's right, Kenna." He sat the tray of food on the edge of the bed. "How are you feeling today? Still sick?"

She stared at her toes, wondering why she'd never bothered to paint them. Trying to recall a Bible verse—anything to anchor her trust in the One who could save her.

You need to get me out of here.

She wasn't going to last much longer.

Doctor Marcus Buzard didn't come too close. He crouched out of reach. "You're looking a little better. Some food will help you have more energy. Anything else you might like? Another book or a magazine?"

A cell phone.

Or a gun.

That would do it. She would appreciate a gun right now.

She had killed this man. Shot him and seen him bleed out, gasping his last breath. And yet, here he was. In charge of this facility—wherever they were. She had no idea. She'd been knocked out in Arizona and woke up strapped to a hospital bed...somewhere. Treated. Assessed. Locked in this cell.

"You just let us know if you'd like anything, all right?" He didn't leave.

Why wasn't he leaving?

"Make sure you eat, Kenna." He straightened to standing. "You need to keep your strength up. For the baby."

The door clanged shut.

Kenna laid her hand on her lower stomach, unsure if this was yet another mind game. The nausea could be anything they'd given her. It could be something in the food. Or the fact she'd been here for weeks with no obvious way out.

No one had come to rescue her. She didn't even know if Jax was alive or dead.

She shifted her hand off her stomach and went to see what food there was on that tray. After all, he was right. She needed all the strength she could get if she was going to get out of here.

She just had to keep fighting.

Keep Reading For...

- Where to find more great Lisa Phillips books.

- How to sign up for Lisa's newsletter and get a FREE book.

- Where to find Lisa on social media.

About the Author

Find out more about Lisa Phillips at her website, where you'll discover more romantic suspense fan-favorite series and heart-pounding thriller novels.
https://authorlisaphillips.com/

If you loved this book, please consider sharing about it on social media. Or leave a review at your book retailer website, on Goodreads, or on Bookbub. Your review will help others find great books to entertain and encourage them!

Signup for Lisa's newsletter by scanning the QR code below
to stay updated on sales, new releases, and
recommendations for your TBR pile. New Subscribers even
get a FREE book!

Find Lisa on Social Media!

facebook.com/authorlisaphillips

instagram.com/lisaphillipsbks

bookbub.com/authors/lisa-phillips

Also by Lisa Phillips

Find out more about Brand of Justice at my website:
https://authorlisaphillips.com/product-tag/brand-of-justice/

Book 1: Cold Dead Night

Book 2: Burn the Dawn

Book 3: Quick and Dead

Book 4: Over the Limit

Book 5: Skin and Bone

Book 6: Dust and Ashes

Book 7: Long Road Home

Book 8 : Dead to Rights

Book 9: Fear No Evil

Book 10: Out of Time

Book 11: Every Which Way

Book 12: One More Chance

Book 13: Storm and Tempest (August 2025)

Other series by Lisa:

Last Chance Downrange

Chevalier Protection Specialists

Last Chance County

Northwest Counter-Terrorism Taskforce

Double Down

WITSEC Town (Sanctuary)

Numerous other titles including several with *Love Inspired Suspense,* find the complete list here (or scan the QR code):

https://authorlisaphillips.com/all-books/